AN UNFORTUNATE COINCIDENCE

An Unfortunate Coincidence

A 1920s Mystery

MICHAEL SINCLAIR

AN UNFORTUNATE COINCIDENCE

Copyright © 2022 by Michael Sinclair
All Rights Reserved

ISBN: 979-8-4263-9571-8

Published by Amazon

Originally published under the title of *The Late Mr. Cary*

Unauthorized Duplication Is A Violation Of Applicable Laws.

This novel is a work of fiction. Names, characters and incidents are the product of the author's imagination. Any resemblance to actual persons, living or dead, is entirely coincidental.

Of all times to travel to upstate New York, Megan Cary told herself as she hurried into Grand Central Station, it was at the height of a blizzard.

It is January 1928. Megan Cary, a young and stylish librarian, is on her way to the state library conference. On the train, Meg meets Janet Faraday who confides that she killed her son's father six years earlier—and got away with it.

With her marriage crumbling, Meg can no longer tolerate her husband Adam's moodiness and philandering. She harbored thoughts of divorce but murder?

During a family visit, Adam mysteriously dies. Meg finds a suicide note and the police want to quickly close the case. So does Adam's mother Helen, the stern matriarch of the family. Skeptical that Adam would kill himself, Meg hires a private detective whose investigation ultimately unravels family secrets as a series of surprising deaths occur over two cold and snowy weeks in Albany. Meg wonders if the deaths could somehow be related.

AN UNFORTUNATE COINCIDENCE is a classic mystery set in the stately home of an upper crust family in Albany, New York in the 1920s, bringing the 1920s to life—amidst a parade of death!

Author's Note

It is true that on January 12, 1928 Ruth Snyder was executed at Sing-Sing Prison for the murder of her husband in 1927. Besides this fact, all the characters and events in this story are imaginary and any resemblance to real people or events is entirely coincidental.

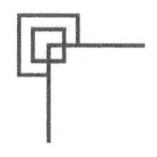

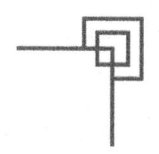

CHAPTER ONE

January 1928

Grand Central Station, New York City

Of all times to travel to upstate New York, Megan Cary told herself as she paid the taxi and hurried into the station, it had to be the height of a blizzard.

She thought she must be foolish to take this trip. Yesterday afternoon, as she finished work at the library and read the notices in the newspaper, the weather prognosis hadn't seemed too bad. Accumulating snow, which already created havoc for the Midwest was slowly approaching the Northeast. By late afternoon, the winds were predicted up to forty miles an hour and winter storm watches were posted. The picture worsened by the hour, along with Meg's mood.

She looked up at the departures board. Then she found the staircase to take her to the boarding platform for the four-forty train to Albany. She shivered at the chill wind, thinking how lonely train stations could feel. She heard an announcement that her train was pulling into the station after a ten-minute delay. Her husband Adam told her he would meet her at the station to say goodbye before she left. He was too busy at the pharmaceutical company and as he put it "just couldn't take time off." She looked at the crowd and could not see him. But then she finally spotted him. He came, after all, to see her off. She called his name, but he was swallowed up in a mad rush of people. She caught a glimpse of his back, retreating up the platform. At that moment, an announcement was made to board the train. Meg turned, walked down the platform, and turned once more hoping Adam might be there. She realized she was blocking other passengers from entering. Abruptly she turned and boarded quickly but then found she had to fight another crowd, only this time in the train itself. She saw an empty window seat. She put her suitcase on the rack above her head and then stretched out in the seat, filled with the mixed emotions of leaving home and her husband.

Megan Cary was on her way to Albany to attend the state library conference. Meg was employed as a librarian at the New York Public Library in Manhattan. She planned to stay with her in-laws who lived in Albany and looked forward to seeing her sister-in-law with whom she attended graduate school at New York University. Both she and Iris, Adam's sister, were librarians. They planned to attend the convention together. Meg enjoyed hearing about the state library where Iris worked, and they often talked shop about their diverse library endeavors.

She looked out the window at the darkness of the underground station, seeing her own reflection. At twenty-five, Meg had been told she was attractive. Although she knew she was not pretty, her golden hair was neat, her white skin and delicate features a source of gratification. She was sensibly dressed in a long skirt and a heavy fur coat to keep warm. She wore a light lipstick, some earrings, and a string of pearls. Overall, as she finished brushing her hair and replaced the brush in her purse, she was pleased with her appearance.

As if in a trance, she continued looking out the train window. The feelings she had experienced prior to boarding suddenly came back, quite strongly. It wasn't the idea of leaving her husband Adam. She thought more than once of leaving him and even considered not returning to New York City after the convention ended. She thought of staying in Albany, making a new life for herself. But she knew she would never be free of Adam. And with her mother-in-law in Albany, that would be foolish.

She tried to shrug it off. It'd be good to get away for a while. She'd go shopping with Iris when she had spare time. Satisfied with her plans, she opened her pocketbook, not exactly sure what she was looking for. Lipstick, her wallet, aspirin, loose change, business cards. She looked through the cards, her hairdresser, a florist, Sloane Sheppard. She looked again at this last card. Her mind raced back several years. She had met Sloane at the New York Public Library when he was there for research. She had helped him find information from the 1920 census for somebody or other, she couldn't remember. He was a private investigator and a librarian, too. Didn't she read how some wives had their husbands investigated if they suspected infidelity?

She saw the New York Times stuffed in the magazine holder in the seat ahead of her. The article on the front page made her look twice and shake her head in disbelief.

Meg read about Ruth Snyder, a housewife from Queens who killed her husband and was put to death yesterday, January the twelfth, for her crime. She died in the electric chair in Sing-Sing Prison! She shivered as she looked at the photograph of Ruth Snyder strapped in the electric chair and the article underneath it. She wondered incredulously how a wife could kill her husband. Did that really happen? Apparently so, she mused and continued reading the Snyder article.

Her reverie was broken by a conductor walking down the aisle and loudly announcing a weather-related delay. Meg sighed impatiently at another delay when suddenly another conductor approached and stopped at her seat.

"Is this seat taken?" he asked Meg and didn't wait for a response before he said, "Here's a seat, ma'am!"

So much for polite conductors, Meg thought. She looked up to see a woman hastily making her way down the aisle.

"Oh, thank you, thank you!" the woman called. She smiled at the conductor, and then sat down rather eagerly next to Meg.

She was hoping no one would sit next to her and that she'd be alone for the entire trip. But with the way the train was filling up Meg realized that was highly unlikely.

She then smiled despite herself as she looked at the woman next to her. She seemed like an agreeable sort, middle age at the most. She had gray hair of a pretty tone and was sensibly dressed in a long skirt, blouse, and a heavy sweater. She had a winter coat on her lap and on the floor near her feet was a rather large traveling bag from which she extracted a ball of yarn. She immediately began to knit. The conductor hoisted her suitcase onto the rack above and then took his leave.

"These trains never leave on time," the woman said, consulting her watch. "We were supposed to leave about fifteen minutes ago."

"I heard someone say the weather up north is worse," Meg commented.

"Oh, don't worry, dear," the woman said pleasantly. "Where are you headed?"

AN UNFORTUNATE COINCIDENCE

"Albany."

"Oh, how nice. Don't worry about the snow. The trains run in any weather!"

"Where are you going?"

"To Plattsburgh. Northern New York is beautiful in January."

"I've lived in New York City my whole life," Meg said, "the seasons are lovely." "New York isn't usually this snowy," the woman commented.

She paused and looked out the window, at the darkness of the underground of Grand Central Station.

"My name is Mrs. Irene Hanson," she said and smiled.

"Megan Cary," Meg said. "You look as if you've traveled by train before."

"Many times, dear," Mrs. Hanson smiled. "I never learned how to drive."

Meg smiled and hoped the conversation would end there. In the somewhat melancholy and reflective mood she was in, she did not feel like exchanging small talk with a stranger. But the woman seemed intent on continuing the conversation.

"Will you be visiting someone in Albany? Or do you live there?"

"Yes, I'm staying with my in-laws and it is for business," Meg said. Before Mrs. Hanson could ask what type of business, Meg added, "I'm a librarian. I'm attending the state library convention."

"How exciting," Mrs. Hanson commented.

"I work at the New York Public Library," Meg said, "I enjoy helping patrons." She thought that wasn't saying much. It seemed to bring an end to the conversation, for Mrs. Hanson smiled, leaned her head back and closed her eyes.

The train now jerked forward, doors were slammed shut and after a delay that seemed to Meg an eternity the locomotive drifted slowly out of the station. She also must have dozed until Mrs. Hanson roused her with another question.

"Is there a cafe car? I should wait till the conductor has checked my ticket." Meg told her she heard a ticket agent mention a cafe car several cars back.

"Do you have children?" Mrs. Hanson asked suddenly.

Meg looked at her curiously and was rather taken aback by her bluntness. Does she have children? What business was that of hers? Just what she needed; a busybody as a traveling companion, prying into things that were not her concern. But then Meg forced a short smile and knew Mrs. Hanson meant no harm by her question.

"My husband and I plan to have children eventually. He's a chemist and is busy with his work."

"I have just one son," Mrs. Hanson commented somewhat sadly as if she either regretted it or regretted not having another.

"Well, Adam had never really wanted…"

Meg stopped suddenly. People passing in the aisle, the train at full speed, the conductors checking tickets; everything you'd expect to see and hear on a train was going on this moment and here she was telling her personal life to a complete stranger.

Really Meg, she thought, you don't know this woman. Yet she seemed so kind with that benign face. Meg felt, somehow, that she could confide her innermost feelings to her, as if all her pent-up frustrations could be understood by the kindness of this total stranger.

"Is there something wrong, dear?" the woman asked sympathetically as though she could read her mind. Perhaps, Meg thought, she could. "Of course, it's none of my business," she continued.

Meg found herself nodding. "Adam, my husband, and I have our problems. He gets moody at times."

She looked out the window. In the glass she saw Adam going up the platform. Why hadn't he tried to get nearer to her? Of course, the mad rush of people. Was that the cause of her apprehension? The fact that she didn't kiss her husband good-bye. That deep down she felt she couldn't trust him? That he may be seeing someone else, especially in her absence. Meg awoke from her reverie to hear Mrs. Hanson ask her another question.

"Did he bring you to the station?"

Meg nodded. "He met me there because he was extremely busy at work. I just missed him in the crowd. We're successful in our own careers." She spoke as if she was trying to convince herself that what she was saying was true.

"Well, I wouldn't know about that, dear. I never had a career. Many years ago, a man caused me great pain. But I took care of it."

Meg asked, "Are you divorced?"

"Oh no, dear." Mrs. Hanson looked appalled at the thought. "He already had a wife, which I didn't know at the time. And was involved with another woman, too. Besides, people in small towns rarely divorced, too scandalous. So, I did away with him."

If Mrs. Hanson had been the type of woman who enjoyed causing an impact, perhaps one that an actress would give upon reading a dramatic line or an army general upon giving orders to attack, then she'd have been pleased at the expression on Meg's face.

"Don't look upset, dear," Mrs. Hanson said pleasantly. She continued knitting placidly.

"It was an accident. Well, at least it seemed like one."

"When did it happen?" Meg asked in disbelief.

"Six years ago," she answered and sighed.

Meg swallowed hard and went white. "I don't understand."

"I've never told it to anyone. Strange how I felt I could confide in you."

Yes, it was strange, Meg thought, because she felt the same way about her.

"He was on trial for murder?" Meg asked.

"Yes, I lived in Kinderhook then. My son's father was accused of killing his girlfriend's husband. He was quite a womanizer. He and the other man struggled with a gun; the other man was shot and died instantly. He said the man pulled on gun on *him* first. I believed he had the gun and they argued, struggled, and the gun went off. He had a great attorney, too."

"Wasn't there proof of his guilt?"

"Hardly any," Mrs. Hanson said rather scornfully. "With his acquittal, he was even more arrogant and wouldn't think of changing his lifestyle. He was drunk, and that morning was nothing new. I fixed some coffee and crushed a few tablets in it to make him sleepy. When we were getting ready to go to the lawyer's office, I told him to go to the garage to warm up the car. It was winter then and cold just like it is today. As we were about to take off, I told him I left my gloves in the kitchen. I waited a few minutes, then returned to close the garage door and went back inside the house."

"You mean he…"

Mrs. Hanson's needles clicked. "Yes, dear, carbon monoxide. It happens all the time in winter. People sit in their cars to get them all warmed up and then fall into a nice, deep sleep and never wake up again. When his attorney called, I pretended I just woke up and then went to the garage. When I went back to the phone, I cried and carried on for the lawyer." She paused. "I regretted doing it at first but when I think of how I suffered because of him, I have no regrets."

"And did the police suspect *you* of killing him?"

Mrs. Hanson shook her head and continued knitting. "No, dear, no breath of suspicion fell on me. It was deemed an accident and was soon forgotten."

Meg was dumbfounded. With her mouth open, she looked at Mrs. Hanson. She didn't know whether to believe the woman. How could she kill someone and get away with it? This sweet woman a killer? She fought a desire to laugh. Did she expect Meg to believe her?

"Please don't tell anyone," Mrs. Hanson whispered. "No one would believe it anyway." She put her knitting in the magazine holder. "But you know, it really is quite easy to kill someone," she added upon reflection. She looked around and then at Meg. "I'm dying for a cup of coffee and a sandwich. Care to join me?"

"No, thank you," Meg said. She watched as Mrs. Hanson walked down the aisle and disappeared into the next car.

She looked out the window, saw the Hudson River covered in snow and wondered where they were. They could not be too far from Poughkeepsie. She would have to contend with this excitable woman for just two more hours. She settled more comfortably in her seat. She decided to put this woman with the overactive imagination out of her mind and she soon fell asleep.

Meg woke up, rather startled. As she stretched, she heard someone say they were close to Poughkeepsie. She looked around. Many people got off at the previous stop. It seemed as if other passengers were either awakened or aroused by people walking up and down the aisle. Meg noticed her traveling companion returned and was also sleeping.

A cold-blooded killer? Meg laughed to herself. Silly woman, that's all she could do to amuse herself, fabricating such crazy stories! But suppose she's telling the truth? Meg had a sudden urge to tell a conductor about Mrs. Hanson's story. But she realized how stupid that would look. He most likely would think *she* was the unbalanced one and not Mrs. Hanson. Meg decided to forget this woman's story of murder. Why think about it anyway? After she'd get off in Albany, she'd never see the woman again, so what difference did it make?

Meg glanced at her watch, saw it was close to six o'clock. She decided to go to the cafe car. Before leaving, she took a book from her suitcase. She glanced at the cover, *The Great Gatsby* by F. Scott Fitzgerald. Although Meg read it upon its release three years ago, she wanted to read it again. It was a title most circulated at the library.

She finally reached the cafe car and saw that it was almost empty. She bought a sandwich and coffee and then sat at a table, looking out the window at the Hudson River. She thought she was alone until she noticed a man at the last table, huddled in the corner, drinking coffee, and reading a newspaper. She could not see his face but when he folded the paper and placed it on the table, she thought she knew him from somewhere. As she looked at him again, she realized she did not know him but, in a way, rather wished she did. The man was about her age, give or take a year and rather dark. He was handsome in an almost theatrical manner. Black hair and eyes, broad shoulders with an overall air of composure and strength. Did she know him from somewhere? He got up as if to leave but instead approached Meg and asked to join her.

"Seems like we're the only ones here," he commented. "I just had lunch myself. Cold weather like this certainly increases my appetite."

Meg commented that it certainly was cold and most likely colder up north. She looked out the window and saw houses and farms in the distance, all snow covered, with fireplaces emitting smoke. She thought of the people inside trying to stay warm. She shivered a little.

"Cold?" the man asked her.

"Somewhat, I guess."

"My name's Ben, by the way," he said. "Ben Faraday."

Meg introduced herself and wondered if he told her his name because he really wanted to or because he saw her shiver, as if telling her his name would be of some comfort. Strangely Meg found that it was. After listening to Mrs. Hanson's story of murder and her apprehension about Adam, she found an unusual solace in a stranger.

"Are you going to Montreal?" he asked her.

"No, to Albany."

"That's where I'm going. I live in Manhattan." Ben smiled, showing a perfect set of white teeth. In fact, everything about this handsome man seemed to be perfect, Meg thought. He seemed so carefree and oh, so worldly! In fact, he was the opposite of Adam. Meg did not often become enthralled with strangers but in a short time found herself doing just that with this unknown man. She put *The Great Gatsby* aside and soon enough, Ben Faraday and Meg were chatting amicably, having a casual conversation between strangers on a train. He told her about his work as an accountant, his life in Manhattan, his apartment on 96th Street, going on and on about this and that. Meg soon found herself entranced, oblivious to everything around her. He continued talking about his career, his travels and all the places he visited. Meg thought she could listen to him talk all day. He lit a cigarette and asked Meg about her plans in Albany. She told him she was attending the state library convention for the weekend and staying at her mother-in-law's house, not far from the state library.

"Although my husband didn't like my going to Albany in this weather."

Meg then told Ben about her husband's career as a chemist.

"You both have your own careers. Must be exciting."

"Oh yes. Quite." Meg had an inexplicable impulse to tell him about her husband Adam. But why should she? Besides, the last time she opened up to someone (and Meg was *not* the type to confide in strangers) was Mrs. Hanson and in return she heard a story of murder! She laughed slightly at the remembrance which made Ben look at her and smile. He asked what was so amusing.

Meg glanced around. In a low voice she said, "A woman sitting next to me told me she killed a man six years ago! Isn't that the most ridiculous thing you've ever heard?" She laughed slightly but then noticed the startled expression on Ben's face.

"I've heard worse stories," he said, not finding it amusing. "People do commit murder, you know." He then added, "I'm sure you read about Ruth Snyder who killed her husband in Queens? She was executed just yesterday."

Meg was surprised. "Well, let's not talk about murder," she said and wondered where this conversation was going. "And yes, I did read about Ruth Snyder."

Obviously, Ben Faraday was not the type to discuss depressing subjects but preferred to talk about upbeat, positive things in keeping with his personality. How nice to be that way, Meg thought; ignore depressing topics and stick to the happy ones. Now if only her husband could be that way.

The attendant made a fresh pot of coffee and rattled cups and saucers. Sleet tapped lightly on the windows. The clouds were extremely low and thick and threatened more snow and sleet as the train progressed northward.

"I'm staying at the Ten Eyck Hotel," Ben said. "It isn't far from Union Station." He looked at his watch. "We should be in Albany soon. Why don't you stop at the hotel on your way to the state library? I'll meet you at the entrance."

AN UNFORTUNATE COINCIDENCE

Meg looked at her watch. She did not realize she had spent so much time talking with him. She hesitated, but then agreed to meet Ben at the Ten Eyck Hotel entrance. Meg then left the cafe car. She wanted to return to her seat, to say good-bye to Mrs. Hanson.

So, she was a busybody with a vivid imagination, but she *was* friendly and very understanding. Meg would probably never see her again. Oh well, the woman was just a passing acquaintance, one of many throughout life. Meg walked up the aisle and saw a head leaning toward her own seat. She must still be sleeping.

"The cafe is still open," Meg said pleasantly once she reached the seat.

"*I* beg your pardon?" the woman, a stranger, said harshly.

"Where's the woman that was sitting here?" Meg stammered as she looked at the woman sitting in Mrs. Hanson's seat. She held onto the back of another seat for support as though she would faint. "She had gray hair and...her name was Mrs. Hanson!"

"I'm *not* Mrs. Hanson," the older woman said even firmer than before. "Are you talking about someone else?"

Meg stopped a conductor and asked if he had seen the woman who was sitting next to her when they boarded at Grand Central. Fortunately for Meg, it was the same conductor who found the seat for Mrs. Hanson.

"Oh her," he said, "I think she got off in Poughkeepsie but I'm not sure."

"Poughkeepsie?" Meg said incredulously. "She told me Plattsburgh!"

"I don't know," he said in the tone of one who couldn't be bothered with other people's business. "But if you're getting off in Albany, we'll be there soon," he added and then continued down the aisle.

Meg stared after him and then reluctantly sat down. She glanced at the older woman next to her, who sat smug and stern and obviously didn't want to be bothered. In a way, Meg missed Mrs. Hanson. She wondered what could have happened to her.

The train arrived at Union Station in Albany at last. Meg got up rather quickly, reached for her suitcase on the overhead rack and moved down the aisle toward the exit. As she got up, the older woman next to her didn't even notice. She followed the crowd into the station. It seemed forever as she made her way up the ramp, through the busy station. She first stopped at a kiosk to buy the local paper.

She came out of Union Station onto Broadway and turned left toward State Street. At the corner of State and Broadway, she turned right up State Street hill to the intersection of State and South Pearl Street. There, before her stood the imposing Ten Eyck Hotel. She crossed the busy intersection and stood at the hotel entrance. By good chance she looked up and saw Ben Faraday standing near the front entrance, smoking.

"Is your mother-in-law's place far from here?" he asked as she came up to him. "I just checked in and came out here, to wait for you."

Meg smiled. "It's just on Willett Street. But in this weather and with my suitcase, it'll be better to take a cab. I'm going to the state library first." There was an awkward silence until Meg finally broke it.

"I can meet you for coffee," she said. "Later tonight, before I go to my in-laws." Ben smiled. "That'd be great! Why don't we meet here in the lobby and then get something to eat? You can call me and if I'm not in leave a message."

AN UNFORTUNATE COINCIDENCE

Meg said she would do that and stepped into an awaiting taxi. She told the driver to take her to the state library, waved goodbye to Ben and settled back in the cab. She sighed rather contentedly. She wondered why Ben Faraday walked to the hotel on his own instead of offering to walk together. But then, that was foolish. They had just met, of course and she didn't know him. Her thoughts then flew to her husband Adam. What would Adam think of her meeting a man for coffee? But on the other hand, why should she care what he thinks? Nothing wrong with meeting Ben Faraday at the hotel in a few hours for coffee. Besides, her in-laws would not be expecting her yet and even if Iris was at the conference, she could make an excuse about meeting colleagues at the Ten Eyck Hotel. She closed her eyes and wondered about the man she just met.

Then her thoughts quickly returned to her husband Adam. The last time she and Adam visited his mother was for Christmas, but that was over a year now. They did not even visit for Christmas just a few weeks ago. Adam vehemently refused to travel to Albany to see his mother. Adam, alone in New York City. She and Adam had few intimate friends. Adam was more introverted and did not care to socialize. As she sat in the taxi on the way to the state library, Meg realized her thoughts had never been so confused and chaotic. Oddly enough, she found herself thinking not only of Adam and Ben Faraday but the woman she met on the train. What was her name again? It was Mrs. Hanson, of course. What a bizarre story! And even stranger for her to get off the train early. Now why would she do that? One moment she was on the train and the next she was off. Did she become ill? Maybe she didn't really get off the train? Perhaps she told that to the conductor and entered another car. But that doesn't make sense! Maybe Mrs. Hanson felt frightened. Perhaps she recognized someone and panicked. Meg then remembered the sense of unity she felt with

Mrs. Hanson. She had never confided in a stranger before. Could she tell Meg was unhappy?

The taxi pulled up in front of the state education building. Meg paid the driver, collected her small suitcase and then stared up at the marble New York State Education Building which housed the state library.

As she climbed the stairs and passed through the marble pillars, a strange uneasiness overcame her, as though she feared she would need all her strength to face whatever lay ahead.

"Hi there, Meg," Ben Faraday said as he got off the elevator in the hotel lobby. He walked toward her, smiled, and seemed glad to see her. "Have you eaten yet?"

It was close to seven-thirty. Meg had called the Ten Eyck Hotel and left word for Ben that she would meet him in the lobby at that time. She walked from the state library as the weather began to clear.

Meg smiled in return and said the first session of the state library convention had gone well. She wasn't due back till tomorrow morning, so she was glad to have dinner with him. They walked over to the hotel restaurant. The hostess showed them to a table and within seconds a waiter arrived with two menus. After eating they relaxed with coffee.

"I'm tired," Meg said, sipping the hot liquid. "I'm going to collapse any minute."

"Was it a long conference this evening?" Ben asked, lighting a cigarette.

"No, not really, just the opening plenary. People I hadn't seen for quite some time. It was good to catch up with them. My sister-in-law, Iris, was there but I didn't have the chance to talk much with her." She paused. "I told her I was meeting colleagues at the Ten Eyck Hotel. I'd be at the house later." She paused again and looked at the handsome young man sitting across from her. "What did you do today?"

"Nothing really," Ben said as he also sipped his coffee. "It's still quite cold."

"I noticed the snow stopped about an hour ago or so."

"Yes, it did. How long is your library conference?"

"Three days." Meg then added, "I leave Monday. You had business to attend?"

"It finished early," Ben said as he again put the coffee cup to his lips. He fidgeted with his napkin and lit another cigarette. Meg decided to be blunt and ask him if something was wrong.

"No, just have a lot on my mind," was his laconic reply. He added nothing more and then said, "So you're leaving on Monday?"

"Yes, in the morning. What about you?"

"I'm not sure yet. I might do some sight-seeing in Albany. It's a nice city."

Meg replied it was a lovely city. She then thought of her husband again. Adam, alone in Manhattan. In her mind, Meg made a note to call him this evening. She could feel her eyelids heavy and stifled a yawn.

"I'm not looking forward to going home," she admitted, which surprised her. "I mean, I do miss my husband Adam. We've had problems, like other couples."

Ben nodded. "Well, things can happen to the best of marriages, I suppose."

She wanted to terminate this conversation. After all, she didn't know Ben Faraday, although he still seemed pleasant enough. "I'm only tired from the train ride, I guess." She paused uncertainly and fumbled in her purse for a much-needed cigarette.

"Well, why don't we call it a night?" Ben suggested.

Meg finished her coffee and she and Ben left the restaurant. The lobby was crowded with people checking in. Meg left Ben's side and sat in a lobby chair, facing several large windows. She had her small suitcase by her side, from which she extracted a pack of cigarettes.

"Things seem busy tonight," he said and sat across from her.

The streets in downtown were busy with cars and the city trolley. As tired as she was, Meg did not feel like going to her in-laws. But then she had no other place to go, unless she stayed here at the hotel, which she told herself was foolish. And besides, her in-laws were expecting her. She found herself thinking a great many chaotic thoughts. Adam, her mother-in-law, the woman on the train. And now the handsome young man sitting opposite her. She wondered; was Ben Faraday married? Was he really on business in Albany? Feeling rather uneasy, she decided to end her casual acquaintance with this man.

"You have a lot on your mind," Ben commented.

It was at this moment that Meg rose from her chair and was staring at something beyond and behind Ben. She clapped her left hand over her mouth. Her eyes were wide opened beneath their raised brows.

"What is it?" Ben asked as he saw the horrified expression on her face.

"Outside!" Meg gasped, hardly getting the word out. She quickly went to the front doors, Ben at her heels.

Once outside, she saw more clearly what she had seen from the lobby. A middle-aged woman was walking down the street, although it seemed she was not actually walking but being *forced* to walk; two policemen were on each side of her. A man in a trench coat was behind them. Ben came up to Meg's side.

"Mrs. Hanson!" Meg shouted causing several heads to turn. But not the head of the woman whose attention she was trying to get.

Mrs. Hanson, the policemen and the man in the coat were far down the street now; swallowed up in the crowd. Meg caught a glimpse of them getting into a police car and drive off. Outside in the cold Meg stood without a jacket oblivious to the weather. Ben was about to suggest they return inside when she turned to him.

"That woman!" she stammered. "She was supposed to have killed a man!"

She looked at Ben and then remembered his reaction when she told him about Mrs. Hanson. He did not laugh, and he had not found it amusing. Something clicked. She spoke hoarsely, *"Do you know that woman?"*

Ben nodded. "Yes, Meg, I do know her. She's the reason I'm here in Albany."

She looked into his eyes, not believing what she was hearing. "But I don't understand!" she said in confusion. "She was going to Plattsburgh. When I got back from the cafe car, she was gone." She shivered. "You never saw her, did you? She was a total stranger!"

"She isn't a stranger," Ben said grimly. "She's my mother."

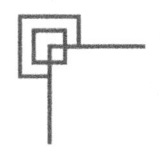

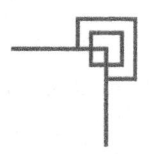

CHAPTER TWO

Shaking fresh snow from his coat, Adam Cary entered the elevator of the mid-town Manhattan building where he worked and told the operator he wanted the ninth floor. A few colleagues, who were also in the elevator, commented on the snowstorm but Adam paid them little attention. He went to a cafeteria for lunch instead of eating in the restaurant on the ground floor. He was in a bad mood already and did not in the least feel like making small talk with colleagues whom he truthfully found to be wearisome and dull.

Before reaching his floor, Adam had to wait while others got off on lower floors. He glanced at his watch, as he had done consistently through his lunch hour, because he planned to return to his laboratory early to finish an experiment. A new project that involved a team effort, something Adam despised, was being given to him for the afternoon.

The elevator reached the ninth floor. As though making an escape he eagerly walked down the hall and entered his laboratory, closing the door with firmness. If he could lock it and keep away from people, he would have preferred that, too. He glanced again at his watch, for he was expecting another chemist at any minute.

As he had little to do until then, Adam paced the floor in his lab. All his life, whenever he wanted anything, Adam had concentrated intently on his goal and proceeded toward it until his purpose was accomplished. If he were working on the project alone, as he preferred, it would already have been completed.

Adam moved over to the long counter in the large laboratory and carefully lifted the test tube from the pan of boiling water, then returned it to the test tube rack. He followed this procedure through various times until a knock came and his assistant, John Evans, entered. He put several beakers on the counter. Adam thanked him and placed them near his microscope.

"You're rather late," Adam said curtly.

"Things were hectic at the other lab." John, a recent graduate of Columbia University, was of medium height, with black hair and large brown eyes. Frequently he annoyed Adam who found his youth and eagerness irritating. "Didn't your wife take a trip today?" he added further infuriating Adam.

Adam grimaced and reluctantly answered. "Yes, I met her at the train station," he explained. *As if it is any of your business.* "She's going to Albany for a few days," he added and then regretted it.

"In this weather? For what?"

"A convention."

"Don't you know what it's about?"

Adam glared at him. "It's about her library work. That's all for now, John."

The door closed and Adam Cary heaved a sigh of relief, glad that he was alone. At twenty-eight, Adam was quite successful in his career. Handsome in a rough sort of way, he could be charming and polite when he wanted. Nearly everyone considered Adam Cary a difficult and strange person, a Jekyll and Hyde personality, with his pleasantness and then total rudeness.

AN UNFORTUNATE COINCIDENCE

He was a research chemist with Pfizer in New York City. He landed the job upon graduation and in no less than two years received numerous promotions. Adam ensured that nothing or no one would come in the way of his career. This included his wife, Meg, who had her own ideas as to what entailed a marriage.

He and Meg were graduate students at NYU when they met. Meg, completing a master's degree in Library Science was introduced to him by his sister, Iris, who was in the same program. Within six months he and Meg were engaged and married two months later. He sometimes wondered why he settled for Meg when he could have had numerous women. He thoughts flew to just ten years ago, when he came down with the flu and had to stay in isolation at his mother's house. That was the year of the flu pandemic and somehow, after graduating high school, he caught the virus and although he recovered it took its toll. It embittered him and he was determined to leave Albany and his mother's house and never to live there again.

Adam momentarily stopped his work and looked out at the snow and sleet that battered the windows. His mind flew to Meg, going to Albany for a conference. The weather would be worse in Albany. His bossy mother, with whom he barely got along, was there. And then he thought of his sister Iris, her husband and his aunt and uncle who all lived in the same house. His mother kept a hodgepodge of people in her house, which included her housekeeper and driver. Another knock came and John entered once again.

"They need you at lab three for a while."

Adam curtly told John that he was extremely busy and would get to lab three as soon as possible. John cast him a dubious look and then left, reminding Adam of the importance of this new project. For a moment Adam reveled in the fact that he was successful, financially well-off, enjoyed excellent health and to outward appearances, had a great life. After all, appearances meant everything.

In less than fifteen minutes, Adam Cary swiftly left the laboratory on his way to lab three and the project there awaiting him.

In the living room of the brownstone house on Washington Park in Albany, Helen Cary sat in an armchair near her fireplace. Ignoring the sleet that battered the windows overlooking Willet Street, she was concentrating on the book she was reading. She glanced at her watch as she was expecting her daughter-in-law to arrive sometime this evening.

Washington Park was once a refined place for families to enjoy a picnic. Nowadays, with young people doing all types of things, it changed. Dance marathons, the Charleston, girls smoking and acting luridly, what else would this generation come up with to amuse themselves? Whatever happened to morals and values, she wondered. And the flappers, as they called themselves, they had all kinds of gaudy ideas in their heads. Helen's thoughts then turned to her daughter-in-law with distaste and even contempt. She looked away from the windows and stared into the crackling fire. Not that she considered herself old, of course. A young fifty and still strong, she was impeccable in her dress and lifestyle.

Helen was one of two children born into a prominent Albany family. Her older sister, Elsie, took the traditional route of marrying after college. After graduating with high honors in political science, Helen intended on a career with the state legislature. It was there that she found her true vocation. And, the first of her two husbands.

Sure enough Arthur Hamilton, an influential politician, encountered young Helen at the state capital. They went to the best restaurants in Albany. It didn't matter that there was a forty-five-year age gap between them (she a mere twenty-five to his seventy) and in a matter of months Helen became engaged.

While her marriage was not a success, she soon found a new friend in Walter Cary, a young executive. While in the State Capital, he literally "ran into" Helen. She was walking hurriedly in one direction and he in the other and upon turning the corner, they collided into each other. Walter Cary straightened up from retrieving his papers. He looked into the eyes of the most beautiful girl he'd ever seen. Helen was tall and slender with a wide forehead and dark brown eyes. She had dignity and composure in her pretty face and a smile that was sincere and alluring. Helen smiled and blushed.

"Sorry," he said. He hurried off, leaving Helen to stare after him. Three days later, Helen saw him in the Capital again and this time made a point to "run into him." He recognized her at once and after exchanging small talk asked her to have lunch with him. Soon she was having lunch and even dinner with Walter Cary and quite often, too, enjoying his company and spending as much time with him as possible.

"What will your husband say if he finds out?" Walter Cary said one sunny afternoon while they sat on a bench in front of the State Capital. "It's rather risky to be seen like this," he added. "I mean, people do talk, you know."

"I don't care what he or anyone else says," Helen retorted.

"What about a divorce?"

"He'd cut me out of his will. Why do you think I married him in the first place?"

Arthur soon fell ill and rather than prolonging his illness, he hung himself in the basement of their home. Helen and Walter were married six months later. She sold the house in Arbor Hill that she and Arthur lived in and then she and Walter bought a handsome brownstone on

Willett Street, the most fashionable address in Albany. It had five floors with tall windows overlooking Washington Park. Helen soon became a mother of two children, Adam, and Iris. It seemed they were the model of family life and respectability in Albany society. Helen soon quit her job at the assembly to devote herself to raising her children while Walter's business prospered beyond his expectations.

Helen Cary's married life to Walter was not everything she expected. In less than five years, she discovered her husband's infidelity. Helen's escape from her once fulfilling but now love-less marriage came in the form of an accident.

Helen told people her husband was involved in a car accident while on business and was instantly killed. She never knew all the details. She was relaxing at home one evening with the children when the call came from the police. Her husband was intoxicated and involved in a car mishap. Helen wasn't surprised; it was almost as though she expected it. After straightening the legal technicalities, she had his body returned to Albany where he was buried in a traditional service. And fortunately, few people asked questions.

Now at fifty, Helen's once jovial face was marred with a few wrinkles, perhaps due more to bitterness. Her lovely brown hair was now mixed with gray, drawn back, and fastened at her nape in a heavy knot. The lines at the corners of her eyes were heavy, even dark, adding to the overall somber appearance on her face.

Her older sister Elsie Thompson and her brother-in-law, Richard, moved into her house ten years ago. During this period, she and her sister had gotten closer. Even Richard was a source of comfort. He was reliable if not cantankerous at times, but then, Helen thought, so was she. She realized Elsie and Richard were lonesome. Childless, they also needed company. They had their own rooms on the fourth floor of the large house and pretty much kept to themselves. The arrangement worked well for Helen. She began to doze when a knock came on the living room door.

It was Ida Munson, Helen's personal maid. Ida was a tall, gaunt woman in her mid-forties who always had a weary, tired expression on her lined face as if she had just woken up from a deep sleep. She had messy gray hair, a lop-sided mouth, and large, beady eyes. She had a perpetually nervous manner and, perhaps because of it, had the irritating habit of stumbling into objects and knocking them over. As she entered the living room, her left foot caught the corner of a coffee table on which reposed a large pile of magazines. The jolt caused the magazines to cascade onto the floor, one after another.

"Now look what you've done," Helen snapped. "Can't you be more careful?"

"Yes, Mrs. Cary," Ida replied and stooped to retrieve the magazines.

Ida Munson served as personal maid to several prominent women in Albany, Boston and Philadelphia. She was from Kinderhook, where she lived with her husband, until he died. She then returned to Albany several years ago. As with most maids, Ida had irritating habits, but Helen overlooked them. She was a meticulous housekeeper and an excellent cook.

"Will you need me further this evening?" Ida Munson repeated.

"What time is it?" Helen asked.

"Almost eight."

"I didn't realize it was so late. Have you seen my sister and brother-in-law?"

"I believe they've gone to bed."

"My daughter-in-law is supposed to arrive today," Helen said clearly irritated. "You have the guest room ready, don't you?"

"Yes, Mrs. Cary."

"Have you seen Iris and my son-in-law? I spoke with her earlier after she returned from the library conference."

"Just briefly. They're in their room and don't wish to be disturbed."

Helen nodded. "Well, goodnight, Ida."

Ida left the living room and climbed the five flights of stairs to the fifth floor. Helen's personal maids always had the fifth floor of the large house to themselves. It was easier for Ida to take the back stairs down to the kitchen in the morning to prepare breakfast so not to awaken the family.

On an impulse, Helen decided to call Adam in New York City. She knew he wouldn't be coming with Meg to the library conference but still it'd be nice to see what he was doing, alone in Manhattan. She picked up the receiver, gave the number to the operator and then waited for the call to go through.

After ten rings, Helen hung up. She wondered where her son could be at eight o'clock on such a cold evening. She then placed a call to his lab and left a message for him to return her call. What kind of a wife would leave her husband alone to attend some ridiculous convention? A married woman should take care of her husband's home. She's ruining Adam, that's what she's doing. She'll ask for a divorce and disgrace this family. I'll get rid of her if it's the last thing I do.

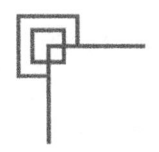

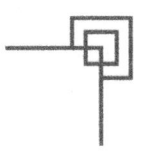

CHAPTER THREE

Was this a nightmare? A nightmare that turned your stomach into knots, until you felt you could no longer breath. A living nightmare, Meg thought.

After Ben disclosed his relation to the woman on the train, Meg felt confused. How could Mrs. Hanson be his mother? She thought of the conversation she had with Ben on the train and how he reacted to hearing Mrs. Hanson's story. She should have seen that. She should have realized there *was* something there, but how could she, really.

First, she read in *The New York Times* the article about Ruth Snyder who killed her husband and now Mrs. Hanson who claimed she killed her lover. Even though she was tired, she did not in the least feel like going to her in-laws. Not yet, anyway. She turned to face Ben again. Light snow was falling now, and it remained bitterly cold.

They reentered the hotel. Meg made a call from a phone booth. She spoke to Ida Munson, her mother-in-law's maid, to let her know that she was with colleagues at the Ten Eyck Hotel and would arrive shortly. Before Ida could inquire further, Meg ended the call and left the phone booth. She joined Ben in the lobby.

"I noticed a diner around the corner," Ben said. They saw the hotel restaurant was now closed. "Why don't we go there for coffee?"

Meg gathered her small suitcase, bundled her winter coat tighter and walked out onto the sidewalk.

Snow blew in her face and she pulled her scarf up around her ears and her hat lower on her head. They crossed onto South Pearl until they came to an all-night diner. Meg's thoughts suddenly flew to Adam, who was alone in New York. And what he was doing and where he was at that very moment. Ben Faraday, the stranger on the train and Mrs. Hanson, who turned out to be his mother. Ruth Snyder, the woman who killed her husband and was executed just yesterday. It was too much for Meg to comprehend. With the library conference tomorrow, she must keep focused on her work. As tired as she was, the walk was doing her good, despite the bitter cold.

A hostess left two menus for them. A waitress approached, and Meg commented that she was not too hungry but would have coffee and a muffin. Ben ordered coffee and French fries. While they waited, Meg's hands and feet were like ice. She looked outside and saw that the snow was now mixed with sleet. It suddenly started to come down even harder and the few pedestrians out were practically bumping into each other as they kept their heads down. Ben took his coat and Meg's coat and hung them on the hanger next to their booth.

Meg glanced around the restaurant, stalling, to find something to say to Ben. She pulled off her gloves and hat. She cupped her frozen fingers together to try to bring back the blood.

The waitress soon returned with their orders. As Meg lit a cigarette and added sugar to her coffee, Ben lit his own cigarette, looked at her ruefully and began to speak. His mother, whose real name was Janet Faraday, killed his father in Kinderhook, where she was living at the time. She had several nervous breakdowns already and was pushed to the limit by what his father had done.

Meg interrupted him. "Your mother told me your father killed a man."

Ben nodded. "He was a compulsive liar. He killed his girlfriend's husband. There was a struggle and the gun went off. But my mother believes he killed him deliberately!"

"How did your mother...?"

"She doped him up and with plenty of booze, he fell asleep at the wheel after starting the car. My mother closed the garage door and waited for him to die."

"Wasn't there an investigation?"

"The police concluded he was drunk and started the car without opening the garage door first. My mother used gloves, so no fingerprints were found. Nobody ever blamed her for what happened."

Slowly Meg understood. Poor Ben. At that moment she wanted to put her hand over his, but Ben suddenly sat up and spoke again.

"After tolerating his mental and physical abuse, it affected my mother in such a way that she saw no way out but to kill him. She told me he never planned on staying with her." He paused. "My mother's doctor treated her for nervous tension and for six years she's lived with her guilt. The other woman from Kinderhook had a child with him, too. So, you can see the kind of man my father was; a womanizer and a cheater."

"How do you know she did it?"

"She told me," Ben said simply. "I was a student at Union College. She found a job as a maid to a large family. That lasted for a few years. I hated her and felt sorry for her at the same time. She'd tell them her name was Mrs. Hanson, like she did with you."

With startled eyes, Meg looked at Ben. "Why was she on the train?"

"I told her to come with me to Albany for a vacation of sorts. We were living in the city. She stayed with me after living on her own for several years. She agreed but I bought her a separate ticket. She insisted on traveling by herself. Her doctor's here in Albany, where he will evaluate her, until she's admitted to the psychiatric center."

"But I don't understand about tonight," Meg stammered.

Ben's face was expressionless. "I told her to meet me in the Ten Eyck lobby for dinner. The doctor arrived about eight o'clock with a policeman. It was cruel, I suppose, when the policeman grabbed her, and they led her down the street. She wouldn't have gone voluntarily. I don't think I have to tell you the rest, you saw it all."

Meg knocked ash from her cigarette. "You told them the truth about your mother?"

"I told them everything."

"Will they prosecute her?"

"I doubt it. They do know why she killed my father. She'll be confined to this institution for a long time."

"I remember how she opened up to me on the train," Meg said. "Did she usually tell strangers about her past?"

Ben wiped his mouth with a napkin. "No, she never did. I panicked when you told me about it. Maybe she believed she could talk to you."

"I felt the same toward her," Meg said ruefully almost as if Mrs. Hanson or Janet Faraday was an old friend. "She was sympathetic when I told her of the problems I've had with my husband."

"I thought I had lost her on the train," Ben continued. "She was extremely paranoid. She thought a man recognized her. She told a conductor she was getting off in Poughkeepsie and then ran to find me. She didn't know I planned to have a doctor evaluate her here. That's why I didn't, or couldn't, walk with you to the hotel. I met her in the lobby of Union Station and together we walked to the hotel. Tomorrow I have to call the doctor to see how she's doing."

Meg finished her coffee and crushed her cigarette. She gathered her coat, hat, and scarf. "It's late, Ben," she said. "I'm going to my in-laws. They're expecting me."

"Are you all right, Meg?" he asked soberly, his eyes looking at her steadily.

"Just tired," she said. "It's been a long day."

Ben paused uncertainly. "I can walk you to their house."

"No," she told him, "it isn't far from here." Ben insisted on paying but Meg offered her half and after giving the money to the hostess, they walked out only to find it still snowing. Meg looked for a taxi and spotted one coming down South Pearl Street. She called for it, the driver braked and then she and Ben crossed the street at the light.

Meg held out her hand. They looked at each other. The snow and sleet stung their faces, but neither was mindful of the weather. There was nothing more that could be said by either of them. She withdrew her hand rather quickly.

"I'll call the hotel tomorrow," she told him. "If you're not in I'll leave a message. I'd like to see you again, Ben. I hope things work out with your mother."

Without waiting for him to answer, she settled in the back seat of the cab and waved goodbye to him. She glanced in the right-hand side mirror and saw Ben still standing on the sidewalk staring after her as the taxi sped off toward Willett Street.

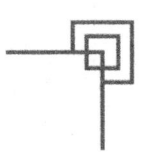

CHAPTER FOUR

The next morning dawned clear but chilly. The precipitation that had plagued the area for several days finally moved away, but not without leaving a havoc of snow and ice. Power lines were down, and motorists and pedestrians had to contend with slick roads and snowy sidewalks.

Iris Cary Bauer was preparing to start her day earlier than usual. Though it was Saturday, she wanted to get to the state library to finish some work and then attend the afternoon session of the state library conference. She figured her sister-in-law arrived late last night and assumed Meg was still sleeping.

She descended the grand staircase slowly, entered the kitchen and rather sleepily sat at the kitchen table. She asked Ida to prepare oatmeal and coffee for her. She just finished her first cup when her husband Bruce entered from the back stairway, sleep still in his eyes.

"I can smell Ida's coffee from upstairs," he said with a smile.

Ida Munson blushed. "I've kept it warm for you!" She quickly took Bruce's favorite mug and filled it with the steaming liquid.

"Where's Mother?" Iris asked, glancing at the newspaper on the kitchen table.

"She hasn't come down yet," Ida explained with concern. "Mr. and Mrs. Thompson left for their usual morning walk, but Megan hasn't gotten up either. She arrived last night after everyone had gone to bed."

"I didn't hear her," Iris said, unfolding the paper. "Did you see her?"

Ida nodded. "I let her in. She met colleagues at the Ten Eyck Hotel afterwards."

"Aunt Elsie and Uncle Richard are foolish to walk in this weather," Iris said.

Ida agreed that it was strange that Elsie and Richard would walk on such a cold morning. Even Helen enjoyed taking winter walks by herself on cold mornings. Ida thought they found the air invigorating.

Bruce glanced out the window. "It stopped snowing," he remarked. He ate a forkful of eggs and took the sections of the paper his wife discarded.

Bruce Bauer was twenty-nine years old, quite tall, and broad-shouldered with brown hair and green eyes. He was an English teacher at Albany Academy and seemed content at his job, although internally he despised the education system and had little patience with uncooperative children and their parents.

"What time does the library conference end today?" he asked Iris.

"About five, I think," Iris answered. "I'm leaving early to finish work at my desk. Then I'll head over to the conference. I hope to see Meg there." She hesitated and looked toward the front hallway. "She hasn't gotten up yet, Ida?"

Ida turned from the sink. "I'll knock on her door."

Iris shook her head. "She's probably tired from the train and the conference." She stood and left the kitchen, stopping to glance at herself in the hallway mirror. Iris was an efficient young woman of twenty-six, who took pride in her professional appearance. She had brown hair and deep blue eyes and dressed rather conservatively. She was active in the suffragette movement in Albany and her library career, too. She went upstairs to dress.

She finished brushing her hair, grabbed her fur coat and headed for the stairs. Before descending, she hesitated. Impulsively she went to her mother's room on the next floor. She knocked softly, pushed the door open slowly and then heard a voice from the pillows.

"What is it, Iris?" Helen Cary said curtly. "I haven't gotten up yet."

Well, good morning to you, too. "I'm leaving for the library," she said, entering the room. "I'll be back later today."

"Is Megan here?" Helen asked, sitting up in bed.

"Ida said she got here late last night," Iris explained. "She's still sleeping in the guest room."

"I didn't hear her come in." Helen paused. She looked at her daughter. Iris could tell something was wrong. She asked outright what it was.

"You're usually up by now, Mother. Something wrong?"

Helen snorted. "I called your brother last night and he wasn't in. I tried several times and couldn't reach him! I left a message at his lab to call me. Where in the world would Adam be on such a bitterly cold night?"

Iris tolerated her mother's frustrated voice. "He does work late at the lab." "Sometimes he doesn't answer the phone," Helen said irritably.

"Especially when Meg isn't there," Iris murmured.

"What was that, Iris? You said something about Megan?" "Maybe Meg's absence will do them good."

I'll bet, Helen thought acidly, thinking of all the men her daughter-in-law encountered in her ridiculous library work. Of course her daughter Iris was a librarian too but that was fine, in Helen's eyes. She was silent for so long that Iris thought her mother had fallen asleep as she put her head back on the pillows.

"We haven't seen Adam in over a year!"

"He hates coming here, you know."

"After I speak to Adam and then Meg, I'll find out if they can visit together, maybe next weekend."

Helen then cleared her throat; told her daughter she would get up soon and dismissed her. Iris kissed her mother goodbye, and Helen looked up and saw Ida in the doorway.

"Do you need anything today, Mrs. Cary?"

"Yes, tell Harmon to bring the car around. I want to do my shopping." "It's quite cold out, Mrs. Cary."

"I don't care, Ida. I've been in all week."

"I'll speak to Harmon, Mrs. Cary."

Helen reached for her robe, stepped into her slippers, and climbed down the stairs and entered the kitchen. She asked Ida for coffee and a muffin to be served in the dining room, where she usually took breakfast. She noticed the morning paper on the kitchen table and took it with her to the dining room.

Ida deposited a tray on which reposed a steaming cup of coffee, a jug of cream, sugar, and a toasted corn muffin. "Will there be anything else?"

Rather irritably Helen said, "Has Megan gotten up yet, Ida?" As though on cue both women heard movement upstairs and someone descending the stairs.

"Tell Megan I'd like her to have breakfast with me," Helen told Ida.

Helen took a sip of coffee. She waited for her daughter-in-law to enter the dining room. She would take care of this irritating young woman her son was foolish enough to marry. For good.

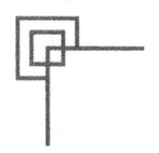

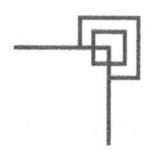

CHAPTER FIVE

"Good morning, Megan," Helen said. "What can Ida bring you for breakfast?" Meg sat across from her mother-in-law. "Coffee. And toast, please." Soon Ida appeared. "Coffee and toast for Megan," Helen told her.

Ida immediately flew to the kitchen and retuned within moments with a tray.

"Are you returning to the state library today?" Helen asked and sipped her coffee. "I'm glad you're here, Meg. We see so little of you." She added, "And Adam."

"Yes, I need to leave soon," Meg said cautiously, ignoring the last comment.

"Iris left for the conference. I'm sure you'll be seeing her there."

"We'll be at a few of the same meetings."

"Will you have dinner with us this evening?"

"I don't have other plans, unless I meet up with some colleagues."

"Like you did last night."

"Yes."

Meg found her patience wearing thin as was usually the case when speaking with her mother-in-law. As she ate the toast and drank her coffee, she wondered how Helen knew she arrived late. Of course, Ida told her but that did not really bother her. What bothered her was Helen's insinuation that she was up to something. Meg knew her mother-in-law was old-fashioned. Didn't she realize Meg had her own career?

Helen put down her cup. "I'd like to ask you and Adam to visit soon. I know you're both busy, of course, but it'd be nice having you here. I didn't see you for Christmas…" She purposely left her sentence unfinished as though to lay a guilt trip on Meg. It did not work.

"I'll ask Adam when I go back on Tuesday. As you said, he's quite busy." She refused a second cup of coffee. The conference was soon starting, and she wanted to leave early to have enough time to get there, what with walking in this cold weather.

"It'd be nice for both of you to visit," she repeated. "I haven't seen you together here for so long. You always used to enjoy visiting here, Meg, so why don't you think about it? We can go out to dinner at one of Albany's terrific restaurants."

Meg wondered what this was all about. She wondered what Adam would think. She was rather impressed by Helen's insistence. Was there something behind it? Was she getting sentimental at her age? Or was senile the better word?

"Did you want Harmon to drive you in the car?" Helen offered.

Meg declined her mother-in-law's offer. She got up from the table, said goodbye to Helen, put on her fur coat, hat and gloves and then abruptly left the house.

In the large basement room of the old brownstone house, Harmon Pendleton got ready for the day. His concern was to take care of whatever Helen wanted, which included grocery shopping and clearing the front steps and sidewalk of snow.

Harmon Pendleton was sixty-five years old. He was a trifle overweight especially in the middle, with smooth brown hair and kind yet shrewd brown eyes. The basement room in which he lived was simple and very mannish. A thick brown rug, deep, comfortable chairs and a couch that had seen better days. There was a kitchenette in one corner, along with a small icebox and a kitchen table for two. Harmon had worked for Helen Cary for several years after serving as butler for another prominent Albany family. He was her personal driver as Helen did not drive. She did not trust these modern cars and when she did venture out on her own, she usually walked. He also helped Ida in the kitchen although he freely admitted he was not a good cook.

Harmon knew Helen's daughter-in-law was in town for some conference and planned to stay at the house. He thought he heard someone arrive late last night. He wondered if that was Megan.

Harmon gathered his winter coat from the closet and hesitated before climbing the stairs to enter the kitchen. Her daughter-in-law's presence could create problems for the household. He knew she was a librarian, like Iris but other than that he knew little else. So why didn't Helen like her? There had to be something he did not know, and she did not say.

If the truth came out that would really shake things up, he thought. With a slight grimace of the weekend ahead, Harmon climbed the stairs to greet Ida in the kitchen.

"Certainly, a cold morning for a walk!" Elsie Thompson exclaimed briskly, her cheeks blotched red from the cold. She stood in the hallway, stomped her boots, and shook her hands to get the blood moving again. She took off her fur coat, hat, scarf, and gloves. She turned to look at her husband, Richard, who was struggling to remove his boots. She asked if he needed help. Richard Thompson glared at his wife with annoyance. After nearly thirty years of marriage, Elsie was used to it.

"No, I don't need help," he replied curtly. "Do I look like an imbecile?"

Sometimes Elsie wondered who was worse, her husband or her sister Helen. She glanced into the living room and noticed her sister sitting in her favorite chair by the fire, reading a magazine. She hesitated to enter and then changed her mind.

Elsie and Richard Thompson lived on the fourth floor, in a large bedroom which also served as a living room. They had use of the two guest rooms on the same floor, which Elsie used as a boudoir and sewing room, respectively. Although there were times when they would have preferred to be on their own, she and Richard were happy living with Helen.

Elsie was fifty-five, quite tall and angular. She had a pretty face with high cheekbones and short brown hair, worn in the bob style, like the young women did these days—although she knew her conservative husband did not approve. She had tried various shades of lipstick, but she preferred the simple red and wore only the slightest rouge.

Richard Thompson was of medium height, with brown hair, gray strands and brown eyes. He was appropriately dressed for a man of sixty, straight pants, comfortable shirt, and brown shoes. Richard was retired from the state taxation department and often spent his days assisting his sister-in-law Helen when and if she needed it (which Richard was glad wasn't too often) or going to the state library.

Childless and without family, except Helen, Elsie and Richard moved into Helen's brownstone on Willett Street about ten years ago, as the housing shortage after the war made it difficult to find their own place in Albany. Helen invited them to stay and after a trial run, Elsie and Richard decided they would make it work. Helen's house was big enough and having the fourth floor to themselves made it feel like their own apartment.

Elsie still worked at the state capital as a secretary and typist. She walked to the state capital, often meeting her niece Iris during the day for lunch, as the library was just across the street.

"What should we do today, dear?" she asked her husband who had made himself comfortable on the couch in their bedroom.

"Well, on a cold day like this, I suppose there isn't much to do. I have the newspaper. There's a program on the radio I want to listen to."

Elsie agreed. "I wanted to go to Whitney's to shop, but I don't think I will." She looked out the windows that overlooked Washington Park.

"I have some sewing to do," she announced, turning from the window. "I'll be in the sewing room, dear." She hesitated. "We haven't seen Megan yet."

Richard looked up from the morning paper. "She was supposed to come here for the weekend. Some conference or other."

"Yes, Ida mentioned she got in late last night." Elsie paused, deep in thought. "I know Iris attended the same conference and got back in a reasonable time."

"Is there something wrong, Elsie?" Richard asked. He knew his wife too well to know when she was perplexed about something. Or someone.

Elsie murmured that there was nothing wrong. She walked to the sewing room, two doors down from their bedroom. As she picked up a dress that needed stitching, she wondered what Adam, her nephew, Meg's husband, was doing in Manhattan by himself. And whether he was alone.

Grace Prescott turned from the oven from which she removed an apple pie. She looked at it favorably and placed it on the counter to cool. She wiped her forehead with her hand, for despite the bitter cold outside it was quite warm in Grace's kitchen. She untied her apron and poured herself a cup of coffee.

Grace was short and rather large with a pink, full face, and a head of gray hair. At fifty, her forehead was prematurely wrinkled, with a great many lines around her eyes but still she maintained a pleasant disposition. Grace was a widow and childless. She did volunteer work at Albany Hospital, and it infuriated her to see Helen Cary there also volunteering.

Grace's mind flew to the Cary family. An Albany family that prospered over the years. And how Grace resented it. She knew some of Helen's secrets, but assumed she had more hidden. With two husbands behind her, there had to be some skeletons rattling in her past. Of course, there was the scandal about her first husband's suicide. And wasn't there a scandal with her second husband's death, too? Grace tried to remember the details. She figured she'd hear about it from her volunteer friends at the hospital.

Grace saw Iris downtown just last week. She commented that Meg, Adam's wife, would be coming up from New York City this weekend. She knew Helen was not fond of her daughter-in-law but did not quite know why. Maybe there was animosity or jealousy. After all, Megan was an attractive young woman.

Once Iris confided in her that she thought her brother was having extramarital affairs. Grace offered the routine words of remorse. But then she thought, Helen finally got her comeuppance. What goes around comes around, doesn't it, Helen?

Grace Prescott paused, deep in thought about Helen and Walter Cary. Well, let sleeping dogs lie. Unless, of course, those who remembered started to talk.

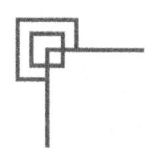

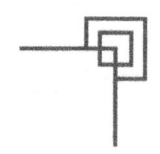

CHAPTER SIX

The conference at the state library was a success, although it ran longer for the Saturday session. Meg met Iris in the lobby of the State Education Building and together they attended several workshops.

"How's the New York Public Library?" Iris asked Meg during lunch, as they sat at a café on Washington Avenue.

"I love it there," Meg said. Iris looked at her as though she could read her mind for she knew she'd ask about her brother.

"How's Adam? Or should I ask?"

Meg wiped her mouth on a napkin. "Adam hasn't changed. He didn't want to come here with me for the weekend. He claimed he had work at the laboratory." She mentioned he wasn't keen on her coming up to Albany in the snowstorm. "Adam can be difficult at times but then you that already."

With compassion Iris looked at her sister-in-law. "I hope he's being faithful, Meg."

What a bold thing to say, Meg thought. She looked at Iris carefully.

"What makes you say that?"

"Well, my brother always had a roving eye. Even before he met you." Iris paused as she realized Meg lapsed into an uncomfortable silence. "I'm sorry, Meg. That was heartless of me to say."

Meg shook her head. "That's all right, Iris." She hesitated. "The food here is quite good, isn't it?" She changed the subject quickly, opened her pocketbook to take out cigarettes. She lit one and offered one to Iris. Iris asked Meg if she had seen her mother that morning.

"Only briefly. I had a quick breakfast. I must have missed you."

"Yes, I had gotten up really early and came straight over. I had a few things to do at my desk." Iris asked the waitress for more coffee. "Do you think you and Adam would like to visit some weekend, Meg? Mother mentioned that it'd be nice since you didn't come here for Christmas."

Meg wondered if that statement came from Iris or her mother. She agreed that it was some time since she and Adam visited. She thought of the arguments Adam and his mother would have nearly every time they were together.

Meg put down her fork and glanced at her watch. "This hour has flown by, Iris. The afternoon session will be starting soon."

Iris signaled the waitress for the check.

"Why don't you go ahead. I want to call someone before the next workshop." Iris gathered her coat from the back of her chair. "A fellow librarian?"

Meg put her coffee cup to her lips. She then decided to tell Iris about Ben and Mrs.

Hanson. After she finished, Iris looked at Meg incredulously.

"You believe her story about killing that man?"

"She turned out to be Ben's mother," Meg told her. "And he confirmed it was true. I want to call him at the Ten Eyck Hotel."

Iris looked at her sister-in-law dubiously. "Suit yourself," she said, shrugged and stood. "I'll see you at the conference." She grabbed her fur coat, scarf, and gloves, walked over to the cashier, paid the bill, turned to wave to Meg and then left the café.

AN UNFORTUNATE COINCIDENCE

Meg searched in wallet, found a nickel, and then left the café in search of a pay phone. Fortunately, on the street, inside a bus kiosk on Washington Avenue, she found one. She deposited the coin, asked the operator to dial the Ten Eyck Hotel and much to her surprise was put through to Ben Faraday right away. He answered on the first ring as though he was expecting her call.

"Meg, I'm glad to hear from you," Ben said. "Are you free today?"

Meg hesitated. What was she doing calling his strange man to ask about his mother who obviously was either delusional or insane or both? She found her voice after a few seconds.

"I have the conference to attend this afternoon. I won't really have any time…"

"My mother's staying at the Albany Hospital for now," Ben said. "She'll be moved to the psychiatric Hospital within a day or so." He paused. "I remember you mentioned you're leaving Albany on Monday…"

"Can you meet me in front of the State Education Building? About five o'clock? That's when the conference ends."

Meg told Ben the State Education Building was on Washington Avenue, across from the state capital. She told him she'd see him then and quickly hung up, allowing an impatient woman behind her to use the phone.

Deep in thought, Meg walked away from the bus kiosk on her way to the State Education Building. She bundled her scarf around her neck and pulled her cloche hat lower. With light snow falling and the chill to the air, Meg walked hurriedly but found herself thinking of Ben. Why did she want to see him again, anyway? She did not know him. But she was interested in his mother, having killed that man in 1922, just six years ago.

She took a deep breath, entered the State Education Building, and brought with her the cold air and a swish of swirling snow.

As she entered the conference room to attend the afternoon session, Meg angrily thought there were times she felt she could kill her husband for his arrogance, meanness, her loveless marriage. Just like Mrs. Hanson and Ruth Snyder, the woman from Queens. It dawned on her she recently became aware of women who killed the men in their lives. Maybe I'll make it a third. And then she was surprised at her own thoughts.

Adam Cary walked briskly down Fifth Avenue until he came to 54th Street. It was almost dusk and still quite cold. He attended to things at his laboratory earlier and decided afterward to make a night of it. He gathered his coat and hat and left the building a little after six o'clock.

Meg would not be home until Monday so why should he stay cooped up in their apartment all weekend? Not that their place was anything drab; Adam and Meg lived in a well-furnished apartment in Manhattan, near Central Park. They recently bought a new radio console, perfect for the spacious living room. The building was complete with a doorman and a garage. But it was boring there, Adam thought, as he turned the corner to walk down 54th Street. And Adam hated to be bored. He came to the place he was looking for, Angelo's, a speakeasy with quite a notorious reputation.

He knocked and a small window within the door opened. An elderly man asked Adam if he had the password. Adam did not have the password but took out from his pocket a wad of bills. He counted out fifty dollars, which he put through the window-door. The latch on the door opened and Adam went inside.

The bar was crowded but he managed to order a strong gin fizz and was soon chatting with a few women, all of whom were talking quite freely with the handsome Adam.

If Meg were in town, he wouldn't be here, he thought and smiled at the red head in front of him. She kept talking, laughing, drinking, and smoking and he realized she was clearly intoxicated. Some men might see that as an advantage, but Adam decided to look around. He was finishing his gin fizz when someone called his name.

"Adam, it's you! Fancy seeing you here!"

It was John Evans, his young associate from the laboratory. Adam just put a cigarette to his lips and had to hold onto it to prevent it from falling. Of all people to see, John, this idiot he worked with. He had to come up with something polite to say to him. Never off guard, Adam composed himself.

"Just dropped in for a short while. What about you?"

"I'm here with friends for drinks," John said jovially, obviously close to the brim of intoxication. "Nice place isn't it?"

The band was playing jazz music and the dance floor was full. What else could happen tonight, Adam thought as he looked at this irritating young fool. Of course, John was single so he would be out on the town. But didn't he live in Brooklyn where there were plenty of speakeasies? Why the hell did he come to this one?

John grinned. "Great to meet the ladies too!" he added rather loudly. "I didn't know you came here."

"First visit," Adam replied laconically. "What about you?"

"I've been here before," John said. He puffed on his cigarette, took a gulp of his whisky and then his gaze traveled to the women Adam conversed with. He turned back to Adam with a sly, coy smile. "Friends of yours?"

"I've just met them," Adam wanted to tell him to mind his own business.

"Do you ever come here with Meg?"

Adam pressed his lips together to refrain from saying something curt. John knew Meg was out of town. Was he implying something? It wasn't any of John's business if he came to this speakeasy or any speakeasy with his wife or alone, so he simply decided not to say anything. There was no love lost between Adam and his associate John. Adam thought John to be a lazy worker, too young at twenty-two to work in the laboratory, regardless of his degree in chemistry. He was careless at work and irresponsible. Adam had tried more than once to get him fired. He looked back at John and forced a smile.

"No, Meg and I have been to other places but not this one," he said in his way of making a lie sound like the truth. He took another swig of his gin and put John off. "I'll see you on Monday, John."

John took another drag of his cigarette; told Adam he would see him bright and early Monday and walked over to another part of the bar. Adam made his escape from John and thought about leaving when he was again stopped but this time by a woman.

She was tall and lovely, incredibly young, brunette and one of the most beautiful women Adam had ever seen. She took a few puffs on a cigarette and sipped a drink.

"What are you drinking?" he asked her and smiled.

"Scotch," she said. "Only thing I drink." She paused. "Do you want to get out of here? There's a party at my girlfriend's place."

What a pick-up, he thought curiously. "What kind of party?"

"A petting party, silly!" the inebriated young woman said and laughed mischievously. "Come on, it'll be fun!" She put her glass and his on an empty table. She grabbed Adam by the arm and led him outside. Adam followed as though in a trance. He could find at a petting party what he could not find at home. And Meg would never know.

It was close to five o'clock and the library convention was wrapping up for the day. People were leaving the State Education Building, chatting among themselves, walking to the corner of Washington Avenue to catch the trolley to take them to their respective hotels.

Meg and Iris exited the building and were immediately swept by the harsh wind and the stinging snow and sleet. Iris buried her chin in her scarf and turned to Meg.

"We should take a cab back home. It'd be too much to walk in this weather."

Meg then looked up and saw Ben Faraday at the bottom of the steps. He smiled when he saw her. Meg came up to him and then turned to her sister-in-law.

"Iris, this is Ben Faraday. He's here in Albany on account of his mother."

Iris shook a frozen hand with Ben, who smiled and looked just as frozen. "I'm on my way to see my mother. Would you like to come with me?"

Iris hesitated and looked at Meg. Why in the world would she want to go see his mother? Hadn't she just met this man? She knew her sister-in-law was a caring person, but this was a little too much for Iris.

"Yes, I'd like to come with you, Ben," Meg said determinedly. She turned to Iris. "Tell your mother that I'll be back soon and not to wait dinner for me."

Iris looked at Meg incredulously. "Are you sure, Meg?"

Meg turned to Ben and told Iris she would see her later. Iris walked off toward Washington Avenue to catch a taxi while Meg and Ben stood on the street, looking into each other's eyes. Ben broke the awkward silence.

"Why don't we get a taxi ourselves? It'll be quicker to get to the hospital."

Meg agreed. They walked off in search of an empty cab and found one in front of the state capital. They arrived at Albany Hospital and soon were in the front entrance.

It wasn't cold inside the hospital, but Meg shivered more out of uneasiness. Ben went to the information desk and was told Janet Faraday was on the fifth floor. In the elevator, Meg wondered what Mrs. Hanson—or Janet Faraday—was like now.

The doctor attending Janet Faraday greeted Ben and explained that his mother would be undergoing a series of examinations. He led them into a small room, obviously a sitting room for patients, and left them alone. In a few minutes, the door burst open suddenly and the doctor returned with Janet Faraday.

She seemed smaller, Meg thought, than when she was on the train as if she had shrunk in size from her horrendous ordeal. She looked strained and tired like she had not slept. Yet she smiled when she saw her son and Meg. The doctor left and they were alone.

"Hello, Megan. I remember you so well. You're so lovely and pretty. I felt so sorry for you on the train, my dear."

"Here, Mother, sit down," Ben said and pulled a chair toward her.

Almost immediately Janet Faraday started to cry, lightly at first but then heavier and steadier. She lifted her eyes toward her son.

"I should hate you for doing this to me. You tricked me, Benjamin."

"I did it for you, Mother."

"For me? All because of your rotten father." She spoke harshly and bitterly.

Meg intervened. "Mrs. Hanson, I mean…"

"Ben's father killed a man," Janet Faraday said, wiping away tears.

"I remember. Ben explained everything."

Janet Faraday spoke remorsefully. "My life has been terrible, just terrible. I killed Ben's father. I couldn't tolerate him any longer. But I have never really escaped. I've been a prisoner." She broke down again. "You can be pushed only so far."

Meg felt a chill run up her spine. She looked at Ben and felt helpless. Janet looked at Meg and asked her a barrage of questions.

"Are you going back to New York soon, dear? Do you like Albany? It's a nice city, isn't it? Why don't you stay in Albany?" She then turned to her son. "What are your plans for me now, Benjamin?"

Ben cleared his throat. "You'll be admitted to another hospital within a few days, Mother." He paused, seeing his mother's flustered expression. "Mother, I'll come back tomorrow."

Janet Faraday then turned angry and hostile. Her temper flared and she demanded to be taken away at once. She told her son not to bother to visit tomorrow and accompanied by an attendant, she left the sitting room in an anxious, overwrought state. The doctor soon returned and explained that mood swings were common in people with her condition.

"Will she be all right?" Ben asked impatiently.

The doctor shook his head. "Within a few days, as soon as they have a room for her, she'll be admitted to the psychiatric hospital as you requested. It'll be the best place for her."

"Thank you, doctor," Ben said and managed a short smile. He and Meg walked to the elevators in silence. They were soon outside getting into a taxi.

Ben told the driver to take Meg to Willett Street and then continue to the Ten Eyck Hotel. She slipped her hand in his. Ben Faraday fell into Meg's arms from weariness, loneliness, and exhaustion. She held him as if he would slip away if she let go.

There's never been a moment like this in my life, Meg thought. Certainly, not with the man she married. She held onto Ben, comforted him, and was filled with love, and tenderness.

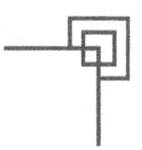

CHAPTER SEVEN

It was just past eight o'clock when Meg returned to her in-law's on Willett Street. She rang the doorbell and was admitted by Ida, who looked at her with concern.

"Mrs. Cary's been worrying about you," she said as she helped Meg with her coat, scarf, gloves, and hat. "She's in the living room with her sister and brother-in-law."

"Thank you," Meg said rather demurely. She truthfully did not want to chat with her mother-in-law but silently hoped with Elsie and Richard there it might not be too uncomfortable. Meg looked in the hallway mirror, tossed her hair a little and then made her way to the living room. Elsie looked up from the newspaper and greeted her pleasantly.

"Hello, Meg! How have you been?"

Meg smiled and approached Elsie. She greeted Richard and then looked at Helen, who also seemed glad to see her. Meg wasn't fooled by her smile, however.

"I'm fine, Elsie, thanks for asking. How are you? And you, Richard?" Pleasantries lasted about five minutes; the storm was dreadful and the snow, how much more could fall! And the cold, too, making it difficult to walk and the messy pavements. Richard said he admired her library work as he spent a great deal of time at the state library.

"Have you read about the Snyder case?" he asked her.

Meg squirmed in her chair. "Well, yes, I believe I have."

"She got what she deserved," Richard continued. "She killed her husband and was put to death only on Thursday."

"Richard, please," Elsie said as she folded the paper and put it on the coffee table. "Meg isn't interested in Ruth Snyder, are you Meg?"

Meg said she had read about it in *The New York Times* but hadn't heard about it on the radio. She glanced at her mother-in-law wondering when she would add to the conversation.

"We missed you for dinner," Helen finally said. "Iris told us you met a man and went to see his mother in the hospital." Her tone carried incredulity.

For a moment Meg didn't know what to say. She didn't feel she needed to offer her mother-in-law or anyone else an explanation. But then she was staying at her house.

She glanced at the comfortable living room, the large Victorian couch, the two easy chairs, the ornate coffee table, and the large radio console in between the two large front windows overlooking Willett Street and Washington Park. The fire had been lit and it was a most inviting and cozy room. She told Iris so why shouldn't she tell the rest of her in-laws? Since Iris mentioned it to her mother anyway, she decided to tell them about Ben. Taking a deep breath, she told them about how she met Ben and his mother and how the woman had killed Ben's father in 1922. She explained how Ben planned to have her committed to the psychiatric hospital in Albany. She also mentioned she wanted to see his mother again to offer support and consolation. When she finished, she looked at Elsie and saw compassion, even a little good humor from her. Richard nodded, and seemed to approve of her decisions. Only Helen looked at her with revulsion and indignation.

"Do you always take off with strangers, Megan?"

Before Meg could reply, Richard and Elsie both spoke, practically at once.

"Meg has a good heart," Elsie smiled. "She'd take an interest in this man's mother. Wouldn't you, Helen?"

Helen glared at her older sister.

"Well, I really don't know," she replied dryly. "With so many murders and assaults happening in Albany nowadays, I find it hard to believe a young woman would trust a man she just met."

Richard coughed. "What did you say this woman's name was?"

"She said her name was Irene Hanson," Meg told them. "Her real name is Janet Faraday and her son's name is Ben Faraday."

"I remember I read in the paper about a man who died from smoke inhalation in his car," Elsie said thoughtfully as she looked at her husband and sister. "It happened a few years ago, in Kinderhook."

"I don't remember it," Richard said.

"It was considered an accidental death," Elsie remembered. "I don't believe they brought a verdict of murder or even arrested anyone." She paused. "Do you remember it, Helen?"

"Helen, is there something wrong?" Richard asked her.

"No, there's nothing wrong. I don't like to hear such stories, that's all."

Changing the subject, Elsie and Richard were talking politics, President Coolidge and his "I do not choose to run" decision for the upcoming election. Richard, being a staunch Republican was adamant that Coolidge was too disturbed over the death of his son to enter the political arena again. Helen and Meg made a few comments but added little else.

"Personally, I like Hoover," he said and began a lengthy discourse on Herbert Hoover and his attributes. Ida entered at that moment and left a tray with coffee and cake. Iris and Bruce also entered. Bruce went over to Meg and commented how well she looked.

"Anyone for bridge?" Iris asked. "Care to join us, Meg?" "Sure, I'd be glad to," she said seeing it as an escape.

"We'll set up in the dining room," Bruce said and helped himself to Ida's rich chocolate cake. "Did you have any, Helen?"

"Too much sugar for me," Helen said acidly and turned to speak to her sister.

Meg joined Iris and Bruce in the dining room to play bridge but couldn't help wondering why her mother-in-law seemed disturbed over hearing about Ben and his mother. Of course, she wasn't used to hearing about such things. With Richard mentioning the Ruth Snyder case, maybe it was too much for Helen. It certainly didn't make for pleasant conversation.

Bruce dealt the cards and the game began. As Meg looked at the cards and concentrated on the game, she wondered what was passing in her mother-in-law's mind.

Sunday was a difficult day for Meg. She woke up early, dressed and then went downstairs only to discover most everyone still not up, except Ida who was in the kitchen, fixing breakfast. She explained that Helen, Elsie, and Iris went to church services and would return shortly. Harmon drove them in the car.

Meg realized with everyone out, except Bruce and Richard still sleeping, she could use the phone freely. But then Ida would say something, of course. Meg asked her if she could use the phone. Ida told her to help herself.

Keeping her voice low, she called Ben at the hotel, who was glad to hear from her. He told her nothing was new with his mother. She told him she'd call him later in the day. She lifted the receiver again and gave the operator her home number. After waiting what seemed an interminable amount of time, the line began to ring on the other end. However, after nearly ten rings, Meg hung up. She replaced the receiver, joined Ida in the kitchen and asked for coffee.

"Finished with your calls?" the maid asked as she poured her a cup of coffee and set a plate of fresh muffins in front of her.

Yes, Meg told her, she was finished with her calls. As though it was any of her business, she thought. She mentioned she tried to call Adam but there was no answer.

"On a Sunday morning?" Ida asked.

Meg grimaced. Even this dowdy maid could put two and two together. She looked at Ida closely. Ugly as sin, nothing stylish, no make-up, no flapper appeal. She wondered if Ida could tell that Adam had other interests outside of his marriage. "The coffee's good," she said to change the subject.

She lit a cigarette and took another sip of coffee. The front door suddenly opened, letting in the cold air. Soon Meg and Ida heard footsteps march down the hallway and enter the kitchen.

Meg turned to see Harmon, Iris, Elsie and Helen, their faces red from the cold and eagerly wanting coffee and breakfast.

Elsie and Iris greeted Meg and invited her to join them in the dining room. Harmon told Meg how glad he was to see her after so long.

"It was a nice service," Helen said as she looked at her sister and daughter. "When the governor's daughter gets married in June it'll be lovely."

"Are you going, Mother?" Iris asked as she spread some butter on her toast.

"Of course, I'll go," Helen said appalled that her daughter would even ask. "I've been invited and it'd be an honor to attend."

That comment brought an awkward silence until it was broken by Elsie.

"Have you spoken to Adam yet, Meg?"

Meg sipped her coffee. "No, I tried him earlier but couldn't reach him."

Helen looked up at Meg. "He wasn't home on a Sunday morning?"

"Well, you know how devoted he is to his work," Meg said making an excuse for her husband. "He does work often on weekends." To change the subject she added, "I'm glad I decided to leave tomorrow instead of today."

A strange silence pervaded until the telephone in the hallway rang, loudly and shrilly. They heard Ida in the hallway, speaking rather excitedly and then she appeared at the dining room entrance.

"Mrs. Cary, it's Adam. He wants to talk to you."

Meg had her coffee cup to her lips and she practically choked on the hot liquid. Adam, calling here? Why would he ask for Helen first? She just tried calling him about an hour ago. Had he just gotten home? And from where? Meg didn't want to think of that.

Helen got up from the table, gave a slight smirk to her daughter-in-law as if to say she meant more to Adam than his own wife and went to the hallway to take the call.

A few moments later, she took her seat at the head of the table. "Adam will be visiting next weekend," was all she said. "And of course, Meg," she added in what sounded like regret. "I called his lab the other night and left a message. How nice he returned my call."

"He hung up already?" Elsie asked in surprise.

"Well, he didn't have much time," Helen said and poured herself another cup of coffee. "It's a long-distance call and the rates…"

Meg wanted to laugh. Since when did Adam care about expenses? Next weekend here again in Albany? She noticed Iris and Bruce looking at her. Their glance conveyed the same thoughts.

Meg wished something would happen to her cold, shallow brute of a husband; that he would have an accident or something. She could no longer tolerate his moodiness, his odd, secretive ways.

At that moment, she realized she did not love her husband. Strangely, she felt as though she never really loved him at all. And if something did happen to him, she didn't think she would really care.

Later in the day, Meg, Iris and Bruce walked to the State Education Building to go to the state museum only to find it closed for restoration.

"Well, what should we do now?" Bruce asked his wife and sister-in-law. They stood at the top of the marble stairs looking down at Washington Avenue. Snow started falling lightly again and it remained cold. "We could take a tour of the state capital?"

Meg laughed. "Bruce, I'm not a tourist. I've seen the capital building before!"

"Let's get out of this cold and get some coffee," Iris suggested.

They crossed Washington Avenue and hopped on the trolley. At the corner of State and Pearl Streets, they got off and walked to the same diner Meg and Ben ate at Friday evening.

"Just coffee for us," Iris told the waitress. They hung their coats on the hook near the table and took out cigarettes. Bruce lit one for his wife and another for Meg.

The waitress deposited three cups, along with cream and sugar. When she was gone Bruce looked at Meg as he puffed on his cigarette.

"How's Adam, Meg?" Before she could answer he added, "I find it hard to believe he actually wants to come here to visit his mother."

Meg sipped some coffee, puffed on her cigarette, and agreed with him. "I haven't spoken to him since I left Friday evening. I tried calling earlier today but there was no answer." She paused. "I don't know where he could have been on a Sunday morning."

"He puts in a lot of hours at the lab," Iris said trying to be optimistic.

Meg stared into space. Her mind flew to Adam again, alone in Manhattan. And to Ben Faraday, and to how much she wanted to see him again.

"What are you thinking about, Meg?" Iris asked.

She cleared her throat and said she was thinking about Ben and his mother, about what would happen to her. Bruce stubbed out his cigarette and whistled.

"Sounds like his mother is crazy," he said. "That loony bin is the best place for her."

"I felt so sorry for her," Meg said sadly, "and for Ben. They've both suffered so much." She paused. "He's still in Albany, at the Ten Eyck Hotel. I should call him."

Iris noticed a pay phone in the corner near the diner entrance. Meg opened her purse and found a nickel. She got up and without saying anything to Iris or Bruce, walked over to the pay phone.

When she deposited the nickel and spoke to the operator, she asked for the Ten Eyck Hotel. The hotel clerk answered and tried Ben's room but there was no answer. She was connected back to the front desk and left a message for Ben, to meet her at Union Station tomorrow morning at eight when she would leave for New York City.

It was Monday morning. Meg dressed and descended the main staircase with her suitcase. She left it in the hallway and joined Ida in the kitchen.

"All-ready for the train trip?" she asked Meg. "I'll fix a good breakfast for you." "Just coffee, Ida," Meg told her.

They heard footsteps on the main stairs. Soon they were joined by Iris and Bruce. Bruce poured coffee, drank it rather quickly, gathered his books and kissed Iris goodbye. He hugged Meg and wished her a safe trip back to New York City. He then left the house by the front entrance. Then Meg turned to Iris.

"Bruce seems devoted to teaching," she commented.

Iris made a wry smile. "Most of the time, until the students act up." She paused. "Let's go into the dining room and have breakfast."

No sooner had they sat at the dining room table with their coffee then Elsie and Richard appeared, apparently still tired, sleep in both of their eyes.

"Usually I don't get up this early," Elsie said as she pulled her robe tighter around her waist. She sat at the dining room table, joining Meg and Iris. "But I wanted to say goodbye to you, Meg, before you left. Are you going in later this morning, Iris?"

"Yes, I already called to let them know I'll be late," Iris said.

Richard also joined them at the dining room table. "Likewise, for me, Meg. I got up to see you off. I hope you have a safe trip home."

"Thanks, Richard," Meg said, sincerely.

Ida entered with a tray containing scrambled eggs, sausage, bacon, and fresh muffins. Richard helped himself to a little of everything, but the women restricted themselves to a muffin each.

"I haven't been to Manhattan in so long," Elsie said rather dreamily. "Perhaps we'll visit you and Adam sometime soon."

Before Meg could reply, Richard spoke up.

"Well, she and Adam are coming next weekend. Isn't that what Helen told us?"

"I'll talk it over with Adam," Meg told them.

"I'm glad, Megan," a voice said from the dining room entrance.

Everyone turned and saw Helen in standing in the doorway, still in her robe and slippers, also looking quite sleepy, but alert in her own distinct way. She helped herself to coffee and a muffin.

"I'm glad you and Adam will visit next weekend," she repeated. "And we'll go out to dinner, too."

Meg was impressed that her mother-in-law could be so insistent. She had never seen that from her before. She realized she was speaking to her.

"We'll go to Keeler's. We'd need a reservation. But I'll take care of that."

Even Iris, Elsie and Richard were impressed by Helen's generosity. There followed the usual strange silence that ensued after Helen spoke. Meg glanced at her watch, realized that time had gone by. She put down her coffee cup and told Iris they needed to get going.

"I'll have Harmon bring you to Union Station in the car," Helen offered. "It'll be faster than waiting for the trolley." She got up rather quickly and went to the kitchen to tell Ida to have Harmon bring the car around to the front of the house.

Meg thanked her and then in the hallway with her coat on and her suitcase in hand, she hugged Helen, Elsie and Richard at the front door and said goodbye to Ida. Then she and Iris walked down the front steps where Harmon waited for them in the car.

"Good morning, ladies," he said as they entered the Packard Twin 6 Roadster.

Meg greeted Harmon, adjusted her cloche hat, and sat back in the car. Iris also adjusted her hat and looked at Meg as Harmon sped off down State Street.

"Is Mr. Faraday meeting you at Union Station?" she asked Meg.

"I left a message with the front desk." She hesitated. "I'd like to see him again."

Harmon dexterously maneuvered the car down State Street hill, avoiding the slushy parts then turned left onto Broadway and pulled up in front of Union Station. Meg said goodbye to Harmon and then she and Iris quickly entered the station.

In the main concourse, it was crowded with people taking local trains to work and others waiting for long distance trains. Meg and Iris looked up at the departures board and saw the Empire State Express train, but it had not yet started to board. Meg turned to Iris.

"Well, I'll see you next weekend, if Adam wants to visit. I can't understand why he'd want to come here but then your mother seems to have that effect on him."

Iris gave a short laugh, but not of humor. "We'll be okay, Meg."

"Meg, I'm glad to see you," a male voice said behind them.

Meg and Iris turned from the departure board and saw Ben Faraday standing before them. Meg felt her heart pound. Iris looked at her sister-in-law and wondered what was going on in her mind. Who was this character and why would she be interested in him? Although, Iris mused, he was rather handsome. Meg introduced Ben to Iris, and they shook hands.

They walked over to a bench to wait. Meg turned to Ben and asked about his mother. He grimaced and said she was slowly accepting her situation, but the doctor advised it would take time. She would be admitted to the psychiatric hospital soon.

"Will you return to work soon?" Meg asked.

Various announcements were made for trains, but Meg's had not yet been called. She turned her attention back to the handsome young man next to her.

Ben nodded. "Soon enough. And you, going back to the library?"

"Yes, tomorrow." She paused. "Where do you live, Ben?"

On a slip of paper, he took from his coat pocket, Ben wrote down his address and phone number in Manhattan. Meg wrote her address and number on paper she had in her pocketbook and gave it to him. Iris looked again at her sister-in-law and thought she was foolish to be trusting this man. She thought of saying so when Ben said something which made her take notice.

"I hope you'll be happy when you get home," he said unexpectedly.

"I'll make the most of it," Meg said resourcefully. "I'm sure Adam will be glad to see me. I'm sure he's missed me."

"You mentioned you and your husband didn't do things together," Ben said.

"Well, I meant a few things." She spoke nervously.

The Empire State Express was called for boarding. Iris gave Meg a final hug goodbye and wished her well. She mentioned she had to get to work, and it was getting late. She told Ben it was a pleasure seeing him and made her way down the platform and into the busy station.

"This is it," Meg said ruefully.

"Would your husband mind if we got together?" Ben asked.

What about Adam, Meg thought suddenly and uncaringly. Well, it was all right, Adam wouldn't mind if she saw Ben, would he?

"Oh, Adam's so busy anyway," came her answer aloud. "He wouldn't mind." Or even care, she added to herself.

Ben moved forward and embraced her tightly. It seemed as if they were alone on the platform. Two young people, each suffering on account of another dominant force in their lives.

"I hope your mother will be all right," Meg whispered. She looked over his shoulder then closed her eyes. She did not want to let go. She felt safe in his arms.

"I'm worried about you," Ben said.

"I'll call you tonight at the hotel," Meg told him. "To find out how your mother is doing," she added as though she felt she had to give a reason.

As she boarded, Meg waved again to Ben. She would see Ben again, yes, she was sure of that. At least she saw him before leaving; she had only seen Adam's back when she left New York City on Monday. But Ben was different than Adam, Meg realized as she settled into an empty seat.

As the train pulled out of Union Station and the skyline of Albany rushed past her window, Meg felt a tranquility settle over her as she repeated those words to herself. *Yes, Ben Faraday was much more different than Adam.*

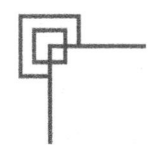

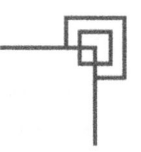

CHAPTER EIGHT

At Grand Central Station, the train pulled in on time. Meg exited with the crowd and came up to the main concourse. Then she spotted her husband behind a guard rope. Adam was there to meet her! She was surprised he even remembered. She hadn't talked to him since leaving on Friday. She waved and briskly made her way over to him.

As they proceeded through the lobby, and up the stairs, Meg explained to her husband what a long weekend it was. While she was talking, she noticed that Adam was hardly listening. His eyes drifted around, to the other passengers milling about. Always, it seemed to Meg, as though he was afraid of being seen in public. They came out onto 42nd Street.

"Where did you park the car?" Meg asked, looking around.

"I didn't," Adam said simply, in his usual curt way. "I took a cab." By the expression on her face, Adam could tell she was surprised. "Easier than parking in a garage."

"I don't mind a cab," she told him. With the crowds, congestion and waiting for a taxi in the cold of course I mind, Meg wanted to say.

"So, how have you been?" Meg asked conversationally. She shivered slightly and bundled her scarf tighter around her neck. Of all days to wait for a cab!

"I've been working," Adam explained in a huff. "Late hours, too."

"Well, I hope you haven't worked every night," Meg said.

"Of course, I've worked every night. Seven days a week."

"You deserve a break," Mrs. Cary said to which Mr. Cary made no comment.

They finally secured a taxi and in no time, pulled in front of their building on Central Park South. Like robots, Meg thought, acting mechanically, without conversation or any sort of interaction. The doorman came over to the back seat, opened it for Mr. and Mrs. Cary, tipped his hat to them and helped Meg with her suitcase. James, the doorman, was always in a friendly and jovial mood. He smiled at Meg and helped with the luggage.

"Can you take your bag in by yourself?" Adam asked impatiently as he put a dollar bill in James's hand and thanked him for his help. "I have to go back to the lab. It's only eleven o'clock."

"Well, I'll manage," Meg said and sighed. "Why don't you come up for lunch? I hate going into that empty apartment alone."

"Sorry," Adam said curtly. "I have to get back to work. Busy time at the lab right now. I'll be home after five." He then turned to the taxi, opened the passenger door, paid the fare, and told the driver to take him to the laboratory on lower Fifth Avenue. The taxi was about to take off when Meg suddenly opened the door and spoke to her husband.

"Adam, wait. Don't you think we should talk about your mother?"

Adam's face was filled with tension. "Not now, Meg, when I get home tonight." Meg noticed his child-like expression, almost that of innocence. She thought now as she had in the past that Adam was like a frightened child. Something was disturbing him. His mother, of course. Helen wanting them to visit so unexpectedly and making demands. It was the invitation to visit this coming weekend.

"I'll be home after five," he repeated. "We'll talk then."

He then closed the taxi door and told the driver to take off, leaving Meg standing on the sidewalk, with her suitcase. She glanced up at the low clouds. It had not yet begun to snow.

Upon entering the apartment, Meg hung up her fur coat, scarf and hat in the hallway closet and then went to the telephone. She picked it up and was about to speak to the operator but then changed her mind and hung up. She wanted so much to call Ben at the Ten Eyck Hotel in Albany. She decided to wait and then entered the large, spotlessly clean-living room and sat down in an easy chair.

Meg and Adam lived in a large duplex overlooking Central Park. The living room was well furnished with a large radio console against the wall leading into the dining room. A wide terrace overlooked Central Park and during the summer, Adam and Meg enjoyed having dinner while admiring the view of the city. The dining room was big, like the other rooms and there was a thick carpet on the floor and an enormous chandelier on the ceiling. She went into the kitchen, took meat from the freezer, put it in the refrigerator to cook later and then put on the kettle for tea.

Satisfied that tomorrow would be better, Meg settled in the living room with tea and *The New York Times*. The day seemed to go by faster than she anticipated because no sooner had she looked at the paper than she woke up from an easy sleep. She looked around, rather disoriented, and realized she had dozed and slept for several hours. She glanced at the windows and saw it was already evening. She then heard a key in the door and soon Adam appeared in the doorway.

"Meg, I'm home," he called. He put down his briefcase and removed his coat, hat, and scarf, and hung them in the hall closet. Then he entered the living room to see Meg looking at him from the couch in a bewildered state.

"I just woke up," she explained. "I must have dozed off." She ran her fingers through her hair and stifled a yawn. "I'll get dinner ready for us." She entered the kitchen and went to the icebox and took out the meat. It would not take too long to cook, and Adam liked a good steak. He entered the kitchen, with a drink in his hand. Meg noticed it was liquor, most likely gin. She did not know where he bought it but then Meg knew Adam had many secrets. She never liked when her husband drank, as he could become moody, at times even violent.

"So how was the weekend with my mother?" he asked as she stood near the kitchen window overlooking Central Park. "How's everyone doing?"

As she lit the gas stove, Meg said that the family was fine. She added nothing more and then took out some frozen vegetables.

"The library convention was terrific," she put in. "And I got the chance to catch up with Iris. We attended several workshops together."

She turned the meat over to brown and at that moment decided to tell her husband about Ben. Why not, she thought. She did not expect him to understand but at least she knew she was telling the truth. She felt she had to anyway, because she knew that if his mother got hold of him, she would make a point to tell him. She figured it was better hearing it from her than his mother, who most likely would add her own embellishments.

She then announced that the steak and vegetables were ready. She emptied the vegetables in a large bowl and placed the meat on plates. She then told him how she had met Ben, his mother and how she had killed Ben's father in 1922 and her commitment to the state psychiatric hospital. Adam sat at the kitchen table and said nothing. He then got up and clearly was not in the mood for eating. He thought of approaching her as she sat at her place but decided against it. He knew she was cold as a fish toward him. But he no longer cared. He had long since made other arrangements in that regard.

"So, you have another man in your life, Meg?"

"Oh, stop it, Adam. Ben Faraday was someone I met on the train."

Adam said mockingly, "You keep in touch with him?" When she did not answer, Meg knew what would happen next. "So you *are* keeping touch with this man? And his unbalanced mother?" He smoothed his hair with an impatient hand and loosened his tie.

"Listen to me," Meg said, keeping her patience. "Listen to what *I* have to say." That was as far as she got. At her first word Adam blew up, going into one of his frequent rages. The symptoms were all there. His eyes were like glass.

"We're going to my mother's this coming weekend," was all he said as if being scolded for doing something wrong. Obviously, it was on his mind. His sudden mood could not be due to just Ben and his mother. But then, given Adam's jealous nature and his instability it could very well be.

"Friday, after work. I won't mind seeing Iris, Bruce and Aunt Elsie and Uncle Richard." He paused. "I'll make the train reservation tomorrow."

Meg noticed he did not include his mother in that list. Adam then sighed in disgust. "I'm going to listen to the radio." He took his plate with the steak and vegetables and went into the living room without another word, leaving Meg alone at the kitchen table. "I've had enough for today," he added.

I've had enough, too, Meg thought acrimoniously, cutting her steak. She could no longer tolerate Adam's moodiness, his odd ways, and his repulsive mother.

There was an escape, somewhere, somehow. There had to be.

◆◇―――◇◆

As five o'clock approached on Thursday, Meg realized it was time to leave work.

She was soon approached by a young man at the reference desk who needed assistance.

"Hey, Meg!" John Evans said and smiled. He was dressed in tailored black slacks, a white shirt and tie, very dapper for a youth his age. "I recognized ya! How are ya?"

Meg could not place him until she remembered he worked with Adam in the laboratory. "Oh, John, of course. Are you done at the laboratory?"

"Yeah, just got off. I stopped to see if you had Gatsby! I really wanna read it!" Meg went to the card catalog and noticed that all six copies were still checked out. She told John to reserve a copy.

"Naw, that's okay! I can check at the Brooklyn Library. I live near there, you know. I just went to Macy's. Thought I'd stop in here." He paused, looking around. "Great place, isn't it?"

Meg commented that it was and that she loved working there. She told John it was a pleasure to see him again, but she was just finishing her shift and needed to get going. As she was walking away, John stopped her again.

"Say, Meg, I saw Adam over the weekend!"

Meg did not know what to say. Since they worked in the same building, she was not sure what he meant. She looked at him as though for clarification.

"No, I mean after work!" John laughed. "At a speakeasy!"

"A speakeasy?" Meg tried to maintain her composure. "You saw Adam there?" Before he could answer she asked without realizing it, "Was he with someone?"

"Naw, but he was talking to the ladies like I was!" John said with a smirk. "Aw, sorry, Meg but I don't think he meant anything by it! Hope I didn't upset ya!"

Meg smiled good-naturedly at John. He was a rather innocent young man, good-humored, cheerful, and convivial. He was far from devious like Adam.

"Thanks, John. I'll see you again sometime." She made her escape to the employee room, where she gathered her fur coat, scarf, and hat. She said goodbye to a few colleagues and left the library.

She walked down the steps, past the lions that flanked the library entrance and saw it was dusk already, with nighttime soon descending on the city. Although cold with a hint of snow, Meg secretly loved this time of year. She looked at the cars and pedestrians on Fifth Avenue. It was busy as the rush hour was in full swing. She joined the crowd on the sidewalk, deep in thought, wondering about Adam.

She dodged a large woman carrying several shopping bags and a nurse with two children. Businessmen bustled by with briefcases, on their way to catch the subway home. A traffic cop was directing traffic as more people erupted out of office buildings, eager to get to their destination.

She walked with more purpose as she approached their apartment building. She glanced at her watch. Yes, she would have plenty of time to call Ben in Albany. If he wasn't in, she'd leave a message that she and her husband were coming to Albany for the weekend and that she hoped to see him. If he were at the psychiatric hospital with his mother, that would be difficult, but Meg kept her hopes up. Either way she knew it would be difficult with Adam around.

She entered the building, nodded to James the doorman, got in the elevator, told the elevator boy what floor she wanted and soon arrived at the apartment. Upon entering, she took off her fur coat, threw it on a chair in the hallway and made for the telephone as though she could not get to it fast enough. Rather breathlessly, she asked the operator to call the Ten Eyck Hotel in Albany. To her disappointment Ben Faraday was not in. He was still registered at the hotel, although the clerk mentioned that Mr. Faraday was at the hospital and would return later in the evening. Did she care to leave a message?

"Yes, please," Meg said. "Please tell Mr. Faraday that Mrs. Megan Cary called and that I will be in Albany this weekend. I'll call him tomorrow evening."

Meg hung up and sighed. What was she doing, calling this strange man, someone she did not really know? She turned from the phone and went into the bedroom to start packing for the trip tomorrow.

Adam arrived home from the lab early and went to bed early after a light supper. Meg was surprised he came home so early. Didn't he have to work late tonight too? She looked at her husband in annoyance as he crawled into bed and quickly fell asleep. But Meg could not sleep as soundly. She tossed and turned, wide awake and got up fitfully, her mind burdened with the trip. She sat in a chair by the window and saw dawn coming. She must have finally dozed because she awoke with a start when Adam shook her rather roughly by the shoulders.

"I'll meet you here after work," he said. "Pack your suitcase and some things for me, too. We'll leave for Grand Central afterwards. I already have the tickets." He said goodbye to her and walked out the apartment, taking his briefcase.

She took out a suitcase from the bedroom closet, threw things pertaining to herself and Adam in it, closed it and had it ready in the hallway for when they returned.

AN UNFORTUNATE COINCIDENCE

Why were they taking this useless trip anyway? Meg had just returned from Albany on Monday and here it was Friday and she would soon be going there again and seeing her mother-in-law, too. She wished she and Adam were not taking this trip to Albany. She hesitated, irresolute, wondering what the weekend held. She then got up, fixed a light breakfast, and left the apartment.

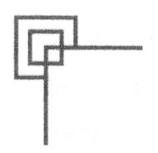

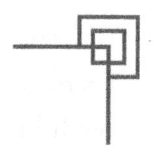

CHAPTER NINE

Grace Prescott looked at herself in her hallway mirror. She applied lipstick, rouge, put on her fur coat, cloche hat and then wrapped her scarf around her neck. She smiled at her appearance. At fifty Grace thought she looked well. A trifle overweight, but she worked on controlling that. She opened her pocketbook, took out gloves and left her house, not bothering to lock the door. In her neighborhood, locked doors were not needed.

Grace lived on upper State Street, across from Washington Park. Her brownstone house was fashionable. She volunteered at Albany Hospital and took an active role in church functions, charity fundraisers and the Republican party. She strongly hoped Herbert Hoover would win the nomination for the upcoming election.

She called Helen earlier in the day and asked if she could visit. From Helen's tone, Grace could tell she wasn't especially pleased to hear from her, but she relented and said around eleven would be fine.

Grace smiled maliciously as she made her way in the snow toward lower State Street. Helen Cary, the woman with so many secrets in her past. And that hideous woman she called her maid and the man who was her driver. Well, she kept a full house. Didn't they crave some privacy, Grace wondered. Of course, the house had five floors, but Grace pondered such a strange living arrangement.

She arrived at Helen's large, imposing brownstone, climbed the steps, and rang the bell. After a few moments, Ida Munson appeared with her usual downcast expression. She peered behind the curtain, opened the door carefully, greeted Grace mechanically and stepped back to allow her to enter.

"Hello, Ida dear," Grace said cheerfully as she took off her coat and gave her belongings to the maid. "Terribly cold out today, isn't it? More snow in the forecast, too, I heard on the radio. How is Helen?"

Ida mumbled something incoherent as was her custom and then brought Grace down the hallway to the living room, where Helen sat before the crackling fire. She was busy knitting, but stopped, and then rose to greet Grace. She seems glad to see me, Grace thought, but knew it was an act. Helen greeted Grace as though she were the most important person in her life, as though it made her day complete. She invited Grace to sit in one of the comfortable chairs by the fire and then asked Ida to bring coffee and cake.

"Thank you, Helen dear," Grace said warmly. "I can't stay too long but I wanted to drop by to see you."

Helen nodded and cleared her throat. "It's nice to see you again, Grace. Terrible weather, isn't it, even for January." Helen had on a long gray dress with a buttoned gray sweater over a navy-blue blouse. No make-up, but a pleasant appearance. I've worn much better, Grace thought, studying her adversary. Ida brought in a tray with coffee and cream.

"I see Iris sometimes," Grace said as she added cream to her coffee. "She seems happy at the state library."

Helen agreed. "And Bruce teaches at Albany Academy."

She asked about Elsie and Richard and was told Elsie had already left for work at the state capital. Richard was still upstairs. Helen mentioned how her brother-in-law spent much of his time at the state library.

"Oh yes, Richard is retired," Grace commented. Changing the subject, she added, "You still volunteer at the hospital, Helen?"

"When I have the time," Helen said. Her tone implied it was really none of Grace's business. She knew Grace also volunteered there and preferred her not to know about her personal life.

"Adam and Meg are visiting later today," Helen said as though to change the subject. "Would you like to visit again?"

Grace, never at a loss for words, stumbled in surprise. "Well, I…"

"We plan to go to Keeler's for dinner. Would you care to join us?"

Grace was so dumbstruck that she momentarily couldn't talk. Since when did Helen go all out for a family gathering and why in the world would she want Grace to attend? She wasn't part of this family. Thank goodness, she thought. But there had to be something she didn't know. After composing herself, Grace cleared her throat.

"Well, Helen dear, thank you kindly, but since it's a family gathering, I'd only be in the way. So, I'll have to decline your generous invitation."

Helen insisted. "Don't worry, Grace. You hardly ever see Adam and Meg." She paused and put her cup on the coffee table. "The reservation is for seven o'clock tomorrow night at Keeler's. Of course, you know where that is, so we'll see you there."

She seemed to have made up Grace's mind. If she played her cards right, Grace could find out exactly what was happening. And add some dimension of her own.

"Thank you, Helen," she said beamingly. "It'll be my pleasure to be there!"

As expected for Friday evening, Grand Central Station was crowded. Meg and Adam finished work early, arrived back at their apartment closer to four thirty, ate a quick meal of salad and chicken and then, suitcase in hand, headed over to the train station. They hailed a cab to take them there.

Adam looked up at the departures board and saw the Empire State Express, in route to Buffalo had a slight delay. He sighed and turned to Meg.

"It's running late," he said, adjusting his hat and fidgeting with his tie. "Should have realized it for Friday."

With people going in all directions, it was a scene of chaotic activity. After a short delay, the Empire State Express was finally called. Adam grabbed the suitcase and then he and Meg walked down the platform for the train to Albany.

As she settled in a seat and glanced around her, Meg was reminded of a week ago when she traveled to Albany and met Mrs. Hanson. And Ben, of course. She was so deep in thought that she didn't realize Adam was speaking to her. He put the suitcase, his hat, jacket, and coat on the rack above their heads.

"Give me your coat, Meg," he said rather impatiently. Meg handed him her hat, scarf, gloves, and coat. After the conductor checked their tickets, Adam took out *The New York Times* from the suitcase and flipped through the pages, seemingly ignoring Meg.

Meg looked out the window at the underground station. She wondered if she would see Ben Faraday this weekend. He was still in Albany. She wanted that very much.

AN UNFORTUNATE COINCIDENCE

Upon arriving at Union Station, Adam and Meg caught a cab to take them to his mother's house. They soon arrived on Willett Street and after Adam paid the driver and collected their suitcase from the trunk, they climbed the snowy front steps, rang the doorbell, and were greeted by Ida.

She opened the door for them to enter and then took their coats. Not much was said other than the usual formalities. Of course, Meg had been here just last Friday, but Adam hadn't been in over a year.

They started to walk down the long hallway, heading for the living room. To their left, a large antique mirror hung on the wall near the great staircase, with its huge ornate banister and thick Oriental rug. There were artificial flowers in a crystal vase on an antique table underneath the mirror. Above their heads hung a huge antique crystal chandelier. Further down the hallway was the entrance to the living room where they could hear a fire crackling. A telephone stand with a bench was next to the living room entrance. She admired how her mother-in-law had preserved the house for so long. She turned to Ida.

"Is Helen in the living room?"

"Yes, I'll take you."

Ida led them down the hall to the double doors which were already wide open.

Helen put down her book and attempted to rise out of her chair.

"Don't get up, Mother," Adam said. He hugged and kissed her.

"Adam dear and Meg," said Helen and smiled.

Meg also hugged and kissed her and then she and Adam sat on the Victorian couch facing Helen. There was an awkward silence between them as though they had just met and did not know what to say. Helen began by clearing her throat and commenting on how well they both looked and how pleased she was that everything was going well for them. And then the terrible snowstorm and oh, wasn't it dreadful? She seemed to be addressing Adam rather than Meg. Of course, she had seen Meg just a week ago compared to the year since she had seen Adam.

The living room was cheerful and rather feminine with a high ceiling and light flowered wallpaper. Everything in the room seemed to be blue and white, the covers on the sofa, the oval rug on the floor. To Helen's right near her favorite armchair was a rather distinguished marble fireplace with a brass fire screen. On the wall behind the couch were two enormous bookcases. A large radio console stood between the windows overlooking Willett Street. And in the corner near the far window was a roll-top desk which Helen used for her correspondence.

As Meg thought a week ago, her mother-in-law was fairing rather well. She watched her as she addressed Adam, her grayish hair, her dark but alert eyes, her wrinkled yet still pretty face. The dress Helen wore was of a dark gray, almost identical to what she saw her wearing last weekend, rather appropriate for winter.

Ida came bustling in with a tray of coffee and cinnamon cake. As usual with Ida, she stubbed her shoe on the corner of the coffee table, nearly knocking the coffee pot onto the floor. Adam saved it by taking the tray from her and setting it on the table. Meg looked from Ida, to Adam, and back again to Ida, wondering what had upset her. Obviously, something did.

"Can't you try to be more careful, Ida?" Helen said irritably.

"Yes, Mrs. Cary. I'm so sorry!" She turned and nearly ran out of the room, her face flushed from embarrassment.

Adam turned to his mother. "You don't have to be so hard on her."

"You don't know Ida. She stumbles into everything! Why the other night she caused my magazines to fall to the floor," Helen said as though that was a crime of major proportions.

"Is Ida a good cook?" Adam asked as he poured coffee for the three of them.

"She is the best."

Adam said that he would look forward to Ida's cooking and then lapsed into silence. Meg fidgeted with her coffee cup and nearly spilled it on her blouse. Helen intervened.

"Iris is upstairs, Meg. I'll have Ida bring your suitcase to the guest room."

Meg thanked her and welcomed the escape. "It was a rather long train trip," she said, feeling rather out-of-place. She excused herself from her husband and mother-in-law and then proceeded out of the living room, into the hallway and up the stairs. When she was gone, Helen turned to her son.

"Well, how have you been, Adam?" she inquired in a rather artificial tone.

"Terrific. My work is great. It couldn't be better!"

"I'm concerned, Adam," she repeated rather tiredly. "I haven't seen you for a while now." She paused and Adam knew she was about to get to the point. "Adam, perhaps it is none of my business but…" She hesitated. "I know you've just gotten here, of course, but Iris told me about a man Meg met along with his mother last weekend here in Albany." She paused. "She also told me, Elsie and Richard. Perhaps she mentioned it to you, too?"

"Yes, Mother. Meg did tell me about this man and his mother." He paused, sipped some coffee. "And I really could care less."

Helen was perturbed. "Well, I'd think you would care!"

"What are you trying to imply?"

"Well, nothing, really."

"I wouldn't worry, Mother," he lied convincingly. "Meg and I are doing just fine." To his surprise she backed down. Adam chuckled, which made Helen even more annoyed. "I didn't realize you cared so much. Meg is not involved with another man, not that I'm aware of." He paused again, abruptly changing the subject. "Why don't you come to the city for a visit? You always liked to go shopping in New York."

"I volunteer at the hospital, you know. Sometimes I just like staying put, Adam." She felt remorse and even sounded sentimental. "At least I have Elsie, Richard, Iris and Bruce here."

At this last remark, Ida entered and removed the tray from the coffee table. She mentioned Iris and Bruce were setting up a bridge game in the dining room. "Elsie and Richard are joining them," she said to Adam, rather flustered. "Do you care to join too?"

Adam hesitated, then said he'd play. "After all, I play a mean bridge game and will skunk them all!"

Ida recoiled from such a comment and even Helen glared at him in distaste.

"I'll get Meg to join us," he said energetically. He left the living room hastily and ran upstairs to the third floor.

Ida looked at her mistress and her face alone was enough to convey her confusion and antipathy. Helen sat brooding, too irritated to even move. Putting her coffee cup to her lips, she concluded this would be a memorable weekend.

AN UNFORTUNATE COINCIDENCE

Meg went upstairs to unpack and freshen up. She put her suitcase on the bed and went over to the windows. She wanted to call Ben to see if he was available.

She came out of the guest room, stood by the stairs, and could hear Adam and Helen conversing in the living room. She was about to return to the guest room when Adam bounded up the stairs, two at a time and full of energy.

"We're starting a bridge game in the dining room," he explained. "Come on, Meg, join us!" He looked at her intently. Meg didn't know her husband was so enthused about a card game.

"First I want to call Mr. Faraday." She was surprised she came right out and admitted her intentions. She was expecting him to blow up but instead he shrugged. He told her he'd meet her in the dining room.

He turned and descended the stairs, Meg following. She glanced at her watch. It was not quite ten o'clock, still too early for sleeping. After Adam disappeared down the hallway to the dining room, she could hear pleasant exclamations, rather loudly, from Iris, Bruce, Elsie, and Richard upon seeing him. With that uproar, Meg quietly picked up the receiver, for she knew Helen was still in the living room and might overhear. She asked the operator to dial the Ten Eyck Hotel and in no time was put through to the front desk, who then connected her to Ben's room.

"Oh Ben," she cried, happy to hear his voice. "I'm back in Albany with my husband at my mother-in-law's house."

"I'm glad you called," Ben said. "We can get together while you're here." "I'd like that, Ben. How's your mother doing?"

Ben explained his mother was well and that she was staying with him at the hotel.

"You were lucky to catch me here," he told her. "I'm going to a boarding house on State Street tomorrow with my mother. She's been released from the hospital and is with me until she's admitted to the psychiatric hospital."

"Where on State Street?" Meg asked.

Ben told her the address and Meg exclaimed that it was practically around the corner from her mother-in-law's house. She gave him her mother-in-law's address and phone number.

"In case you need me," she told him sympathetically.

"Maybe we can see each other this weekend," he repeated and sounded hopeful.

From the dining room entrance Meg suddenly heard voices as though someone was approaching. "I'll call you later, Ben," she whispered. She hung up rather quickly; just in time for Adam entered the hallway, looking rather annoyed.

"What's wrong?" Meg asked him.

"Well, are you joining us for bridge?" he asked rather impatiently.

Meg forced a smile. "I just spoke with Mr. Faraday. His mother's doing fine." Like Adam cared about Ben or his mother. She added, "I may call him later tonight."

Adam sighed impatiently. "Join us in the dining room."

Upon entering the dining room, Iris, Bruce, Elsie, and Richard greeted Meg warmly, beckoned her to sit and enjoy a round of bridge.

"And this time I'll be the winner!" Elsie exclaimed triumphantly. Once Adam and Meg were settled, Bruce shuffled the cards, dealt them out, and the bridge game got underway.

Later in the evening, close to midnight, they retired to the third-floor guest room. It was a simple room, with two beds. A portable typewriter on a stand, with a chair in front, stood to the right of a closet door. A comfortable room, albeit small, but Meg supposed it suited the purpose of having guests. She assumed her mother-in-law didn't have many guests.

She kept her voice low as she knew Helen's bedroom was across the hall on the same floor. As she prepared for bed, she turned to Adam who sat moodily in an easy chair near the window, looking out at the blackness of the night.

"I tried calling you when I was here in Albany," Meg said as she turned down the bed. "John Evans told me he saw you at a speakeasy Saturday evening." She paused. "You called and spoke to your mother while I was here."

"No, I didn't try to reach you last Friday," he said without remorse. "I worked extremely late Friday night and Saturday. And yes, I did go to a speakeasy Saturday evening." He then added, "And had a good time, too."

Adam simply looked at her and without blinking an eye, crawled into bed. You have a good sleep, she thought angrily. Maybe a permanent one. Meg was startled. What made her think that? Janet Faraday and how she managed to get rid of the man in her life. Mrs. Snyder, too. But they both suffered because of it. Was it worth it? A lifetime of mental anguish?

But as she turned off the light on the nightstand, she thought that perhaps it was worth it indeed.

Meg tossed and turned and finally fell asleep after what seemed hours. As she awoke, she glanced at the bed next to her and saw it was empty. Adam already got up. She put on her robe, slippers, and opened the guest room door. She could hear Harmon and Adam downstairs, chatting in the dining room. Elsie and Richard were also there as were Iris and Bruce. And where was Helen? Meg glanced at her door down the hall and saw it still closed, so she assumed she was also asleep. She closed the guest room door, climbed down the stairs, walked down the hallway, and entered the dining room.

"Good morning, Meg," Iris said pleasantly. "Sleep well?"

Bruce was buttering toast, Richard was absorbed in the morning paper, Elsie was sipping tea and Adam was eating cereal. Meg greeted everyone and told Ida she'd like coffee and a muffin. Adam ignored her as he ate.

"I'm fine, Iris," Meg said. "Is Helen up?"

Elsie shook her head. "No, she hasn't gotten up yet. She's tired, poor dear."

"Good morning, everyone," came a raspy female voice from the dining room entrance. "How nice to have everyone here!" Helen swept into the room and sat at the head of the table. She told Ida coffee would be fine, and toast, too.

"How are you, Adam? And Meg, dear? Did everyone sleep well? I hope so because we have big plans for tonight!"

Even Richard took his eyes off the paper to look at his sister-in-law. "Big plans?"

Helen sipped her coffee. "I made a reservation at Keeler's tonight. Seven o'clock. The food is delicious and Grace Prescott will be joining us. I'm looking forward to it."

"That sounds nice, Mother," Iris said. "I haven't been to Keeler's in years! What's the occasion? Anything special?"

Helen shook her head and smiled. "No, dear, it'll be a nice evening and I believe there's a dance band there, too."

Elsie and Richard made approving comments as did Bruce. Even Adam showed his approval. Meg was silent wondering what her mother-in-law was up to and why she would invite Grace Prescott.

Iris asked Meg if she'd like to go to Whitney's Department Store to shop for hats. Meg came out of her reverie and told her yes, she'd like that very much, anything to escape this hideous house. She glanced at Adam, never knowing how to read him, or what machinations he had in store. She told Iris that they'd eat lunch at Whitney's lunch counter while there.

Afternoon quickly came to an end and darkness encroached on the city as four thirty arrived. Meg and Iris bustled in about that time, with a hat box each. Iris proudly displayed her new cloche hat to her husband as he sat in the living room with Adam, Richard, and Elsie.

"How many hats do you have now, Iris?" her husband asked, keeping the disapproval out of his voice. Soon she'd have an entire bureau full of them, he thought.

Iris ignored it. "Not enough," she exclaimed and tried it on in front of a mirror in the living room. She turned to look at her audience. "What do you think?"

Elsie spoke up first. "It looks lovely, Iris. Perfect with your outfit, too."

It was a white cloche hat with tan trim and very chic. Meg also had a new hat, similar in style only navy blue with light blue trim.

"You know how to pick a nice hat," Richard said and smiled.

Adam then coughed and spoke with a cigarette between his lips.

"Nice hats," was his laconic reply.

They were sipping coffee, with the radio console tuned to a jazz station. Bruce got up and added another log to the fire and Elsie refilled Richard's cup.

"Isn't it nice that Mother invited us for dinner at Keeler's?" Iris said to no one in particular. She sat next to her husband and took a cup from Elsie.

Bruce was about to comment when Helen came into the living room just then cutting off any further conversation. Meg thought her mother-in-law had that effect. She looked at her closely. Helen walked slowly and looked lopsided and ill at ease in a black evening dress. She looked quickly around at her family and appeared to be in a thoroughly foul temper, in contrast to her happier mood from this morning. That Helen Cary was rather moody was an understatement.

"We'll be leaving soon for Keeler's. I invited Ida and Harmon, too."

Meg showed surprised. Even Iris looked at her mother as though she had gone mad. Inviting servants to dinner at a fine restaurant like Keeler's? Meg knew she was close to Ida and Harmon but didn't think she'd include them in a family outing. But then she asked Grace Prescott to attend, too.

"We should be leaving soon," she added.

"I'd like to change my dress," Elsie said and got up from the chair. She and Richard left to change into more formal wear.

Ida said she'd clean the kitchen and then change into a dress. Adam cleared his throat and mentioned he also would change his suit and get ready for the dinner. Meg watched her husband, as he slowly got up, ignored her completely and then walked out of the living room.

"You'll enjoy the dinner tonight, Meg," Helen said to her daughter-in-law. "The food at Keeler's is the best. And there's a band. I might even dance if I feel up to it."

Meg thanked Helen for her generosity, wondering what the battleax had up her sleeve. She didn't trust her but was rather taken aback by her pleasantness, even if it was phony to an extent.

"I'll check on Adam," she said to Helen. "I'll change my dress, too."

AN UNFORTUNATE COINCIDENCE

Meg went upstairs to see Adam and to change clothes. Afterward she tried to remember everything that transpired during the evening but could not.

◆◇

At close to seven that evening, Harmon pulled the car in front of the house and with their coats on and scarves wrapped around their necks, Helen, Elsie, Richard, Iris, Bruce, Meg and Adam made their way down the front steps and into the car. Ida locked the front door and then joined the group, sitting in the front seat while Harmon drove.

As Harmon drove down State Street and approached the state capital, the traffic was heavy, and they had to wait for the bottleneck to clear before arriving at the bottom of State Street. As he pulled up in front of the restaurant, a valet approached and offered to park the car. Harmon handed the keys to the young man, got out and entered the elegant restaurant with the rest.

Meg had never been inside Keeler's. It had an excellent reputation and attracted politicians, businessmen and well-to-do families. Upon leaving their coats with the attendant at the cloak room, Helen was greeted pleasantly by the head waiter who ushered them to a reserved table in one of the large dining rooms, where already people were enjoying a fabulous meal and dancing to the music of a swing band. It was a festive atmosphere, with much laughter and sparkling conversations.

The dining room was of exemplary sophistication and painstaking perfection; the blue tiled floor was pristine and the large crystal chandelier was exquisite.

Meg looked around in approval. What a great place! And the music was certainly inviting. She looked elegant in a white evening dress, with lovely pearls and silver earrings. She sat next to Adam and took a menu from the waiter. Iris, Bruce, Elsie and Richard also accepted a menu and gazed at the dinner entrees. Even Ida and Harmon appreciated the food offerings and the ambience. Helen looked up from chatting with Elsie and Richard and saw Grace Prescott make her way over to their table.

Grace was severely although appropriately attired in a long gray dress with black trim at the waist. Helen rose and went forward to greet her. "Grace, I'm *so* glad to see you." They hugged and then Grace took an empty chair next to Adam.

"Grace, you remember my daughter-in-law, Megan."

"Of course, Megan dear. I haven't seen you in so long! And Iris and Bruce!" She paused.

"Adam, you're looking nice this evening." She glanced further down the table. "Oh, Ida and Harmon, what a pleasure to see both of you!"

Shock was the better word, Meg thought, as she looked at Grace's startled face, obviously wondering like everyone else why Helen would invite her servants to a fancy restaurant. But then Grace merely shrugged and accepted a dinner menu from a waiter.

On a pad another waiter was busy scribbling the various dinner choices. Conversations ensued and pleasantries continued in earnest. The food was exceptional, and they enjoyed a hearty meal.

The band continued playing and the rhythm was enticing. It wasn't long before Iris, Bruce, Richard and Elsie were dancing with everyone else, first the Charleston and then the Lindy Hop. The music was lively, and the dance floor was full. Richard finished dancing with Elsie and he soon asked Meg to dance, which she graciously accepted. Harmon and Ida were also on the dance floor, obviously enjoying the music.

Elsie mentioned to Adam if he'd like to dance, but he puffed moodily on his cigarette and declined.

Harmon returned to the table with Ida. He asked Helen if she'd care to dance. She got up and met him in the center of the dance floor, while Meg sat down after dancing with Richard. Bruce and Iris were still dancing while Richard and Elsie got started once again.

"Look at Mrs. Cary and Harmon!" Ida exclaimed in amazement, from behind Meg. "You'd think they were Vernon and Irene Castle!"

Meg looked toward Helen and Harmon, who were indeed enjoying an intimate fox trot. Adam remained at the table and although he ate plenty and appeared in good spirits earlier, now seemed irritable and smoked one cigarette after another. Meg briefly turned to her husband as though to ask him to dance but changed her mind. Helen and Harmon returned at the conclusion of the fox trot. Elsie, Richard, Bruce and Iris also returned to the table after dancing.

Helen cleared her throat. "I'm glad to have my son and daughter-in-law here, especially since I haven't seen you for so long." She smiled and appeared in a better mood than before leaving the house. "And Iris and Bruce. I cannot remember when we were all together like this!"

Meg wanted to say that she remembered when they were last together; last Christmas when Adam and his mother quarreled at the dinner table. Didn't her mother-in-law remember that?

"I'm so fortunate to have my sister and brother-in-law here, along with my faithful Ida and Harmon. And the rest of my wonderful family!"

Meg wondered what the point was, if she was making one, except that she got sentimental in her middle-age. Everyone murmured appreciation. The waiter approached with chocolate cake and more coffee. He filled everyone's cup and began handing out dainty white plates of the rich cake.

"When I made the reservation, I specifically requested the chocolate layer cake," Helen beamed as everyone appreciated the texture of the dessert. "Walter and I ate here years ago. It was delicious!"

Meg stopped with her fork almost in mid-air. Walter Cary, her husband, who died years ago. Strange, she never mentioned him. Wasn't there some mystery to his death? She took a drag on her cigarette and looked at Adam. This time he met her gaze. As usual she couldn't read him but saw something different. A melancholia, a certain sadness, almost as though he missed something or someone. She didn't think Adam was the sentimental type. He drank more coffee and dug into his piece of chocolate cake.

Dancing then continued and Iris and Bruce again rose to join in the fun, along with Elsie and Richard. To Meg's surprise, Adam asked Helen to dance. She joined him in a swing dance. Observing Adam, Meg didn't realize her husband could dance so well. Ida excused herself for the powder room, while Harmon and Grace danced too, leaving Meg sitting alone. She was watching the dancing for quite some time and enjoying the music, her back to the table, when a male voice suddenly called her name. She turned. Standing near her was Ben Faraday, along with his mother.

"Ben," she said in complete shock. "Wh-What are you doing here?"

"Well, we were walking around and wanted dinner." Ben looked at the dance floor. "The music's great, isn't it?"

"Ben, I'm here with my husband and in-laws," Meg said still in shock. She looked at Mrs. Hanson or Janet Faraday or whatever name she used. Meg thought she looked older and more shrunken, almost sickly.

"Nice to see you again, Meg," Janet Faraday said and smiled faintly.

By this time, the music stopped, and people returned to tables scattered around the large dining room. Iris, Bruce, Elsie, and Richard sat down, having enjoyed the dancing and the music. Helen and Adam also came back. Ida returned from the powder room and sat next to Helen, while Harmon and Grace also returned from the dance floor. Adam finished his coffee but did not sit. He glared at his wife and the young man next to her. He was clearly in a bad temper.

Seeing Ben, a light bulb went on in Adam's mind. He looked at his wife and then at Ben and could figure out who the handsome young man was who stood next to her. Meg felt her heart lunge.

"Is this that friend of yours, Meg?" he asked, a cigarette dangling from his mouth. He glanced at the small, dowdy woman standing next to Ben.

"Oh, how nice to have unexpected company!" Grace Prescott beamed. "I always say a full table is the best!"

"So, you *are* the guy with the crazy mother!" Adam said mockingly, looking at Ben. "Meg told me all about it." He blew smoke from his cigarette.

"Meg, did you invite him here?" Helen asked as she glanced at Ben. Helen didn't see his mother behind him, but her gaze returned to her daughter-in-law.

"I'm sorry if I've disturbed your party," Ben said and moved closer to the table where everyone could see him. He looked at them anxiously, with a puzzled, disconcerted expression.

"Would you care to join us?" Iris asked Ben and then glanced at her mother. She regretted saying it.

"No, thank you," Ben said uneasily.

"It just so happened you found my wife here," Adam said and took a step closer to Ben. "Did you arrange to meet here? It's just a coincidence?"

Meg got between the two men. There was a moment of shocked silence while everyone looked at Adam. It was obvious he was angry;

his face became red. Realizing Adam was upset, Helen rose and immediately took control of the situation.

"Who are these people?" she demanded harshly. "Why are they at our table? Meg, did you arrange for them to be here? I'll call the waiter and have them removed!"

"You're here to meet my wife," Adam persisted. "You could've gone to any restaurant, but you came to this one! You knew she'd be here!"

"No, I didn't come here to meet Meg," Ben explained. "My mother and I are staying at the Ten Eyck Hotel just up State Street."

There ensued an awkward silence as Adam continued glaring at Ben and Janet Faraday, huddled behind him. Music started again and the band beckoned more dancing, but no one at the table got up.

"I don't believe you!" Adam said rather loudly causing several people at other tables to look his way. He was indignant.

"Adam, control yourself!" Iris said, attempting to calm him. Even Bruce attempted to control his brother-in-law, but it was to no avail.

Adam ignored them. Meg, who knew her husband could be dangerous when angry, held her breath. She continued standing between Adam and Ben. Everyone looked at Ben Faraday in stunned silence expecting an answer. But by then it was too late. Like a wild man Adam lunged for Ben, knocking the latter off balance. A struggle ensued but Ben regained himself and fought back. Adam delivered a blow to Ben's left side and Ben retaliated with a swift jab in the ribs. Chairs went over as more punches were thrown. Arms, legs, bodies twisting and turning; it took Harmon, Bruce, and several waiters to break the men apart. Cursing, Adam was led out of the dining room by the head waiter to another dining room. Ben got up and attempted to pull himself together, straightening his shirt, tie, jacket, and ruffled hair.

Adding to the confusion and causing more mayhem to the already chaotic scene, Janet Faraday suddenly gave a sharp cry and slumped forward in a dead faint. At the same time, Helen, unaccustomed to such an intrusion, frantically put her hand to her chest, gasped for breath and collapsed, taking half of the tablecloth with her, knocking over cups, saucers, plates and silverware.

"Mother!" Iris screamed and went quickly to aide her. She grabbed her wrist and felt for a pulse. "Someone, call an ambulance!"

Ida rushed to the head waiter and pleaded for him to call for help, while the manager entered and demanded to know what the ruckus was about. Harmon explained what happened. Meg, Iris and Elsie tried to resuscitate Helen. Ben pulled his mother aside and shook her face a bit to try to bring her around.

After verifying the home address with the ambulance service, Ida soon returned from the hallway. Other people were coming in and out of the dining room, approaching the table, asking if they needed assistance. Meg thought she heard someone ask for smelling salts, but no one had any.

After a few moments, Meg looked around. Fortunately, the music started up again. She was grateful as it seemed to divert attention from their table. And what had become of Ben? As if in answer to her thoughts, he appeared with a glass of water.

"I thought this might bring her around," he said. He handed it to his mother, who was slowly regaining consciousness and sitting up. He lit a cigarette, took a long puff of smoke, and looked at Meg feeling a trifle embarrassed. "I guess I did the wrong thing by coming here."

"You didn't know I'd be here, Ben. Don't think of that now."

"What about your mother-in-law?"

"Ida asked them to call an ambulance," Meg explained.

"My mother faints easily," Ben said looking down at her. His glance then went back to Helen who remained on the floor near the table. Harmon appeared and told them the ambulance arrived. At that moment three men in white uniforms entered the elegant dining room.

At first, they didn't know which woman to attend to until Iris, sobbing, told them to assist her mother. They lifted Helen onto a stretcher and took her out to the ambulance. Ben went for more water leaving Meg alone momentarily with Janet Faraday.

Meg looked at the dishes, cups, saucers and utensils on the floor, the chairs overturned, and the tablecloth pulled halfway off by Helen as she collapsed. Her gaze went to the other people in the dining room, either leaving after witnessing such a horrid scene or deciding to stay, enjoy themselves and ignore it.

Meg then thought of Grace Prescott and turned expecting to see her. She looked at the toppled cups and spilled coffee and realized Grace Prescott was not in the room. Where had she gone? In the pandemonium, she paid no attention to the Prescott woman. Had she left? There came a quiet sobbing. Meg realized it was Janet Faraday calling her name. She had regained consciousness but was still lying on the floor. Meg bent down and put her hands over hers. They were cold and clammy as if death had settled over her. She whispered hoarsely to Meg.

"My son, Meg. Please. He's a good man…"

Meg got her to sit up completely while Ben returned with more water. With Ben's and Meg's aide, she steadied herself by leaning on the table. She looked around and smiled.

"Oh, such a lovely dining room! And the music is wonderful!"

"Are you okay, Mother?" he asked her.

Janet Faraday finished the water. "I'll be all right, dear. Just a little shock and excitement. I'm so sorry, Meg, for interrupting your dinner party."

Iris came over and expressed her concern for Ben's mother. She mentioned that she and Bruce were going to Albany Hospital, along with Elsie and Richard.

"I'm sorry," was all Ben could say again.

"Don't think about it," Iris reassured him. "Mother should pull through."

Harmon approached them, clearly shaken and upset.

"I asked the manager to call a taxi for you and your mother," he told Ben. "Did you want your mother to go to the hospital, too?"

Ben thanked him and said the hospital wasn't necessary. With Meg's help, Janet Faraday walked to the entrance. Meg told Ben she'd call tomorrow at the hotel then returned to her in-law's table.

"This shouldn't have happened to Mrs. Cary," Ida said, clearly upset, by Harmon's side, wiping away a few tears. She also wanted to go to the hospital to see Helen. She had collected their belongings from the coat check. They were putting on their coats when suddenly Elsie spoke.

"Where's Adam?"

Everyone looked around at once. No one knew what became of Adam. In the ensuing chaos, it was as if they momentarily forgot about Adam.

"Where's Adam?" Elsie repeated somewhat impatiently.

"He went into another dining room," Richard said. "A waiter brought him there."

"Yes, he was brought into another dining room," Bruce remembered.

Iris and Bruce volunteered to look for Adam. But at that moment a waiter, a young man of no more than twenty, rushed up to their table, flushed and out of breath. His dark hair was falling over his forehead, his eyes bulging with fear, confusion and anxiety.

"The gentleman at your table!" he sputtered incoherently, barely getting the words out. "In the other dining room! He won't talk or move and…and he's dead!"

This time it was Meg who pitched forward and clutched onto the tablecloth as darkness descended upon her and everything went black.

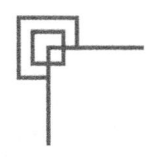

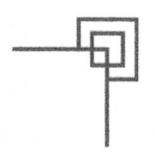

CHAPTER TEN

The scene at the restaurant was indeed grave and chaotic. Richard helped Meg up and settled her carefully in a chair. A waiter brought coffee and it helped to revive her. Richard felt her pulse and patted her face a little, to try to bring color and life back to her. Meg slowly blinked, looked at everyone near her and managed a faint smile.

"What happened?" she asked weakly. "Adam? What happened to him?" Then the memory of what occurred came flooding back and once again she felt weak. Richard gave her the coffee and encouraged her to finish it.

"Do you want us to call a doctor, Meg?" Elsie asked.

Meg shook her head. "I'll be all right, Elsie, thanks."

"We'll stay here with you, Meg," Iris said with concern. She had her coat on and was getting ready to leave the restaurant with Bruce, Elsie, and Richard.

Meg shook her head. "I'm fine, Iris." She stood slowly and Richard helped her up. Bruce and Harmon returned their faces ashen white. They looked helplessly at the group centered around Meg and neither spoke. It was Meg who broke the awkward silence.

"Is Adam really dead?"

Harmon cleared his throat and looked at her and then at the rest of the family. Slowly, he nodded. "Yes, the waiters found him on the floor in the other dining room."

"But how did he die?" Meg asked incredulously.

Harmon shook his head. "We don't know."

Meg listened to Harmon, not believing what she heard. "He seemed fine an hour ago," she mumbled rather incoherently.

Harmon again shook his head. "I don't know what happened. Maybe his heart."

"His heart?" Iris interjected. "Adam didn't have a heart condition!"

The restaurant manager returned to the dining room, again perturbed at the events occurring in his place of business. He told them rather curtly that he would call another ambulance, this time for Adam and then asked if Meg wanted to go to the emergency room.

Meg shook her head and stood, assisted by Harmon. "I'd like to go to the hospital to see Helen."

Protests erupted. She needed to rest, and Ida would take care of her. But Meg insisted. Before leaving, Meg wanted to see her husband. Harmon cautioned against it, but Iris also wanted to see her brother. The family walked to the other dining room, which was empty of customers. Upon entering, they saw a figure on the floor, covered by a white sheet. The waiter who found him was speaking to the manager, who assured the family the ambulance was on its way. He was not in least happy that another ambulance would arrive at his restaurant. At first, nobody moved, until Meg went forward followed by Iris and Bruce. She bent down and lifted the sheet slowly.

Adam was lying on his stomach, his face pressed into the carpet. His lifeless body did not move, or breath. Meg felt for his pulse and found none. She replaced the sheet and stood, looking at Iris and Bruce. The ambulance crew entered and were directed to the dining room, where they carefully lifted Adam's lifeless body on a stretcher. The family watched as the ambulance left the restaurant, on its way to the hospital and the morgue.

"Come on, Meg," Bruce said. "There's nothing more you can do here."

Ida helped Meg on with her fur coat and the party then descended on the front entrance, where the valet brought the car around and Harmon got behind the wheel.

Meg clenched and unclenched her hands as she sat in the cold car. A few tears came to her face. She felt so alone and confused but tried to maintain her composure. She reached for Bruce's hand and squeezed it, looking for support. They soon arrived at Albany Hospital. Iris helped Meg out of the car, along with Elsie and Richard. There were few people in emergency at this hour. The nurse told them the doctor would speak to them shortly. Meg inquired about Adam. The nurse called the morgue and was told his body arrived. She gave Meg a form to complete, with name and address. She assured Meg the morgue would contact her shortly.

Finally, after what seemed an eternity, a young doctor in a white coat came out to address them. A sharp, intaking of breath, a hunching of shoulders, a tensing of muscles. They were expecting the worse.

The doctor cleared his throat. "Your mother experienced a slight heart attack," he explained, "most likely induced by severe shock." He paused grimly. "Her condition has stabilized. She should be fine to leave tomorrow."

They looked at the doctor uncertain as to their next plan of action. The doctor turned to address Meg, who appeared calm although shaken by the earlier events.

"What is your relationship to Mrs. Cary?" he asked.

"I'm her daughter-in-law," explained Meg.

"Was she upset by something this evening?"

Harmon cleared his throat. "We had a slight commotion earlier this evening. Mrs. Cary collapsed. We were out to dinner and the restaurant staff immediately called for an ambulance." The doctor nodded. Harmon continued reluctantly. "And her son…he was involved in the fight with the fight."

The doctor shook his head, wondering what kind of people he was dealing with. Meg looked at Bruce, Iris, Elsie, and Richard and could see embarrassment, even disgust. Only Harmon and Ida managed to appear in somewhat control, perhaps in their roles as servants, they were used to such disturbances. Although Meg rather doubted it included a fist fight and sudden death.

"Disturbances could trigger an attack," the doctor told them somewhat awkwardly. "There's nothing more for you to do tonight," he added as though he could not wait to take leave of them.

Meg thanked the doctor. "I'll call in the morning."

Iris stopped at the nurses' station and filled out the appropriate forms. The nurse there told Iris she would call in the interim if needed.

Meg and Iris then reluctantly left the hospital, supported by Elsie, Richard, Bruce, Harmon, and Ida.

On the way back to Willett Street, she stared out the window at the snowy streets. Did Ben plan that? But then he did not know she and the rest of the family would be at that restaurant. Strange, how his mother seemed a part of everything. If that woman had not sat next to her on the train trip, Meg would have never gotten involved in this whole mess. She was thinking of Adam when she realized Bruce was talking to her.

"We're here now" he told her.

He helped her out of the car. Once inside, Elsie and Bruce settled into chairs by the fireplace, gazing absently at the deep armchair that belonged to Helen. Iris scurried off to the kitchen to help Ida, while Bruce turned on the radio console to find a station playing soothing music. Ida soon entered with a tray with mugs, a coffeepot and a jug of cream.

"I'm too tired to stay up," she said wearily.

Iris entered just then and announced that she also was tired.

"I'll just have some coffee first," Elsie said and poured cups for herself and Richard. Bruce and Iris declined as did Meg. Iris hugged Meg and then turned and left the living room, followed by Bruce. Harmon also went to bed.

Elsie gave Meg a reassuring hug. "You need me to come with you upstairs?"

Meg shook her head, thanked Elsie, and then turned and walked out of the living room. Up the stairs and to the guest room, she sat down on the bed and turned on the nightstand light. As she changed into her nightclothes, she noticed a piece of paper on top of the bureau. It was typewritten, explicit in its content.

I CANNOT GO ON. I CAN ENDURE NO LONGER.
I SEE NO OTHER WAY OUT.

Meg read it several times, confused, not understanding it. How did it get here? Who left it? But most importantly, why?

The next morning, Meg decided to not say anything about the note until after breakfast. The mood was solemn. Hardly anyone spoke, except Iris who inquired about Meg. They would be leaving for the hospital. Would she care to go with them?

"Of course," Meg said. "I have to call the hospital morgue to make funeral arrangements for Adam." As Ida cleared the dishes and returned to the kitchen, Meg told the family about the note she found on the bureau before going to sleep last night.

"Do you have it?" Richard asked.

Meg took it from her robe pocket, unfolded it and handed it to Richard, who in turn handed it around the table. Iris, Bruce, and Elsie each read it numerous times, not understanding it.

"It must have been typed on the typewriter in the guest room," Elsie said and handed it back to Meg. "Sounds like a suicide note." A dreaded hush fell over the table, for that thought was present in their minds.

"You think Adam typed it?" Bruce asked.

"Adam wasn't suicidal," Meg said. "If he wanted to kill himself, I don't think he'd chose a restaurant in Albany to do it." She paused. "Although he was upset after meeting Ben Faraday and his mother."

"I never thought Adam was a suicidal type," Elsie said.

"No, I didn't think so either," Richard agreed. He then called to Ida. "Ida, did you clean the guest room prior to Meg and Adam arriving?"

Ida looked her usual haggard self and was taken aback by Richard's question. She looked at the family and wondered what she could have done wrong.

"Yes, of course. Fresh linen, too."

Elsie smiled. "We're asking because of this note Meg found on the bureau last night." Elsie asked Meg for the note again and handed it to Ida. The maid read it several times and then returned it to Meg. She shook her head.

"I don't know anything about it. Perhaps Adam typed it."

Richard thanked Ida and dismissed her. The family sat in terrible silence, which was only broken by the ringing of the phone. Harmon entered the dining room and said the hospital called. Helen was awake and asking for her family.

"We'll go to see Helen after lunch," Richard said, taking control of the situation. Elsie agreed. "We'll need nourishment first." She cast a concerned eye on Meg. Meg finished her coffee and then left the dining room, climbing the stairs to the guest room, with the strange note tucked in her robe pocket.

Ida stood at the kitchen sink, humming softly as she washed and dried the coffee cups and breakfast dishes. The tune she hummed was Helen Kane's "I Want to be Loved by You," which she heard frequently on the radio. She liked it but found that she was not able to concentrate on the melody; it was rather a diversion to keep her from crying again.

She opened the broom closet and looked at the various brooms, dust pans and the carpet sweeper, along with a few cans and boxes of food on the shelves. She already swept the kitchen floor so there was no need to do it again now. She glanced at an old sewing machine stored on the top right. She didn't know why Elsie stored that heavy sewing machine there, but it was out of the way. She heard a key rattle in the front door and Harmon bustled in. He walked down the hallway and stop at the kitchen doorway.

"Ida," he said with concern. "What are you doing?"

"Nothing really," she answered him. "How is it outside?"

"I've shoveled the steps but there's no use! It keeps piling up!"

"Want more coffee?" she asked him.

"I can never refuse your coffee, Ida," Harmon said congenially. He settled into a chair at the kitchen table. Ida turned from the counter with a cup and saucer, along with cream and sugar. She sat across from him and sighed deeply.

"I called the hospital," she explained and told him everything the doctor said.

"We'll have to wait to tell her about Adam." He paused and stirred his coffee.

"When do you want to go to the hospital to pick up Helen?"

"They agreed after lunch." She paused and told Harmon about the note Meg found on the bureau last night. Even Harmon did not understand it.

"Who left it?" he asked as if Ida knew the answer.

"I don't know. But Mrs. Cary will be home today."

Harmon nodded. "Do you think this is a police matter?"

Ida shuddered. "Policemen! I don't want them trampling through the house!"

"Ida, please," Harmon said rather firmly. "In cases of sudden death, the police are always called." He looked at her gravely. "I need to buy gas for the car."

He offered to rekindle the fire in the living room. Ida said she would do it herself and walked with him to the front door. She descended the snowy steps to see him off.

He rolled down the driver's side window and said something about staying safe and locking the doors but with the wind blowing so strongly she barely heard him. She just nodded her head, stood on the steps until the car disappeared around the corner and then went back into the house and closed and locked the door with firmness.

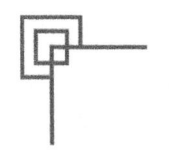

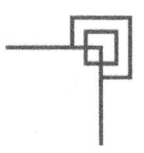

CHAPTER ELEVEN

Iris admitted to herself that she was not in a good humor. While the rest of the family was preparing to leave for the hospital after lunch, she decided to wander around the streets of Albany, mindless of the snow and ice.

Iris wondered about the note left in the guest room. It indeed sounded like a suicide note. Maybe Adam typed it before they left for the restaurant? But if he did take his own life, why would he wait till they went to the restaurant? And he didn't put his name on it, either. Strange.

She went back to the fight between her brother and that Ben character. Adam's behavior was totally uncalled for. And then poor Mother. Of course, violence was not something she was used to. And that other woman fainting. Now why would *she* faint suddenly? She looked like a sickly person, almost as if she were on her deathbed.

Iris stopped on the corner of State and Willett. Her mother's house was just a block down to the left. She glanced ahead to Washington Park and thought how pretty it looked with the snow covering the tree branches. Her face lightened as a new idea entered her mind.

"Of course!" Iris exclaimed. "Grace Prescott! She remembers everything!"

With a firm step, Iris hurriedly walked up State Street. She came to a distinguished looking brownstone house, at the junction of State and Western Avenues. She rang the bell and waited. Iris was about to turn away when the door opened a few inches.

"Grace," she said and caught her breath. "I hope I'm not disturbing you."

Grace Prescott set her mouth firmly. "Well, Iris dear, this certainly is a surprise. Not that I mind, of course. What brings you here this time of day?"

Iris explained she was taking a walk to clear her mind over what happened last night and decided to call on her, hoping she might be of some help. Grace wished she could. She asked about Helen, but Iris mentioned her mother's condition was not the problem.

"You don't know the worst," Iris added grimly.

Grace eyed her carefully and then opened the door allowing Iris to step into the hallway. She took another look at her as she helped her out of her coat.

Iris followed her down a long hallway and at the end entered a large and rather old-fashioned living room with an antique sofa, an elaborate chandelier hanging from the ornate high ceiling and a small fireplace that warmed the room nicely. A radio was playing soft music in the corner. Grace, always the perfect hostess, went to the kitchen and soon returned with a tray containing coffee and a slice of apple pie.

"Just what you need," she said cheerfully.

"I'm not hungry," Iris told her, but her hostess insisted.

She sat on the antique sofa, took the plate, and started to eat. After a few bites, she admitted it was quite good which pleased her hostess. But then she put down the plate and turned to Grace with a grim look upon her face.

"Grace, I must speak to you."

"Your coffee, dear. It'll get cold."

"Oh."

Iris lifted the cup and saucer to her lips, swallowed some of the hot liquid and then began drinking it steadily finding it was doing her good. She finished it and then addressed the woman next to her rather firmly.

"Grace, I need to speak to you, about last night." Grace sipped her coffee, avoiding Iris.

"Did you see anything that happened?"

"Well dear, when your mother collapsed, I was quite startled."

"Like the rest of us," Iris said.

"I worried over Helen. I went to the bathroom when…"

"When what?"

"Iris, I saw Adam in the other dining room. I didn't understand but didn't want to intervene. He appeared sick and confused."

Iris grabbed her arm encouragingly. "That's the part I haven't told you! Adam died last night! The waiter came to our table to tell us!"

"Oh, my dear," Grace said with sympathy. She hugged Iris tenderly and then held her off. "I'm so sorry, Iris. I had no idea about your brother. How terrible for you." She paused and then added, "How did he die, dear?"

"We don't know yet," Iris said. Then she told Grace about the note Meg found in the guest room on the bureau.

Grace frowned. "A suicide?" she pondered.

Iris shook her head. "I don't believe my brother ended his life. Somebody left the note for Meg to find when we returned." She looked at Grace again. "Did you leave right away?"

Grace nodded. "I decided to leave after Helen collapsed."

"You did the right thing," Iris said simply. "It was chaos in that dining room." She got up restlessly and went to the windows overlooking State Street. She was silent for a while.

"Adam is dead and the worse of it is that Mother doesn't know! She's still in the hospital but comes home today."

"Will you tell her today?"

"I don't know," she said as she sat down.

Grace said soothingly. "You have to tell her, Iris. You can't lie to your Mother, you know that."

Iris looked at her carefully. She thanked Grace for the coffee and pie. Grace told her to stay, to calm herself but she refused.

"Thank you, Grace. What you've told me has been helpful."

Returning her look, Grace met her eyes. "Perhaps your brother did take his life." As much as she liked Grace Prescott, she felt she could not tolerate her motherly warmth anymore and had to get away from it. She shook her head vehemently. "No, of course not. Adam didn't kill himself!"

"Did the police come to your house?"

Iris sighed wearily. "Elsie called them, and they plan to come this evening. They'll probably want to talk to you, too."

"Of course, dear, if I can help in anyway."

She walked down the hallway and helped Iris into her coat. They embraced and Grace smiled at her with reassurance. She then grabbed her fur coat from a chair in the hallway and told Iris she would walk with her. "I need the fresh air, dear," she told her.

Iris said she preferred to walk alone. Through a window in the hallway, Grace watched her walk down State Street. When she could not see Iris any longer, she returned to the kitchen thoughtfully.

Scandal was nothing new to Helen Cary. The secrets that rich battleax has in her past! Her first husband's suicide. And of course, her second husband. Now another suspicious death in the Cary family?

AN UNFORTUNATE COINCIDENCE

Despite the snow, a few breaks of an uncertain sun were trying to seep through the low clouds. Those who saw a brief glimpse of it were encouraged that the snow would diminish and eventually come to an end.

Little of this sunlight found its way into the small but comfortable room at the Ten Eyck Hotel where Ben and his mother were staying. Ben blinked several times, trying to orientate to his surroundings. He sat up in bed, reached over for his watch on the bedside table and saw it was almost nine o'clock. He swung his long legs out of the bed, sat immobile for a few minutes and ran his fingers through his wavy black hair.

What a night he had been through! His mother's doctor recommended a walk around Albany and dinner out would do her a world of good. Of course, it was a bitterly cold night but when he suggested it, she seemed eager at the prospect. Neither Ben nor his mother knew Albany, so upon leaving the hospital, they returned to the hotel by taxi and decided to walk around downtown.

So began the adventure, Ben thought as he rose from the bed and proceeded to dress. It had been a long night, especially for his mother. And Meg's mother-in-law, too. He ran a comb through his thick hair. Well, he did see Meg but did not count on her husband making a fool of himself. Accusing him of arranging to meet her?

What an idiot to start a fight in public. As if he were supposed to stand there and take it! He prided himself on lifting weights in college. It came in handy! He looked at his mother, sleeping in the other bed. She stirred slightly, raised her head, and greeted her son with a small smile.

"Are you all right, Mother?" he asked, sitting near her on her bed.

"I'm fine, Benjamin." She sighed. "How is Megan?"

"I've been thinking of calling her." He paused. "Ready for breakfast?"

Janet agreed, got out of bed, and went into the bathroom to prepare for the day. He locked the door and mother and son made their way to the elevator. They entered the dining room on the first floor of the hotel. Ben and Janet helped themselves to coffee from the sideboard. Ben unfolded the morning paper, which lay on the empty chair next to him. Just then the waitress entered with a smile. She was middle-aged, stout, and full of energy.

"Good morning! What can I get for you?"

Ben ordered cereal while Janet asked for coffee and a blueberry muffin.

He put the paper aside and looked around. The room was rather large and decorated in a rustic, Colonial design. There was a fireplace on the wall leading to the kitchen in which danced a bright, warm blaze and to the left a large Colonial bureau. Ben asked his mother if she was relaxing and enjoying Albany.

"Well, it's pleasant," Janet replied, sipping her coffee.

Another woman entered at that moment, brushing snow from her coat. She exclaimed rather breathlessly that she went for a walk but soon returned due to the weather. She introduced herself to Ben and Janet. She was from New Jersey but was in Albany with her husband on business. Ben exchanged a few trifle words of small talk and hoped it would end there but then she totally took him by surprise.

"I heard someone died at a restaurant not far from here last night."

"Oh really?" Ben did not know what else to say. He assumed that Albany had its share of crime, with gangsters and speakeasies like in

Manhattan and Brooklyn. Janet remained quiet and continued drinking her coffee.

The woman nodded. "A woman walking her dog said something about ambulances at Keeler's, anyway…"

"Someone died there last night?" Ben interrupted, trying to maintain composure. The woman nodded. "A son from a family from Willett Street. And two women collapsed, both at the same time, and in the same restaurant!"

Ben and Janet sat frozen. Someone died? Janet's heart lurched. Even Ben felt a peculiar mixture of dread and anticipation and something close to pain.

The death, whoever it was, must have happened after they went back to the hotel. Ben wondered how Meg was coping. Someone died in the restaurant last night. A son. Did she mean Adam?

The waitress then bustled in with Ben's and Janet's orders. She placed the plates in front of them, refilled their coffee and then turned to the woman. Ben began to eat but soon found he lost his appetite. He looked at his mother who also could not eat. He was totally oblivious to the woman sitting opposite at the next table, who kept making small talk about the weather, traveling and her family.

A death at the restaurant last night? As he finished his coffee he glanced again at his mother. He wondered if this was not the end of things happening but the beginning.

Harmon hesitated before inserting his key into the front door. He got the car from the garage and parked it in front of the house on

Willett Street. It was close to noon and the family should be ready to go. He paused, deep in thought.

He shrugged his heavy shoulders in annoyance. Poor Helen, he thought sadly. Why should he think like that? Her prognosis was good, and she would pull through! But she would have to be told about Adam. That, Harmon thought in despair, was what worried him. Her son dying on the day he came to visit. Harmon shook his head in disbelief. He opened the door, entered the hallway, and saw Bruce with Meg behind him, followed by Elsie and Richard.

"While we're at the hospital, I want to go to the morgue," Meg told them as she stood in the hallway. "Arrangements have to be made for Adam."

"I'll help you," Elsie said to her. "You shouldn't have to face that alone." Richard and Bruce agreed. "When we finish with Mother, we'll go to the morgue for Adam's arrangements," Bruce added.

"Does anyone know where Iris went?" Bruce asked them.

"I saw her go out," Richard said.

"We're ready," Ida told them, wiping away a few tears. She was dressed as if she were in mourning, a severe black dress with a small black winter hat.

Suddenly the front door opened and closed with a bang. Everyone looked and saw Iris, her face flushed and out-of-breath.

"Where have you been?" Bruce said. Not one to lose his temper, he found it difficult to do so now. "We're leaving for the hospital!"

Iris entered the hallway demurely. She looked at her husband indifferently.

"I went for a walk."

"In this weather?"

"I stopped to see Grace," she explained.

"We're going to the hospital," said Harmon, intervening. He then addressed Iris. "Your mother comes home today."

"We were just leaving," said Ida and put on her heavy coat.

Everyone started to move about. Harmon locked the house and started the car. Meg shivered and Ida looked at the house remorsefully. She started to cry again, and Meg reached over to comfort the older woman.

"I'm afraid now," said Ida as she dabbed at her eyes with a handkerchief. "I'm just afraid! I'm afraid to stay in that house!"

Meg shuddered inwardly as the car drove away from the brownstone. Silently she agreed with Ida. She, too, felt afraid to stay in her mother-in-law's house.

At the hospital they took the elevator to the eleventh floor and were soon greeted by Helen's doctor. He said she could see them provided she did not become upset.

"Her vital signs have improved," the Doctor said. "She's fine to return home today."

Iris turned to the doctor anxiously. "Doctor, I think there's something you should know. My brother Adam died last night. It happened after my mother collapsed. She doesn't know about it."

"Would she have another attack?" Bruce asked.

The doctor turned to him. "It's possible."

It was agreed then that no one would mention Adam. Meg knew that was ridiculous. Helen would most likely demand to know where Adam was and why wasn't he with them.

Solemnly, they entered the room in pairs and stood around the bed in silence as though Helen had the last rites performed and was near death. She had her eyes closed at first and then became aware of people near her. She opened them quickly and cast a rather disapproving glance at each of them.

"Well, how nice that you're all here," she said acidly.

She was propped up in bed, her head resting on several pillows. Her face was drawn and her skin pallid, but she was still the same, Meg thought wryly. Even a slight heart attack would not change this woman.

"Ida, you look like you're going to a wake. Did you have to wear black? It's too depressing. Thank goodness I leave here today!" She paused as she realized for the first time someone was missing. "Where's Adam?" She looked at each of them.

Helen sat up in bed and demanded to know what was happening. Only Meg, whose nerves were remarkably calm, approached the woman in the bed.

"Mrs. Cary," she began but Richard's stern voice stopped her.

"Remember what the doctor told us," he warned.

"Let's just have a nice conversation," said Harmon trying to act cheerful. "Mrs. Cary is doing better and…"

Meg looked up at Elsie, Richard, Ida, and Harmon helplessly. She looked at Helen again and wondered if the news of Adam's death would really be the end of this tough woman. With all that she had endured in her wicked life, the battleax could survive this latest tragedy. Meg looked at her mother-in-law differently now and her eyes filled with compassion.

"Mrs. Cary, you suffered a terrible attack last night. You need to rest!"

Helen became impatient. "Why don't you tell me, Ida? Or you, Harmon?" Helen looked at them and felt helpless. "Elsie, Richard, what is going on?" She knew she did not have the advantage in the situation, but she pressed her point further. "Something has happened to Adam."

"Adam had an accident," said Meg impulsively. "He's dead," she added bluntly. There was a terrible silence for what seemed an eternity. Helen then sat up, trying to take control of the situation.

"What do you mean he's dead?" She was calm but alert. She hesitated because Meg was silent. "I insist you tell me what happened!"

The doctor began to intervene, but Helen insisted. Much to the doctor's chagrin, Meg told her mother-in-law about the strange note left on the bureau. After she finished, a strange sort of calmness swept over her. And even Ida and Harmon felt differently. In a way it was rather a relief to get it out in the open. Elsie and Richard both appeared calmer and more in control.

"Adam didn't kill himself," said Helen tearfully.

"He may have gotten sick on the food, Mrs. Cary," said Ida.

Helen was flustered. "Sick on food? What more do you know, Meg?"

"I know nothing more," Meg said honestly. "Perhaps if we hadn't come here this weekend Adam would still be alive."

"Just what do you mean by that?"

Meg had enough. "I've finished here," she said. "I'll be at the morgue to see about Adam." She walked out of the room. Helen called to her, but Ida gently pushed her back onto the pillows.

The doctor repeated that Helen could leave today or tomorrow. They would call a hospital driver if the family wished. Helen spoke from the pillows and said she was ready to leave today, without hesitation.

At about the same time that Helen's entourage arrived at the hospital, Ben and his mother also arrived at the hospital, to see Janet's doctor. They dusted snow off their coats, then stepped in the elevator. They arrived at the ward, and Ben inquired at the nurses' station for Dr. Stevens and was told the doctor would be with them shortly.

Ben was restless and he paced up and down the corridor. His mind was racing over the events of the past two days but all he could think of was Meg. He wanted desperately to call her or even drop by her mother-in-law's house but decided against it. He wondered how she was holding up with the death of her husband. He assumed it was her husband although he wasn't sure.

"Mr. Faraday?"

Ben turned sharply. "Oh, Dr. Stevens. My mother and I are here to see you." He nodded to his mother, who sat in the waiting room, flipping the pages of a magazine.

"Let's go to my office. We can talk there."

They walked down the corridor and then entered a rather large office containing a desk, file cabinets and chairs.

"How are you feeling today, Janet?" he asked her.

Janet Faraday smiled. "I'm fine, Doctor, although last night I fainted."

The doctor looked at them both and then his eyes rested on Ben. "Fainted?"

Ben cleared his throat and explained to the doctor what happened last night at the restaurant. The doctor shook his head.

"Unnecessary disturbances are not a good thing for someone in your mother's condition, Mr. Faraday."

"Well, it happened rather quickly." He looked at his mother and smiled. "She's doing better now." Janet returned the smile and assured the doctor she was fine.

"You and this man had a fist fight?" The doctor's tone was incredulous. "That, of course, would cause your mother to collapse. Any display of violence would affect her in a bad way." He paused and looked at Ben and at Janet. "Is there anything you're not telling me, Mr. Faraday?"

Ben shifted in the chair. He explained what happened at the restaurant last night; the fight he had with Adam, his mother fainting and Meg's mother-in-law collapsing.

"Are you related to this Mrs. Megan Cary, Mr. Faraday?"

"No. My mother sat next to her on the train coming here. She told Mrs. Cary how she killed my father."

"You brought Mrs. Cary here to see your mother."

Ben nodded. "My mother wanted to see her. Mrs. Cary has been a great help to me while I've been in Albany."

"But she didn't help in any way last night?"

Ben hesitated. "Her husband accused her of being unfaithful. Then he started throwing punches."

Dr. Stevens coughed somewhat impatiently. "I've made arrangements for you to be admitted to the psychiatric hospital here in Albany," he turned to Janet. "Thursday of this week was the earliest they could take you." He paused. "You will be comfortable there and have your own room. In the meantime, you are free to spend time with your son," he added awkwardly.

Janet simply nodded but said nothing. Ben mentioned they would arrive at the hospital on Thursday morning, for Janet to be admitted.

From the lobby, they went outside and got into a taxi to take them back to the hotel, where they would spend their last night before checking into the boarding house.

"Mother," Ben said affectionately as they sat in the taxi. "How are you feeling?" Janet Faraday gave a short sigh.

"A terrible shock, Benjamin."

"I know, Mother. It's too upsetting."

"But Benjamin you don't understand…"

"I don't want to talk about anything that'll upset you. The hospital is the best place for you."

Janet squeezed her son's hand. "How is Megan after last night?"

They looked out the taxi window at the big, white flakes that seemed to blow in all directions.

"I don't know," Ben told her. "Is there something you're not telling me?"

Janet looked at her son with raised eyebrows. "What do you mean, dear?"

"There's something about last night. That fainting spell…"

"Well, I wouldn't worry, dear. I had a terrible shock last night."

"I know," Ben said slowly, still unconvinced. "I don't know why Meg's husband started to fight."

"He thought you were interested in his wife" she said wearily. "Then everything happened at once and he attacked you and…"

"Let's not talk about it. You're much too weak to talk."

"Benjamin, you should know…"

The taxi pulled up in front of the Ten Eyck Hotel. Ben paid the driver and they got out. Janet turned to her son as though she was about to speak but changed her mind. Ben ushered her into the hotel, where it was warm and friendly, with the desk clerk greeting them congenially. They got into the elevator and asked the attendant for their floor.

Ben felt as though he had not accomplished anything. He wanted to talk to her further about whatever was troubling her. They entered their room and Janet announced she wanted to rest.

"The past, Benjamin, the past! The past is wicked! Seems like yesterday! I never forget a face, never …"

Ben told his mother she was safe. He then wondered if she would eventually come to a bad end. He would later realize how prophetic his thoughts proved to be.

Sunday evening came quickly to Albany as it does during winter, with closed curtains and pedestrians rushing home to escape the cold.

Ben and his mother decided to eat at a restaurant recommended by the front desk clerk. They caught the trolley to go up Central Avenue. They walked until they came to an Italian restaurant.

"This is the place," Ben said and opened the door for his mother. The Faradays sat at a corner table, decorated with a red and white checkered tablecloth and a small candle in the center. Ben ordered lasagna and Janet enjoyed a plate of spaghetti and meatballs. Afterwards, they relaxed with espresso and dessert. Ben noticed his mother was enjoying herself and appeared calm and at peace.

"I'm glad you're more comfortable being in public, Mother." He paused. "Tomorrow we leave for the boarding house," he told her, trying to sound encouraging while sipping his coffee. "Thursday, we'll be at the hospital."

"I don't mind," Janet said and smiled at her son. "After all, I know you want the best for me." She hesitated. "I suppose we should've traveled together on the train. I was just so afraid, Benjamin. I was afraid someone knew me and what I had done six years ago! Then what would've happened!" She paused, fear in her eyes. "But then I wouldn't have met Megan. And I'm glad I did."

"Mother, was there something you wanted to tell me about last night?"

Janet looked down at her coffee cup. "Well, your father," she hesitated.

"What about my father?"

"I killed him by closing the garage door. He was overcome by the fumes."

"I know that, Mother."

"But I never forget a face, Benjamin." She looked thoughtfully at her son. "No, I don't forget a face."

Ben didn't know what she was referring to and realizing his mother was becoming melancholy and sentimental, he didn't pursue it. He finished his coffee and asked the waitress for the check.

"Are you going to call Megan?" his mother asked. "Such a pretty girl. I liked talking to her. Strange meeting someone you don't even know, and you feel a bonding."

"The evening paper might have something about last night," Ben said. As the waitress brought them the check, he asked if she had a copy of the Albany paper. By good luck she returned with *The Albany Evening News*. He opened it and looked through the local section but saw nothing about the events from last night. They sat silently until Ben asked his mother if she was ready to return to the hotel. Janet finished her coffee and put on her coat while Ben paid the bill. They then walked out of the restaurant, to catch the trolley downtown to the hotel.

"Lovely evening, isn't it, Benjamin?" Janet remarked, linking her hand through his arm as they walked among the crowd. It was still cold but tolerable and it was a pretty scene, with streetlamps illuminating the snowy sidewalk and the buildings brilliantly. Ben admired his mother, for despite her past deeds, she had been through absolute hell. He respected her bravery and courage.

AN UNFORTUNATE COINCIDENCE

At the corner of Central Avenue and Northern Boulevard, a trolley approached to pick up more passengers. Ben and his mother moved forward with a rather large crowd and were waiting for it to stop, when suddenly, Janet fell forward just as the trolley was near them. A woman screamed. Ben tried to catch his mother, but it was too late.

The wheels were upon her, crushing her, leaving her mangled and bloodied. And the hideous remains of Janet Faraday were a heap on the ground, all life gone from her.

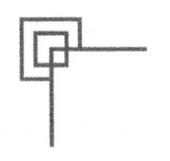

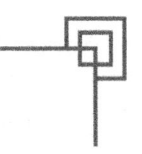

CHAPTER TWELVE

Several hours earlier, the police were concluding their inquiries. The atmosphere in the living room was tense. Lieutenant Taylor was a shortish, stout, middle aged man with a firm, no-nonsense manner about him, who came directly to the point when speaking. Inspector Harris, on the other hand, was more subtle, tall, and athletic for a man of about fifty with fierce, determined brown eyes. He closed his notebook, after making a few final notations on what they learned from the people assembled.

Meg sat on the Victorian sofa next to Ida. She was composed but tired and wanted nothing more than to go upstairs and be by herself. Ida was still distraught but slowly beginning to retain her composure. Iris and Bruce tried to avoid the policemen's eyes. Harmon, near the front windows, refused to sit down. He paced back and forth, restless. Elsie and Richard also were standing, unable to sit still. The Lieutenant broke her thoughts.

"From what we've heard this evening, and from the evidence of the note left in the guest room, Adam Cary committed suicide." The lieutenant looked again at the strange note Meg found that evening in the guest room. "This clearly is a suicide note." He looked at Meg steadily. A silence followed until she spoke, hoarsely.

"I don't understand why Adam waited until he came here to end his life! Or why he killed himself at all! He never showed any signs…"

"Many suicides don't," Inspector Harris said.

"But how did he die?" Elsie asked and stopped pacing. She looked at the policemen as though they had the answer.

"We don't know yet," the Inspector said. "His body is at the hospital morgue and an autopsy will be to be performed to determine how he died."

Elsie explained how Helen collapsed and then the other woman also collapsed, at almost the same time, after Adam swung at Ben and the men started fighting. She mentioned her sister returned earlier today and was upstairs in her bedroom, resting quietly.

"Is there anything more you'd like to add before we leave?"

There was a ripple of fear that spread around the room as if they wanted to look at one another but hesitated. Bruce suddenly spoke.

"Perhaps you should speak to the wait staff at the restaurant. Adam was brought to another dining room and was out of our sight for some time. We only knew that he died when a waiter rushed to our table to tell us."

Iris agreed. "For a while we didn't see Adam. The waiter brought him to the other dining room so that he could pull himself together."

Inspector Harris turned to Harmon who was still by the front windows. "Did you, Mr. Pendleton, by any chance remember anything unusual, other than the fighting and the women collapsing?"

Harmon cleared his throat. "Of course not, Inspector. I would have said if I had, naturally."

"Naturally," the Inspector echoed faintly, drawing the conclusion that the people before him were either exaggerating the truth or lying.

"We'll need to speak to Mrs. Prescott and that other gentleman. What was his name?" He flipped through his notebook. "Oh yes, Benjamin Faraday. He's staying at a boarding house on State Street, Mrs. Cary?"

"Yes, but I don't know what he can tell you."

"You mentioned Mrs. Helen Cary came home from the hospital today. We'll need to speak with her, too."

"Mother is resting now," Iris said.

The policemen said they'd return later when Helen was awake.

"Thank you for coming," Meg said. She showed them to the front door, while Iris and Bruce were busy at the phone in the hallway. Meg said good night to the policemen and then turned to face them.

"I called the hospital," Iris told Harmon and Ida, as they entered the hallway.

"They want to see Mother tomorrow." She looked wearily at Meg.

"I'm glad Helen regained her strength after all she went through." Meg told her. She said goodnight to Iris and Bruce and then returned to the living room, to join Elsie and Richard.

"We'll find out what happened," Elsie said to Meg as she sat on the sofa. "It'll come out soon enough."

And that is exactly what I'm afraid of, Meg thought wearily. Closing her eyes as Elsie continued talking, she wished she had never taken this trip and this nightmare would never had happened.

Throughout his adult life, Ben Faraday felt he was living a lie. He never knew what his mother would do next as she had become increasingly unstable. As a result, Ben's life had been anything but normal. He rarely developed relationships with people and the few acquaintances he had were always kept at bay in fear of his mother.

Ben waited for a doctor to come over and explain her condition. He was a tall, heavy-set middle-aged man with wavy brown hair and a firm chin.

"Your mother seems to…" the doctor hesitated, trying to choose his words carefully. "Your mother died, Mr. Faraday. There was nothing we could do; her injuries were too severe." He paused. "What exactly happened?"

Ben opened his mouth to speak. He was in denial and he knew it. He could not talk.

"She died from her injuries," the doctor continued. "An autopsy will be performed. That is, if you agree to it, Mr. Faraday."

Ben looked at the doctor in a haze of confusion and fear. How did this happen?

"I'm sorry," he said, rather awkwardly. "We were waiting for the trolley to take us downtown and she fell in front of it. She must have slipped on the snow and ice and fell underneath the wheels. May I see my mother?"

The doctor hesitated. "She will be brought to the morgue." He then mentioned if Ben needed him further, he would be available later in the evening. He walked away, leaving Ben alone in the hallway until a nurse approached him.

"Excuse me, Mr. Faraday? There's a woman and her husband here to see you." Ben turned and saw an elderly woman in a fur coat and cloche hat, heavily made-up, but apparently in a state of great distress, hastily making her way down the corridor, her husband trailing behind her.

"Oh, sir, I'm so glad to see you," she exclaimed, out of breath as though she had run the length of the hall. "I'm Mrs. Kelly and this is my husband." A gray haired distinguished looking gentleman approached and nodded to Ben. "I came here just to see you!"

Ben looked at this woman in confusion. Did he know her from somewhere? As if reading his mind, she started to talk, non-stop, in rather excitable, high-pitched tones.

"I realize you don't know me, but my husband and I were at the corner of Central and Northern Boulevard waiting for the trolley at the same time as you. Was that your mother with you? Anyway, as the trolley pulled up and everyone surged forward, I saw someone push your mother!" She hesitated as though for dramatic effect. "I screamed when I saw it!"

Ben looked at her, uncomprehending yet at the same time startled at what he heard. "You saw someone push my mother?" was all he could say.

Mrs. Kelly nodded. "Oh yes, my husband and I both noticed it, didn't we, Henry?" Mr. Kelly nodded and seemed content to let his wife continue her narrative.

"I couldn't see who it was, but someone pushed her!" She finished and gave a deep sigh. "It was just horrible! We came here straight away to find you!"

"Thank you, Mrs. Kelly," Ben told her. "Maybe we should go to the police?"

Mr. and Mrs. Kelly agreed. "I will call them when I get home," she assured Ben. Ben forced a short smile. He gave her the name, address, and phone number of the boarding house on State Street and Mrs. Kelly commented that she and her husband lived not far from there on Hudson Avenue. They wished Ben well and supplied their address and phone number if he needed them further.

Ben went to the nurses' station, told them the address of the boarding house, and decided there was nothing more he could do at the hospital. He then took a taxi back to the Ten Eyck Hotel. Upon entering the room, he shared with his mother, he took off his coat, jacket, and tie. He sat down on the bed, removed his shoes, rubbed his tired feet, and lit a cigarette.

The phone rang, startling Ben. He hoped it was Meg as he wanted so much to speak to her. He looked at watch. It was close to eleven o'clock.

"Ben, is that you? It's Meg."

Ben's sadness suddenly turned into relief upon hearing Meg's voice.

"Meg, are you all right?"

"No, not really, Ben."

"We need to talk, Meg. I have a lot to tell you."

"And I have a lot to tell you." Meg wiped away a few tears. "I'm at my mother-in-law's house still. There's been an accident—Adam is dead!"

"I thought so," Ben said. He explained about the woman he met in the hotel dining room yesterday morning and how she heard about the events at the restaurant. He suggested they meet sometime soon.

"Tomorrow," Meg said abruptly. "I'm staying for Adam's funeral." She paused. "I'm taking the week off from the library." She then asked him how his mother was doing, and Ben hesitated.

"Meg, my mother passed away tonight." He told her about how Janet had fallen under the passing trolley.

"I don't believe it," Meg cried, shaken.

"Tomorrow I'll be at the boarding house on State Street. You mentioned that it isn't far from your in-law's house. Can we meet tomorrow?"

"Yes, here's the address," Meg said. "Tomorrow morning is fine, around eleven, when everyone is out."

AN UNFORTUNATE COINCIDENCE

Monday dawned bright and chilly. The usual routine of breakfast and small talk ensued, although an undercurrent was obvious among everyone seated at the dining room table. Helen was there and looked remarkably strong. She doesn't look like she just came out of the hospital, Meg thought. Helen commented she needed to see her doctor this morning. The family agreed to take her to his office at the hospital after breakfast.

Iris hugged Meg as did Elsie and then Bruce and Richard wished her well, telling her if she needed anything to let them know. Meg smiled weakly and thanked them, then watched from the front door as they piled into the car and took off. She entered the living room, sat on the sofa, and waited for Ben.

After about an hour or so, the doorbell rang quite suddenly. She opened the door and smiled when she saw him.

"It's still cold out there," he said breathlessly as he stepped inside the warm hallway. "Have you been out yet?"

Meg closed the door and then turned to face Ben. She did not know what he was feeling but at that moment she simply reached out for him and he was there for her.

"Oh Ben," she cried. "Ben, I'm so afraid!"

She felt secure and sheltered in his warm; tight embrace as though no harm could ever come to her. Ben hugged her for a few moments then held her off.

She led him down the hallway to the living room. There was a fire dancing in the fireplace and the curtains were pulled back to let in the cold January sunlight. Ben lit a cigarette and exhaled a great puff of smoke.

"Oh Ben, I'm so sorry about your mother. She understood when I told her about Adam." Meg hesitated then started to cry again. "The police believe Adam killed himself because of a note I found upstairs." She showed Ben the strange note she found on the bureau. Ben put his arm around her. He nodded, not sure what to say. He spoke tenderly.

"What will you do now, Meg?"

Meg rose from the couch fitfully. She strode over to the windows restlessly.

"Arrangements will be made for Adam's funeral this week." She turned to face him. "And what will you do, Ben?"

Ben gave a tired smile. "After the autopsy…"

"Why do you need an autopsy?" Meg interrupted.

"Because in cases of sudden death like my mother's, the doctor recommends it." Ben paused, uncertain how to proceed. "And you will have the same for Adam?"

Meg nodded. "We don't know how he died."

Ben looked at her steadily. "I can't help feeling my mother was holding something back. She wanted to tell me something. Of course, it's too late now." He paused. He then told Meg about Mrs. Kelly, who claimed she saw someone push his mother in the line of the trolley.

"Do you think your mother was pushed, Ben?" Meg asked. "By whom?" "At this point, I don't know what to think," he said.

"Strange how Adam and your mother died almost at the same time," Meg observed with a sad expression. She paused, looking at Ben. "Adam on Saturday night and your mother last night. Isn't that a strange coincidence?"

Ben nodded, stubbed out his cigarette in the ashtray on the coffee table and rose from the sofa and approached Meg. He tried to give her a confident smile.

"We'll have to be patient and wait."

"Of course," Meg said tenderly. "Adam was already dead when we got to the dining room, lying face down on the floor."

"Try not to think of it now, Meg" Ben said soothingly.

Meg nodded. "Helen wasn't nice to me in the hospital yesterday. If Adam did commit suicide, she assumed I led him to it." She hesitated, uncertainly. "Ben, in just two days my life has been just hell! I couldn't believe Adam would come here to Albany to kill himself, after having a fight with you!"

"I had to defend myself, Meg."

"Of course, I'm not blaming you. But why did your mother faint?"

"I suppose she wasn't used to seeing a fistfight. She always suffered from fainting spells, anyway."

Meg nodded uncertainly. "Strange that she'd collapse and then Helen would collapse, too. Of course, such a display of violence…" The fighting caused the women to collapse, of course, Meg told herself. She sighed impatiently. So many unanswered questions. At this point she didn't know what to think, either.

"Who would push your mother in front of the trolley?" Meg repeated. "And why? It makes no sense, Ben!"

A clock on the mantel chimed softly. Ben looked at it and said he had better go. He wanted to return to the boarding house, where he had just checked in, to wait to hear further from the doctor, the autopsy results and to arrange for Janet Faraday's body to be returned to New York, where she would be buried.

"I'll call you tomorrow," Meg said. "I'll be here all week. Take care, Ben."

Ben pulled open the door and stepped out into the snow.

"Mrs. Cary, you must eat," Ida said with concern. "Why don't I fix you a tray?"

Helen relinquished. As the family settled in the dining room for dinner, she was alone in the living room with a tray, the radio tuned to a soft jazz station. Helen, having regained strength to fix her hair and even go walking in the park, put down her fork and stared into the fire. This morning her doctor commented her vital signs were excellent, but she still needed to remain calm. Helen sighed in disgust. Remain calm? Too much happened at once.

Oddly, her mind flew to her first husband. Arthur, who hung himself in the basement of their home. She never imagined another suicide in her life. It was bad enough with Arthur that she was never able to live that down. She was chastised from the Albany community and it took years for her to regain its acceptance. But then came Walter's death and she had to explain that, too, how both husbands died so tragically. People whispered behind her back about Arthur Hamilton's apparent suicide but then she had to contend with Walter's death.

It took a few years, but eventually she won to a degree. People always talk, as Helen knew, and Grace Prescott was one who talked constantly. But with every passing year the gossip grew less and less interesting. So, the talking soon died off, and people forgot.

Helen, too, forgot but not completely. She remembered how she fought to become someone who was looked up to as a good wife and mother and an asset to the community. Now there was Adam's suicide that threatened to ruin her normal, placid life into one of shame and disgrace. Iris appeared and asked if she enjoyed the meal.

"I'm afraid I've hardly touched any," Helen said.

Iris smiled, took the tray from the coffee table, and returned it to the kitchen. Meg and Elsie came in then and sat down near Helen. Bruce stuck his head in the doorway and said he and Richard were taking a walk in Washington Park and asked if they cared to join them. The women declined and continued listening to the radio.

"I'll take another walk later," Helen said to him. "Helps clear my mind."

She rose from her chair, told Elsie and Meg she would return shortly and walked into the hallway to the telephone. She asked the operator to place two calls for her. The first was to Grace Prescott. The second was to the hospital morgue.

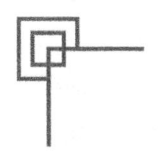

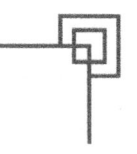

CHAPTER THIRTEEN

"Mr. Faraday, I'm so sorry about your mother."

Ben looked up at Mrs. Perry, the proprietor of the boarding house. He had checked out of the Ten Eyck Hotel on Tuesday morning and took the trolley to the corner of Washington Avenue and Dove Street. From there he walked on Dove, turned right onto State Street until he came to the boarding house. He was pleased with his room and the place itself; spacious, clean and comfortable. Mrs. Perry was a competent, pleasant middle-aged woman with wavy brown hair, blue eyes, dressed in an apron over her gray dress. She offered breakfast to her guests at no extra charge.

"I'm really sorry to hear about her death," Mrs. Perry said again. "I read about it in this morning's paper." She held the paper out to him, and Ben read the small article for himself. It specified how Janet Faraday, waiting at the corner of Central and Northern Boulevard, was struck and killed by a trolley. It mentioned how trolleys needed to exercise more caution when maneuvering through the city and that a police investigation would take place.

"The police are getting involved," Mrs. Perry said.

Ben looked up from the paper, adjusted his tie and ran his fingers through his hair. He looked tired and drawn, despite having slept last night, and knew he had to contact the police soon. He figured Mrs. Kelly, the woman he met at the hospital and an eyewitness, had already done so.

Ben sighed, thanked Mrs. Perry for letting him read the paper and went back upstairs to his room. He sat on the bed for what seemed hours until a knock came on his door. Mrs. Perry slowly opened it and smiled.

"There's a phone call for you," she told him. "I think it's the hospital."

Ben looked up, startled. He followed her downstairs and to the phone in the hallway. It was the same doctor he spoke to over the weekend in the emergency room, calling with the autopsy results. He explained the nature of Janet's injuries, internal bleeding, and broken bones. Ben asked him if he could tell whether his mother had been pushed instead of fallen.

"Pushed? No, I wouldn't say she was pushed. Is there a reason you ask that?"

Ben told him about Mrs. Kelly, who claimed to have seen someone push his mother in front of the moving trolley. The doctor was silent and then recovered himself.

"No, there was no way to tell that, I am afraid."

Ben thanked the doctor again, asked if he could have a copy of the autopsy results sent to him at the boarding house and hung up. He realized Mrs. Perry was speaking.

"Do you think your mother was pushed?" she asked him.

"I really don't know." Ben reached in his shirt pocket for cigarettes, lit one and immediately felt somewhat better.

"Frankly, Mr. Faraday, Albany has seen its fair share of crime recently. I'm even afraid to walk alone in Washington Park. But you can't jump to conclusions."

"Except that she may have been murdered," Ben said, clearly aggrieved.

Mrs. Perry was aghast. "The police will investigate."

Ben gathered his coat from the hallway closet, where guests were welcome to leave them, and hastily put it on.

"The police? A lot good they'll do," Ben said with some sarcasm. He walked over to the door and practically flung it open.

"Mr. Faraday, where are you going?" Mrs. Perry could clearly see that Ben was shaken by his mother's unnatural death.

"I'll go to see Mrs. Cary. She might know." He told Mrs. Perry about Meg, how they met and how her husband died on Saturday evening at the restaurant.

"But what else can she tell you about your mother, Mr. Faraday?" Mrs. Perry asked, attempting to help.

But Ben had already left the boarding house.

Tuesday brought the news in the paper. Ida took it into the dining room where the family was having breakfast. Richard took the paper from Ida and unfolded it until he came to the local news.

He frowned, looked around the table at Elsie, Helen, Iris, Bruce, and Meg and then read out loud the article that appeared in the Albany news section. The article mentioned Adam's death as suicide. They discussed Adam's illustrious career in pharmacy, his marriage to Meg and his father's death in a car mishap, which was several years ago. It mentioned Adam's wealthy mother, Helen, who suffered a heart attack at the same restaurant where her son died. And the article finally concluded that Adam Cary, while under a great amount of duress from his work, took his own life on Saturday night.

Richard folded the paper again and passed it around for everyone to see. Iris read it in complete shock, her face a mixture of remorse and anger. Bruce, after reading it, got up from the dining room and went into the hallway, speechless and in shock. Elsie maintained her composure but was attuned to her sister's attitude. Helen stared at the article as though she could not speak, her eyes a glaze as though she was on the verge of collapsing again.

Upon being handed the paper by Elsie and reading it, Meg threw it down on the dining room table in disgust. Helen looked at her daughter-in-law curiously.

"Are you all right, Megan?"

"We haven't gotten the autopsy results yet," Meg said, her voice a mixture of pain and anger.

"Have you decided what to do next?" inquired Helen with concern. "It was suicide, after all, Meg."

Iris entered with her fur coat, hat, and scarf. She picked up the paper Meg left on the coffee table.

"I'm going to the state library," Iris said to them. "I'll return in a few hours." They heard the front door open and close, letting in swish of cold air that traveled down the hallway to the dining room and kitchen.

Elsie turned to her sister. "Are you feeling better, Helen?"

Helen smiled wearily. "Actually, I'm feeling worse. That article rather upset me." She pulled the sweater she wore even closer around her shoulders and shivered slightly.

"Will you stay the rest of the week?" Richard asked turning to Meg.

Meg nodded. "I arranged for someone to cover my work in my absence."

Elsie smiled understandingly. "We've all been under a tremendous strain. I have someone covering my work, too."

"Have you been in touch with Mr. Faraday?" Helen asked unexpectedly.

Meg was taken aback by the question. Now why would she ask about Ben? Even when she appeared to relent in her attitude toward her, Meg found her mother-in-law could still be manipulating and unpredictable.

"Why yes, I did speak to him on the phone." Meg decided to tell them about Ben's visit to the house yesterday and his mother's sudden death.

"Well, it's unfortunate what happened to his mother," Elsie lamented. "These trolleys can be so dangerous, especially in the winter."

"I don't know any more about it," said Meg wishing to change the subject.

"I'd like to rest now, dear," Helen said with a tired smile. "Perhaps you can tell Ida to fix me a cup of tea."

Meg said she would tell Ida her wishes and then proceeded out of the dining room with Elsie to the kitchen. Helen then left the dining room, with Richard, in route to the living room. Meg and Elsie entered the kitchen and saw Ida busy at the sink.

"Helen would like a cup of tea, Ida," Meg told the maid. "She's in the living room with Richard."

Ida turned and gave Meg and Elsie a weary smile. She was busy cleaning the kitchen and looked tired. "Of course. Would you be needing anything?"

Elsie shook her head. "Thanks anyway, Ida." She glanced at the wall clock and saw it was only ten-thirty. "It's still early but I think I'll go upstairs to read."

"Do you need anything, Megan?" Ida asked as she washed the breakfast dishes.

"No, I'm just eager to hear from the hospital regarding Adam," Meg answered. "The doctor told me he'd call with the autopsy results."

Ida shuddered. "I don't even like to think about it."

"I'll also go upstairs," Meg told her. "If the hospital morgue does call, Ida, please come and get me."

Ida assured her she would come and get her the minute the hospital called. Meg wanted nothing more than to get away from Ida who, although helpful at times, could be tiresome and irritating.

What a strange woman Ida was, Meg thought climbing the stairs to the guest room. By some twist of fate, she worked cleaning house for others, cooking their food and even answering to their every whim. Meg wondered how she could tolerate Helen's bullying for so long. And wasn't her name Mrs. Ida Munson? She must have had a husband at one time. Several hours passed before Meg heard the phone ring downstairs. Ida climbed the main stairs and appeared at the guest room doorway, her face full of concern and apprehension.

"Megan, it's the doctor with the autopsy results. He wants to speak with you."

As she climbed down the stairs with Ida behind her, Meg felt her heart pounding. After what was a long discourse on Adam's autopsy, Meg replaced the candlestick phone on the hallway table and turned toward the living room, in shock. She managed to walk into the living room, where Elsie, Richard and Helen were still talking and listening to the radio console. Iris had returned from the state library and she and Bruce also joined them in the living room. Harmon, who had been helping tidy the kitchen also entered. Soon enough, Ida, wiping her hands on a dish towel came in and looked at Meg with concern.

"That was the doctor about Adam's autopsy," Meg said slowly. She went white and fought back tears.

"What did he say, Meg?" Helen insisted, seeing her daughter-in-law clearly upset. Meg took her time and replied, looking at the people assembled before her. "The doctor told me Adam died of arsenic poisoning."

A stunned, shocked silence pervaded the living room. Only Richard was brave enough to speak.

"Arsenic? Is he sure about that?"

"I asked him several times," Meg told him, clearly upset. "He's certain. Adam died from arsenic poisoning,"

"Well, the only thing we drank was the soda and the coffee with the dessert," Elsie remarked. "He put it in his soda or coffee?"

"If he did," Meg said.

"Meg, please," Helen spoke up. "Please don't insinuate something else."

"I don't know, Mother," Iris put in. "Adam didn't give the impression of taking his own life."

"What will happen now?" Elsie asked Meg.

"The police will be notified, and they'll come here to see us."

"What more can we tell them?" Harmon said, almost angrily. He stood by the windows overlooking Willett Street and then came over to Meg sitting on the sofa. "We didn't see him put arsenic in his cup."

"No, none of us saw anything," Helen said.

"Meg, why don't you rest?" Elsie said. "This has been a lot for you to endure in such a short time period."

Meg nodded. "First, I'd like to call Ben Faraday. He should know."

In the hallway, Meg once again picked up the candlestick phone, and asked the operator to put through a call to the boarding house on State Street. Upon answering, Mrs Perry assured Meg she would fetch Ben, who apparently just returned after walking for several blocks, despite the wind and cold. He was glad to hear her voice.

"Ben," she said in an exhausted voice. "I'd like to see you again. I have things to tell you."

"Meg, I have more news about my mother," he said gravely. He related to her what he knew about his mother's death, how Mrs. Kelly claims she saw someone push her into the trolley before it stopped. Meg was horrified.

"Ben let's meet again, tonight. I may return home sooner than I expected. I need to sort my thoughts and I want to see you before I leave…"

"Where? I don't know Albany."

Meg thought hurriedly. "Let's meet on State Street. I know where the boarding house is located. Is it still snowing?" She glanced out the hall window but could not tell for sure. "About seven o'clock?"

Meg hung up rather quickly, eager to leave the hallway before Ida should enter. She glanced at her watch and saw it was only six o'clock. She would meet Ben and talk to him about his mother's strange death. And her own precarious situation. She turned and walked down the hallway to the kitchen to see Ida.

"Ida, I'm going to see Mr. Faraday," she told her.

Ida turned from the stove where she was busy preparing lamb for the evening meal. Harmon also had joined her in getting things ready for dinner.

"Are you sure, Meg?" he asked her.

"Yes, I need to get out for a while."

Harmon and Ida looked at each other not knowing what to say.

"You should tell Mrs. Cary," Ida told her with what sounded like fear.

Meg walked out of the kitchen and over to the living room, where Helen sat knitting in her favorite chair by the fireplace, listening to the radio console and chatting with Elsie and Richard.

"I won't be joining you for dinner. I'm going to meet Mr. Faraday and expect I'll be back late."

Helen, Elsie, and Richard stared at her for so long Meg thought they were statues incapable of speech. Finally, Elsie cleared her throat and spoke.

"Please give Mr. Faraday our condolences."

"Be careful," Helen said. "A girl walking by herself at night is not a good idea." Meg smiled faintly at Helen. "I'll be careful."

As she stood before the hallway mirror, adjusting her fur coat, cloche hat and scarf, Meg did not realize she was looking at her husband's death from the wrong angle, and that Adam's death was more complex than she thought.

Ida entered the living room, carrying a tray with a steaming cup of tea. It was early evening, dinner was over, and the family had dispersed into various parts of the large house. Ida deposited the tray on the coffee table in front of Helen and handed her the cup and saucer.

"You know how much I enjoy tea in the evening. You're so thoughtful, Ida!"

"Of course, Mrs. Cary."

Helen sipped the scalding liquid and nodded her approval. She asked Ida to fetch her knitting from the table underneath the mirror next to the radio console and proceeded to unravel it when she noticed Ida hovering nearby.

"Well, what is it, Ida?"

"I'm so concerned about everything that has happened! I feel so frightened!" Helen gave a short smile. "There's nothing to fear, Ida. I managed to come to terms with Adam's death. We all have to; even you."

"I can't help thinking of poor Megan and Iris when they saw Adam's body on the floor of the dining room! How upsetting for them!"

"Ida, you must not talk about this until we have more answers. You are not to mention it to anyone. Do you understand?"

"Yes, Mrs. Cary."

Helen eyed her irritably. "It doesn't do any good to talk without having the facts. And to spread rumors about something other than suicide, like Megan hinted at, is just too much." Helen sighed. "Megan told me that woman who was there with her son died, too. Apparently, it was rather sudden."

"Oh, how sad for that young man."

"Well, that doesn't concern us." Helen dismissed the subject of Janet Faraday, someone without status. She looked at the crackling fireplace and her gaze returned to Ida. "Where are Iris and Bruce?"

"They're playing bridge in the dining room," said Ida.

"Meg has other plans," Helen said contemptuously. "Her husband is dead not even two days and already she takes off with another man!"

"Yes, Mrs. Cary."

"Disgraceful," Helen added with tight lips.

"Yes, Mrs. Cary."

"Ida, tell Iris and Bruce I want to see them. And Harmon?"

"He was shoveling in front of the house earlier."

"I asked Mrs. Prescott to drop by around eight o'clock," said Helen and Ida showed surprise. She added, "I want to ask her what she remembers about that night."

"Yes, Mrs. Cary."

"Now, go get my daughter and son-in-law."

"Yes, Mrs. Cary."

Ida went to the dining room to tell Iris and Bruce that Mrs. Cary wished to see them. They were busy playing bridge, although neither seemed to be enjoying themselves. They looked up as the maid stood in the doorway.

"Your mother wishes to see you."

Iris looked annoyed. "What happened now?"

"Nothing. I believe she simply wants to see you."

As they left the dining room, Iris wondered what the future held for the Cary family. Her thoughts flew to her father, Walter Cary. For years she wanted to talk about him, but her mother always remained tight-lipped. She and Bruce entered the living room and were greeted by Helen, who told them to sit by her so they could talk.

Iris wondered why her father's name conjured up such disagreeable memories. There must be something in the past that was too unpleasant to mention.

Meg stood for a moment looking at Washington Park and saw the rather sinister illumination of the night sky. Snow, snow, snow would it ever stop snowing? It had reached the window ledges and even drifted halfway up the outside kitchen door. Before Meg left, Ida joined her at the front door.

"It's awfully cold out," the maid warned her.

Meg promised she would not be long. She then opened the door quickly and made her escape. She walked on trying to block the events of the past several days from her mind.

For a weekday evening, State Street was busy, with crowds going to restaurants and, Meg assumed, speakeasies.

The snow came down more steadily and as Meg observed, it was deep around lower State Street. She spotted Ben, standing near the front of the boarding house, smoking a cigarette, and waiting for her. "Ben!" she called as though she was afraid of losing him.

He turned with a tired but welcomed smile. "I just came outside, Meg. I knew you'd be coming." She came up to him and looked into his deep, warm, compassionate eyes.

"The owner, Mrs. Perry, is such a nice lady. She'll make coffee."

Before she knew it, he was leading her up the steps. They shook snow from their shoes and coats in the foyer and then entered the gracious dining room. It was a charming brownstone house. The fireplace was lit and the warmth in the room cheered her. Was it the fire that was making her feel so content? Or the mere presence of the handsome young man sitting near her? Mrs. Perry came out from the kitchen with a smile.

"I thought I heard you, Mr. Faraday." She asked if she could get them anything to drink or eat. Ben introduced Meg to Mrs. Perry and then asked for coffee. As she departed back to the kitchen, he sighed out of sheer weariness.

"Ben, tell me about your poor mother," Meg said.

They sat at the dining room table, overlooking State Street, where customers ate breakfast. There was no one else there at this time of night. Ben then told Meg everything he knew, about the trolley accident and Mrs. Kelly who claims she saw someone push his mother. Mrs. Perry entered with two cups of coffee and a jug of cream. Ben thanked her and she returned to the kitchen. Meg then looked at him ruefully.

"Do you really think she was pushed?" she asked.

"I don't know," Ben said, almost harshly, puffing at a cigarette.

"Maybe she slipped on the ice," Meg said logically, adding cream to her coffee. "Or the crowd could have pushed her by accident?"

"Meg, my mother is dead, and I don't know why," Ben stammered. He stirred his coffee absently. "Just like you don't know why your husband died."

"And you think her death is related to my husband's death?"

Ben took a big swallow of coffee. "I don't know." Meg could tell he had a lot on his mind. "But it all seems to add up, doesn't it? My mother was in the dining room that night at the same time as your husband."

"I don't see how they tie in at all," Meg admitted. "Adam didn't know your mother. He never saw her before in his life."

He shook his head. He lit another cigarette, took a few puffs and finished his coffee. Meg also lit another cigarette and finished the coffee. Mrs. Perry entered at that moment, asking if they needed anything else.

"No, we're fine, thank you," Ben told her. "I want to show Meg some souvenirs of Albany." Mrs. Perry smiled, removed the coffee cups and returned to the kitchen.

Meg, overcome with grief, loss, and confusion, followed Ben up the staircase to his room overlooking State Street. Once the door was closed, he reached for her hand and then she was in his strong arms. The pent-up emotions of weeks gone by overwhelmed them. They embraced urgently, until it was too late for decisions, because both had suffered a loss so great, so unbearable, they found solace in each other.

Almost an hour later, Meg realized time had gone by since she first left her mother-in-law's house. As though afraid of being reprimanded, she quickly put on her fur coat and reached for the doorknob.

"I have to go," she told him anxiously. She hesitated as if she really wanted to stay. She looked at Ben somewhat anxiously.

"I'll come with you," he told her. "Mrs. Perry may have locked up. Besides, you shouldn't be walking at night by yourself."

Meg assured him she was perfectly well to go by herself. "I can see myself out. Besides, it isn't far. I'll call here tomorrow."

"Good night, Meg," Ben said tenderly.

"Good night, Ben," Meg whispered back, as she closed the door behind her.

Ben sat up in bed, smoking a last cigarette.

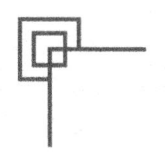

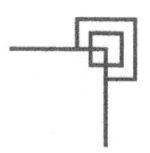

CHAPTER FOURTEEN

Wednesday morning brought the police once again to the house on Willett Street. This time, Inspector Harris and Lieutenant Taylor had the chance to meet Helen and immediately offered their condolences.

The family was sitting in the living room, with the radio console playing softly in the background. Ida offered coffee to the policemen, but they declined, as they wanted to get to point of their visit. Inspector Harris opened his notebook, sat at a chair against the wall and along with Lieutenant Taylor, addressed the people before him.

"Mrs. Cary, I understand your son died Saturday evening. The autopsy showed he died of arsenic poisoning. You daughter-in-law showed us a note she found, a suicide note." He paused and looked intently at Helen. "What do you think?"

Helen sighed wearily. She wore a black dress, low at the waist, with black shoes, perhaps to mourn Adam, although Meg thought she usually wore that color anyway. "I really don't know. Adam decided to take his life, although why he waited to come here to do it is beyond me."

Elsie agreed. "It seems like we'll never know." She looked pretty, if rather plain, in a gray dress, with a white collar and pearls.

"Where would he get arsenic?" Inspector Harris said.

The family looked at each other, not knowing how to answer. Only Iris ventured to speak.

"He must have had it with him. We don't keep poisons here in the house." "There are other ways to get arsenic," the Inspector commented dryly. "Such as?" Elsie asked.

"Have you had rodents here in your house, Mrs. Cary?"

Helen looked appalled at such a question. "Well, we've had our share of mice on occasion, Inspector." She looked at Ida. "Do we still have any rat poison, Ida?"

Ida, her face showing fear and anguish, looked as though she would collapse any minute. Bruce almost went over to help her, but she managed to compose herself and rather demurely went into the kitchen pantry to check.

"Were you aware of Adam's intentions Saturday night?" the Inspector asked.

"I don't believe Adam killed himself," Meg spoke up boldly. She also wore black but looked more becoming, with some powder and rogue and a touch of perfume. She looked at the policemen and then at the family, who equally looked at her, shocked at her suggestion.

"You're allowing your feelings to get the best of you," Richard said tenderly.

A hush fell over the room, as though everyone present could think of a multitude of reasons for killing Adam, but no one dared speak. Only Iris, rather formally dressed in a dark suit and gold collar, was brave enough to speak.

"We hadn't seen Adam since Christmas 1926, over a year ago. This weekend was our first time in seeing him since then."

Helen cleared her throat. "I don't believe anyone killed Adam." Her tone implied the case was finished and need not be discussed any further.

AN UNFORTUNATE COINCIDENCE

Lieutenant Taylor asked them to relate again the events leading up to the dinner, what occurred at the dinner and the discovery of the body. Richard spoke up first. He explained how Helen had invited them all to Keeler's for dinner and dancing, how after dinner they danced to the wonderful music of the band, they enjoyed coffee and the specialty chocolate cake afterwards and everyone appeared happy, having a fine time. That is, until Ben Faraday and his mother appeared.

"Mr. Faraday and his mother," Inspector Harris looked again at his notes. "We received word that his mother died Sunday evening, having been run over by a trolley on Central Avenue."

"How is that related to Adam's death?" Elsie asked.

"I'm not saying it is," the Inspector continued. "But Adam and Ben Faraday fought at the restaurant, as you mentioned, which caused quite a scene."

"Yes, it did, Inspector," Helen agreed. "Adam was removed by a few waiters who settled him in another dining room, and it was there that he died."

"From the arsenic poisoning," Elsie put in.

"About how long was Adam in the other dining room before you went to check on him?" he addressed Meg and Iris.

"At least half an hour," Meg said, turning to Iris who nodded.

"Before coming here today we went to the restaurant and spoke to waiters who were there Saturday evening. When they saw him again, he was in convulsions on the floor, writhing, then he stopped breathing and died."

The Inspector looked at his partner. "We're handling this as a suicide. We don't have proof that there was foul play."

"Where would Adam get arsenic?" Iris asked the room at large. No one knew anything about arsenic and as if on cue Ida entered at that moment, holding a small box.

"We do have an old box of rat poison." She held the box out to the Inspector who took it and opened it.

"It's hard to tell if it's been used recently. You've had this for a longtime?"

Ida nodded. "I've used it to kill mice in the kitchen."

"Please throw that away," Helen said to the inspector. "I don't want it in my house!" Her tone bordered on hysterics and Elsie leaned forward and placed her hand on her sister's arm.

"No, it doesn't prove anything," the Inspector agreed. "But I'd like to take this with me." Helen did not offer any resistance to his taking the box of rat poison. "We are currently investigating Mr. Faraday's mother's death as well. Does anyone have information on that?"

No one had information to offer the policemen about Janet Faraday. He mentioned Helen fainting before the fight began.

"Must we go over that again, Inspector?" Helen said with a tired expression.

"The fighting was too much for my sister," Elsie spoke up in Helen's defense. "She isn't used to such a violent display of emotions." she paused. "And for the other woman, too, I'm sure."

"There may be something that comes back to you," Inspector Harris said, addressing the family, before leaving. "In cases like this, it may be days before a flashback occurs to clarify things."

With Harmon to see them out, the policemen left the living room, to the hallway and out the front door, into the cold light of day.

"I'll be leaving Saturday," Meg told the family at dinner that evening.

The afternoon passed slowly, after the policemen left, and the inhabitants of the house found themselves at a loss at what to do. It was dark out now and bitterly cold, but the snow had finally paused. The family was still grieving, and their mourning took different forms.

Iris, Bruce, and Elsie took time off from work to assist Helen and Meg, while Harmon helped Ida in the kitchen in preparing meals and fixing coffee and desserts. Adam's wake was arranged for Thursday evening and the burial for Friday morning. Helen, along with Elsie, made the funeral arrangements as Meg was too disturbed to handle such matters.

Richard spent most of his time in the living room, reading the papers, listening to the radio and conversing with Helen. They were at the dining room table, digesting a rather heavy meal. As Ida served coffee, Meg announced her departure Saturday. Iris asked if she could help her with anything.

Meg was grateful for her sister-in-law. "I do want to call Ben Faraday again before I leave. Also, there's a librarian here I know." She looked at Iris. "You may know him, too. His name is Sloane Sheppard."

"Sloane Sheppard?" Iris said the name questioningly. "No, I can't say I do."

"I met him at the New York Public Library once when he was doing research. He's also a private detective. I'd like to call him before leaving Saturday."

"What do you want with a private detective?" Elsie said. Her tone held disapproval.

"I'd like his advice on Adam's death," Meg replied simply. "The police think he killed himself, but I don't believe Adam was suicidal."

"You imply Adam was murdered," Helen said.

"I don't know," came Meg's answer. "But there are a lot of unanswered questions. Perhaps Sloane Sheppard can help clarify them for me."

"That's nonsense," Elsie said and even Richard agreed.

"Well, I plan to speak to him anyway," Meg said, and her voice held conviction. She finished her coffee and stood. "I'd like to use the phone, Helen, if you don't mind." Without waiting for a reply, Meg went into the hallway and to the telephone.

"Meg seems determined to investigate Adam's death," Bruce commented. "She isn't content to leave it as it is."

"And what about Mr. Faraday's mother?" Iris asked.

"Who cares about her?" Richard said and his voice was somewhat harsh, and Iris was taken aback. "We didn't know her and personally. I could care less."

In the hallway, Meg called the boarding house and spoke to Mrs. Perry, who immediately went upstairs, knocked on Ben's door, and told him it was Meg calling for him. He came downstairs and picked up the phone quickly, eager to speak to Meg.

"Ben, I'd like to see you again tomorrow," Meg said hopefully. "I'm leaving Saturday morning to go back to New York." She paused. "How about tomorrow morning for coffee? And if you're leaving to go back to New York too, perhaps we can take the same train on Saturday?"

"Yes, I'd like that, Meg," Ben told her. "Tomorrow I have to arrange for mother's body to be returned to New York. I need to call the psychiatric hospital to let them know what happened. Let's meet at ten o'clock tomorrow at that diner on Pearl Street."

It was early evening. As was her usual routine, Helen retired to the living room, along with Iris and Bruce. She picked up her knitting and began to work, while Iris and Bruce listened to the radio and chatted among themselves.

Elsie and Richard entered the living room, wearing their coats and preparing to go out. Helen asked them where they were going on such a cold night.

"To the theater!" Elsie exclaimed. "I need to get out before I go out of my mind!" Helen looked at her sister, appalled at her behavior.

Richard gave Helen a wry smile and told her they would be back later. They walked out of the living room and to the front door, where they met Ida.

At the same time, Grace Prescott was just about to ring the doorbell. She greeted Elsie and Richard, who passed her on their way out. She then smiled at Ida, who welcomed her into the house.

"Hello, Ida dear," Grace said cheerfully. Ida closed the door and took Grace's coat and then led her down the hallway to the living room.

"Grace, how nice to see you," Helen said as she entered. "Coffee or tea?"

"Coffee is fine," said Grace warmly.

She then looked at Helen who looked sad and unhappy. After all, Adam committed suicide at that restaurant. But then Grace saw that look on Helen Cary for years, so it was really nothing new. Her glance went to Bruce. Grace knew little of Bruce Bauer except that he was rather laconic. The quiet type always masks a darker side, Grace thought. Her gaze went to Iris who looked as if she had not slept for days. Of course, with her brother's death and her mother's attack, who could sleep? Grace looked up as Ida came bustling in with a tray and several cups of coffee. As usual with Ida, the maid nearly knocked the tray off the coffee table, but Grace helped her and received a demure thank you in return. Grace gave her a careful look, which apparently Ida found embarrassing. She left the room rather abruptly and hurried off to the kitchen. Helen smiled faintly.

"You must excuse my maid, Grace. She's taking Adam's death in a peculiar way. We each have our own way of dealing with death and its aftermath."

Grace nodded. "How are you holding up, Helen? You have my sympathy."

Helen thanked her. "My family has been helpful." She smiled faintly at Grace. "Perhaps you can tell us what you remember from that evening. I fainted when Adam and that other man, Ben Faraday, started fighting."

"I don't remember much," Grace said. "Iris told me about Adam."

Iris looked at her mother. "Mother, you should talk to Ben Faraday. He was there with his mother."

Helen's face was grave. "Perhaps. Mr. Faraday's mother died. It happened suddenly." She explained how Janet Faraday had been run over by a trolley on Sunday evening. Grace acted as though she didn't know, when in fact she read it in the newspaper on Monday.

"Grace, is there anything more you remember?" Iris persisted.

Grace sipped her coffee. "I wish I could, Iris. I left after the fight started." She paused. "I'm not used to fighting, you know."

"Well, perhaps something will come to you," Iris said.

Helen sighed impatiently. "What *do* you remember, Grace?"

"Well, Adam and that other man started fighting," she said choosing her words carefully. "Then that other woman collapsed. Of course, you collapsed too, Helen."

"I know all that," Helen said irritably.

"Well, as I walked past the other dining room, I glanced in and saw Adam sitting in a chair. I didn't stop as he seemed almost asleep. I did notice a waiter had approached him, but other than that, nothing else." She paused. "I then walked to the main exit and left."

"Why didn't you let us know you had left?" asked Iris.

Grace looked at her with something close to mirth. "How could I with all the confusion going on?"

Iris nodded. Her dark eyes were bright and alert. "Perhaps someone put the arsenic in Adam's coffee. Or he could have put it in himself."

"He died after the fighting took place," Bruce commented.

Helen cleared her throat. "This is too much to listen to. Just speculations."

Iris turned to Grace anxiously. "Would you tell me about my father, Grace? Mother hardly ever mentions him."

"Well, dear, our concern is for Adam."

"Do you remember him, Grace? My father?" Iris persisted.

Grace felt bad for the younger woman. She was having a difficult time coping with her brother's death. It was understandable. She put the elegant cup and saucer on the coffee table and suddenly, Helen gasped for breath, put her hand to her chest and turned white. Grace went to her aide while Bruce calmed Iris. From the corner of the room, they could hear Iris talking about Adam.

"She's too upset," Grace murmured to Helen.

"Perhaps my daughter is taking it too hard," said Helen ruefully.

Grace patted her hand. "Old skeletons never resurface unless we let them, Helen." Helen looked up into Grace's cold, calculating, clever eyes. She then turned to leave when Bruce stopped her.

"I apologize for my wife's behavior. Why don't you stay a bit longer?"

"Yes, please stay, Grace," said Helen. "I'll have Ida bring in more coffee." Grace thanked them but declined. Bruce led her to the hallway while Iris fetched her belongings. Harmon offered to drive her in the car if she wished. She declined that also, saying the walk would do her good. Bruce and Harmon returned to the living room to check on Helen, leaving Iris to show Grace out. She opened the front door for her, but Grace hesitated in the doorway.

"I wouldn't worry, dear. Everything comes out in the open sooner or later."

Iris gave a wry smile. "Sometimes I wonder."

Grace finished putting on her gloves, wrapped her scarf around her neck and put on her cloche hat. There was a strange mixture of sympathy and malice as she looked at her rather intently.

"Indeed, Iris dear, it always does. Would you like me to be your real mother?"

"What do you mean by that?" asked Iris, bewildered.

But Grace Prescott merely gave a short laugh as she walked down the snowy steps leaving Iris to stare after her.

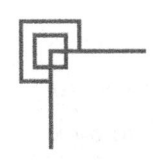

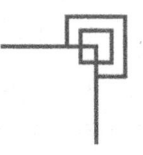

CHAPTER FIFTEEN

Thursday morning, Ben came wide awake and got up rather quickly. His mind was crowded, tumbling with images of the past and present. He tried to calm his inner being, to relax and get hold of his emotions and feelings, but no matter how hard he tried, it was not working.

He glanced at his watch restlessly. Seven o'clock. He called the police yesterday and was to meet with them this morning before meeting Meg at the diner at ten o'clock.

He looked in the mirror, at his beard which was a messy stubble. As he filled the sink in the bathroom with water to shave, his thoughts flew to his mother, who was crushed underneath the trolley wheels. Mrs. Kelly was nice enough to relate what she saw to him. She would call the police to tell them what she witnessed. That brought its own confusion, because if that were true, then his mother was murdered, deliberately pushed in front of the trolley. But who would do that to mother?

Ben sighed in frustration as he finished shaving, washing his face with a towel. He then put on his vest, straightened his tie, grabbed his hat, coat and gloves. He walked down the hallway, to the tall staircase and met Mrs. Perry in the dining room.

"Good morning, Mr. Faraday," she said pleasantly. "Ready for breakfast?"

Ben returned the smile, although it was an effort. "I'm going to the police station first," he told her. "I may not have time for breakfast today." He told Mrs. Perry he would be back later in the day and took his leave.

When he opened the door, cold wind and snow stung his face. He tugged the door shut behind him and turned left onto State Street.

Sleet struck sharply against the back of his neck, bringing with it a sobering touch of cold reality. He knew he had to leave Albany soon to return to work. He crossed Washington Avenue at Dove Street and caught the trolley to go uptown. He got off at the corner of Central Avenue and Quail Street. He crossed to the police station and went inside. He was directed to a small office to the right. He expected a long wait but to his surprise the policemen entered the small room almost immediately and introduced themselves to Ben.

"Mr. Faraday, my partner and I are investigating your mother's death," Lieutenant Taylor said, as he got straight to the point. "We want to help you as much as possible." He cleared his throat. "At the moment we have no leads regarding your mother's death."

"She was pushed," Ben said bluntly. "Mrs. Kelly was a witness. She told me she saw someone push my mother in the line of the trolley!"

"We've spoken with Mrs. Kelly," the Inspector told Ben. "And we have a statement from her. We're hoping others will come forward with any new information." He paused. "Do you remember anything that can help us, Mr. Faraday?"

Ben shook his head. "We ate dinner at an Italian restaurant and then walked down Central until we came to Northern Boulevard. We crossed at the intersection to wait for the trolley to take us back downtown. There was a large crowd. As the trolley approached, my mother fell in the line of the wheels! I tried to grab her, but it was too late."

"Was it icy on the sidewalk?" the Lieutenant asked.

"Of course, it was icy," Ben said abruptly almost losing his patience. "This is January, after all!" He looked at Inspector Harris with mounting anger. "Why do you ask if it was icy? Do you think Mrs. Kelly is lying?"

"We have to check all possibilities."

Ben rose from the chair. He looked out the one window to see cars, trollies and people walking in the snow. It was overcast and the bleak weather did nothing to help overcome his somber mood. He turned to look at the policemen.

"I want to know what happened to my mother," he told them forcefully. "I plan to leave tomorrow. I live in Manhattan and need to return to work soon."

Lieutenant Taylor gave Ben a short but reassuring smile. It did not help to alleviate his chaotic thoughts, but he spoke sincerely as he got up and went over to him.

"We're continuing this investigation and will arrive at an answer soon enough."

Ben nodded. He then gave the policemen his address and phone number in Manhattan where he lived on 96th Street.

"I understand your frustration and concern. My partner and I will do everything to arrive at a conclusion to this case. You must be patient."

"I can't be patient," Ben said and moved aside. He had enough of the police and their lackluster attempts to investigate his mother's death.

"We've spoken to the trolley driver who worked Saturday night. Unfortunately, he didn't see anything out of the ordinary, except for when your mother fell in front of the wheels."

"Mrs. Kelly is a credible witness," Ben said to them.

"Yes, she supplied us with a great deal of information. However, at this time we don't have a definite answer."

"People just don't push people in front of a vehicle!" Ben paused. "It seems like you don't have anything to go on."

"I'm sorry, Mr. Faraday," Inspector Harris said.

Ben paced restlessly. "Are you investigating the death of Adam Cary?" Lieutenant Taylor and Inspector Harris showed surprise. "Well yes, we are," said the Inspector. "What does that have to do with your mother's case?"

Ben told them how he knew Meg and the fight that had occurred between he and Adam in the dining room that evening.

"We were told about the fight," the Lieutenant said and added nothing more.

"Something strange is going on with the Cary family," Ben said thoughtfully.

"Do you think my mother's death and Adam Cary's death are somehow related?" "Related?" the Inspector said. "Did your mother know Adam Cary?"

"No, of course she didn't know him. But it's unusual that Adam Cary died Saturday evening and my mother died Sunday evening. From what Meg told me, he died of arsenic poisoning." He paused. "Two homicides in less than twenty-hours."

"Mr. Faraday, as investigating officers we are doing everything we can to arrive at a solution to your mother's death. We don't know if we're dealing with homicide or in your mother's case, an accident."

Ben was not satisfied. He felt the policemen were attempting to pacify him rather than take any definitive action.

"There have been two deaths under strange circumstances," he said gravely. "Someone knows something that can clear up my mother's death." He paused and cleared his throat. "And Adam Cary's death, too."

"We've already reached a conclusion of suicide on that case, Mr. Faraday," the Lieutenant said with gentle firmness. He paused and then added, "We intend to speak to Helen Cary again later today."

"Perhaps she will be helpful," Ben said. "Maybe someone knows something but isn't telling the truth."

With that, Ben turned to leave. Without saying another word to the policemen, he left the small room, walked hurriedly past the officer at the front desk and then went outside to get the trolley downtown.

By ten o'clock, Meg and Iris were seated at a booth at the diner on Pearl Street, waiting for Ben. They had ordered coffee and were lighting cigarettes when the diner door opened, and Ben bustled in. The hostess looked at the tall, handsome young man who just entered in his appealing Ulster coat. Ben mentioned he was looking for someone and then soon spotted Meg and Iris. He made his way to their booth, sat down, and lit a cigarette.

"Hope I didn't keep you waiting," he told them, taking a long drag on his cigarette. "I just came from the police station."

"Did you find out anything helpful?" Iris asked.

Ben shook his head. "They spoke to Mrs. Kelly, the woman who saw someone push Mother into the trolley. Other than that, they have no leads." He paused, with his cigarette at his lips. "They're investigating Adam's death, too."

"They spoke to us yesterday," Iris said. She was dressed in a simple yet becoming dress of pale blue, with white collar and cuffs. Pearls accentuated the whiteness of her skin, the auburn hair, and the pretty green eyes. Ben nodded and turned his attention to Meg.

"Saturday, we leave for New York," Meg told him. "I've already changed my ticket. Did you plan to do the same?"

Ben nodded. "After leaving here, I'll go to Union Station to make the change. There's really no point in staying in Albany any further. I gave the police my address and phone number in New York for them to contact me and I've arranged for mother's body to be returned to a funeral parlor there, too." He paused, lit another cigarette, and sipped some coffee. "I called the psychiatric hospital to let them know what happened to her as well."

"So much in just two days," Iris said sadly. "It's really too much!"

"Did you find out anything from Grace Prescott?" Meg asked her.

Iris shook her head. "That woman is full of secrets. I asked her about my father." Meg looked at her in surprise and Iris continued. "Mother never talks about him and I'd like to know more about him."

"What's that to do with Adam's death?" Meg asked.

"Nothing, really, I guess."

The waitress soon came with menus and they ordered breakfast and relaxed afterward with coffee and more cigarettes. Ben asked Iris if would be returning to work on Monday.

"Yes, Aunt Elsie also is returning to work. My husband Bruce returns to Albany Academy. We took the week off to help mother." She hesitated. "Adam's wake is this evening and his funeral is tomorrow morning."

Meg turned to Ben. "I called a private investigator here in Albany. His name is Sloane Sheppard. I met him once when he came to the New York Public Library and I helped him with research. He gave me his business card. Perhaps he can be of some help to us."

"What do you think he can do?" Iris asked her, flicking ash into an ashtray. "The police concluded Adam killed himself. I don't believe he did."

Both Iris and Ben looked at Meg, startled and speechless. Ben crushed his
cigarette and sipped some coffee.

"Then what do you think happened?" he asked her.

"I think someone put arsenic in his coffee. The table was empty for a long time while everyone was dancing. Anyone could have done it."

"Who would want to poison Adam?" Ben asked.

Meg and Iris looked at each other. Their thoughts were identical. Only Meg found the courage to speak.

"Adam didn't make friends easily. We had a rocky marriage. He wasn't too nice to his sister and brother-in-law. I don't think Elsie and Richard were fond of him, either."

Iris agreed. "Some years ago, he borrowed money from Uncle Richard and never paid him back."

"Must have been before I met him," Meg commented. "I don't remember Adam ever mentioning borrowing money from anyone."

Ben was deep in thought. "Two deaths, one right after the other. Do you think they're related somehow?"

"How could they be?" Meg asked. "Your mother didn't know Adam. She had never seen him, except for the night at the restaurant."

"You're right, Meg," Ben said and had another cigarette to his lips. "Strange that two mysterious deaths occurred in one weekend."

Iris agreed. "As far as arsenic goes, Ida found a box of rat poison in the kitchen pantry. She gave it to the police. Mother became terribly upset when she saw it."

"Rat poison?" Ben said. "The arsenic came from that?" "We don't know yet. The police are still investigating."

"That's why I want to talk to Sloane Sheppard," Meg said, helpfully. "He may be able to answer a lot of these questions." She finished her coffee and suggested they leave.

Iris, Meg and Ben contributed to the tab and then went for their coats. Walking onto Pearl Street, Meg asked Ben what he planned to do for the rest of the day.

"Nothing, really. This is my last night in Albany." He paused and looked at the two young women. "Perhaps we can meet again tonight, Meg?"

"I'll ask my mother if it'll be okay for you to come over," Iris spoke up, holding onto her cloche hat as the wind picked up, almost blowing it away. "You're staying on State Street, right? Well, we're just around the corner on Willett."

"Do you think she'd mind?" Ben asked, also holding onto his hat.

"She'd like to speak to people at our table. Since you and Adam fought, she should speak to you."

It was then decided that early in the evening, Ben would stop by to see Helen, whether she liked it or not, Iris added. As they came to the corner of State and Pearl Streets, Ben announced he was going to Union Station to change his ticket. Meg told them she had her appointment with Sloane Sheppard, just across the street at the Home Savings Bank Building. Iris mentioned she was returning home, to get out of the wind and cold. She crossed State Street to get the trolley uptown.

She watched Ben walk down State Street on his way to Union Station and Meg cross to the other side of Pearl Street, to see that private investigator or librarian or whatever he was. Iris hoped her sister-in-law was doing the right thing and was not putting herself in any danger.

AN UNFORTUNATE COINCIDENCE

Albany's newest skyscraper, proudly proclaimed the tallest in the city, was the Home Savings Bank Building. Recently completed, it was a nineteen-story art deco masterpiece, with marble floors and high ceilings.

Meg went to the wall directory to look for the office of Sloane Sheppard. She saw he was located on the tenth floor. She entered an elevator and told the attendant what floor she wanted. He then closed the gates and soon the elevator was on its way upward.

Upon arriving at floor ten, the attendant opened the gates and Meg got out. She looked to her right and then left to try to find Sloane Sheppard's office. She turned left and saw a small sign that read *Sloane Sheppard Detective* on a nameplate to the right of the door. She knocked but got answer. So, she turned the knob and walked in.

Meg saw a well-dressed man, perhaps in his late thirties, with wavy brown hair mixed with a few gray streaks, pleasant blue eyes and a charming if not handsome face and appearance. He sat behind a desk, with a multitude of files and papers in front of him. He was well-dressed in a white shirt, dress tie and suspenders, black trousers, and Oxford shoes, overall a pleasing and professional appearance.

He had a cup of coffee and a roast beef sandwich to his right and was eating it while reviewing some papers. There was no waiting area, except a few metal chairs and a small table with some magazines in the far corner. It was not a large room and Meg gathered from looking around that it was a one-man operation, no secretaries, or associates just the man behind the desk. He looked up at her again and smiled.

"Mr. Sheppard? Thank you for seeing me at short notice." The voice faltered and quivered slightly. "My name is Mrs. Megan Cary. You may remember me from the New York Public Library several years ago when you were there for research. I assisted you and…"

Sloane smiled encouragingly. "Of course, Mrs. Cary, I remember you. I gave you my business card, too."

"You mentioned if I ever needed your services if in Albany, to call on you."

He motioned Meg to sit in the metal chair in front of his desk. Sloane paused in remembering his visit to the New York Public Library in 1925, just three years ago. He remembered the attractive, bright young woman whose assistance with his research project proved invaluable.

"Yes, I do remember you," he told her. "How have you been?"

"I'm afraid things aren't going well," Meg said ruefully. "That's why I'm here. You told me you were a private investigator."

"Yes, I'm a private investigator and a librarian," Sloane added with a smile. "Which we have in common."

Upon hearing Sloane's comforting words, Meg nodded and gave a brief smile.

After a few moments, she composed herself and spoke hoarsely.

"Mr. Sheppard, my husband is dead. Poisoned with arsenic! The police think he killed himself, but I don't know if that's what really happened." She paused uncertainly.

Sloane interrupted kindly. "First, please call me Sloane, since we're old acquaintances." He closed a folder, wrapped the remains of his sandwich, put it in a drawer and looked carefully at Meg.

"I need to get to the bottom of Adam's death. I don't believe he killed himself. And neither does Iris, my sister-in-law."

Sloane nodded. "Why don't you start at the beginning and tell me the details of the events of that Saturday evening?"

Meg prepared herself for a rather hard recount of the past week. She related to Sloane what happened to Adam, ending with the strange note she found that evening in the guest room. She supplied Sloane with the names of the policemen who investigated and then she remained quiet as though her narration had sapped her of all her strength.

Sloane remained silent for a few moments. Then he looked down at the notes he had written.

"Seems to me that your husband had little reason to end his life," he said.

"He had an excellent career as a chemist," Meg said. "We live on Central Park South in a beautiful apartment, but I've always felt Adam wasn't really happy. He may have had other women in his life. He certainly knew how to look for them."

"Do you think he was cheating on you?"

"Adam didn't like to be tied down. He was appealing to women."

"And yet you married him?"

Meg sighed tiredly. "Looking back, he wasn't really the marrying kind."

Sloane reflected on the situation. "Why would your husband pick a fight with Mr. Faraday? Did he think you were involved with him?"

"Possibly. He was the jealous type."

"How was he before dinner that evening?"

"He assumed that Ben and I were involved." She then gave a short laugh.

"Adam was so clever. He could tell a lie right to your face and not blink an eyelash."

Sloane looked at Meg and could detect the bitterness in her voice. "In order for your husband to have ended his life, there had to be a reason. Your marital problems did not seem that they'd drive him to suicide." Sloane paused. "You found what sounds like a suicide note later that evening. Is there something else you're not telling me?"

Meg was rather taken aback. "No, of course not. If Adam had secrets, I didn't know about them. He was reclusive and spent most of his time in the lab."

Sloane then asked for her mother-in-law's address and phone number. He jotted it down and then closed the notebook.

"I'll investigate your husband's death, Meg. I'll speak to the policemen who handled the case and reach my own conclusions. I will need, of course, to speak to the entire family, too."

"Actually, I'm returning to the city tomorrow," Meg told him. "I go back to work on Monday. Can you visit my in-laws later today? My mother-in-law is always home."

Sloane looked at his calendar and did not see anything else planned for the rest of the day. He would call Helen Cary, introduce himself and mention he would like to visit this evening if she would be available. He would first call Lieutenant Taylor and Inspector Harris and speak with them to learn more about the case. He explained to Meg his fees and payment methods. Meg assured him she would pay by check upon completion of his investigations.

"Thank you for offering to help," she said sincerely. She shook hands with Sloane and gave him her address and phone number in Manhattan.

Sloane opened his office door, thanked Meg for coming to see him, and watched as she pressed the button for the elevator. He eyed her rather appreciatively; the appealing scent of her perfume, her expensive fur coat and the sleek cloche hat that fitted her lovely head so well. An impressive young woman and an intelligent one. Yes, he would assist Megan Cary in learning more about her husband's death.

The attendant closed the gates as soon as she stepped in and the elevator began its descent to the lobby.

AN UNFORTUNATE COINCIDENCE

At dinner, Meg announced that she spoke to Sloane at his office that afternoon. Helen looked up from her after dinner coffee and mentioned that he had called, and she invited him to the house at six o'clock. She reminded her daughter-in-law that they would leave shortly after for Adam's wake. Ida cleared the dinner and dessert dishes and offered more coffee. Elsie and Richard declined, but Iris and Bruce had second cups.

"I can never resist Ida's coffee," Bruce smiled as he added more cream and sugar to his cup. He started on another piece of cake.

In the living room, Helen sat in her chair near the fireplace, knitting. Iris, Richard, and Elsie listened to the news on the radio, Richard had the evening newspaper in his lap. Elsie had a book in her hand and was about to start reading. Harmon entered and threw another log in the fireplace. The fire danced brightly for a few moments and offered more warmth to the room.

Meg sat on the Victorian sofa and looked at Helen. "I'm leaving tomorrow, Helen. I have to go back to work at the library."

"Of course, Meg," Helen said. "You must get on with your life."

"I'd like to speak to you," Meg said rather boldly. Helen looked up and the two women locked glances for a moment. "I've mourned my husband's death, but my life has to continue."

Helen looked at Meg with a tired expression and sighed.

"Your library work, where you meet strange men? How shameful."

"I'm sorry you feel that way," Meg said. She was surprised she had the patience to listen to such gratuitous insults. "My career as a librarian…"

"A married woman's acceptable employment is looking after her husband's home."

"You have such ancient ideas about women. My work is important, and I need to get on with my life. That's why I hired an investigator to clear up any remaining questions concerning Adam's death."

"Remaining questions? I believe none of this would have happened if you hadn't spoken to that sickly woman and then gotten involved with her son."

"This has nothing to do with Ben."

"You refer to him by his first name?"

"It makes no difference. I have confidence in Sloane Sheppard."

"And how do you know this Mr. Sheppard and where is he from, my dear? Another casual acquaintance?"

"He's from Albany. I met him when he was at the New York Public Library to research a project."

"You become acquainted with two men and your husband isn't dead a week?" Helen scowled and Meg fought hard to keep her thoughts to herself. She felt her temper rise but kept it at bay. Her glance then returned to Helen.

"I'll speak to this Mr. Sheppard when he comes, but I don't know what I can tell him." She paused. "The police have already closed the book on Adam's death. And I have accepted it as suicide. I do intend to get on with my life just as you intend to."

"Ben Faraday may also come here tonight," Meg said. "I think it's a good idea for you to speak to him, since he was at the restaurant that night."

"Yes, I'd like to meet him," Helen said to Meg's surprise.

Elsie looked up from the book she was reding and asked Helen if she wanted anything else. Meg had momentarily forgotten she was even in the room, along with Richard.

"Thank you, Elsie. Meg and I were just concluding our discussion." She smiled at her sister and brother-in-law.

AN UNFORTUNATE COINCIDENCE

Elsie mentioned she would get ready for the wake. She and Richard left the living room to return to their room to prepare for the service.

Meg decided to remain in the living room, looking at magazines, awaiting Sloane's arrival.

Helen excused herself from Meg and went upstairs to prepare for the wake. A gentle knock came on her bedroom door after about a half hour. Helen had been sitting on her bed, deep in thought for so long she was not aware of the time that had gone by. She looked up and saw Ida in the doorway.

"Mr. Sloane Sheppard is downstairs in the living room, Mrs. Cary."

Upon entering the living room, Helen saw Meg and another man sitting on the sofa, deep in conversation.

"Helen, this is Mr. Sloane Sheppard," Meg said and introduced her to the man on the sofa, who rose to shake her hand. "Mr. Sheppard, this is Mrs. Helen Cary."

It was a hard face, Sloane thought, as he shook hands with Helen. As though she had been through numerous events in her life and still carried the burdens of yesterday. He quickly sized her up and realized she was doing the same. Helen forced a smile, motioned for Sloane to sit down again, and sat at her chair by the fire. She came straight to the point.

"I've spoken to the police and have told them everything I remember." She then added, "My son's wake is this evening, Mr. Sheppard. I cannot speak with you too long." She finished speaking abruptly as though closing the book on the subject.

Sloane chose his words carefully. "Thank you for seeing me, Mrs. Cary. Please accept my condolences on the loss of your son. Meg's asked me to investigate her husband's death. She feels there are still some loose ends to be tied up before she leaves Albany."

"Loose ends," Helen remarked acidly. "I've accepted Adam's death as suicide. The police have concluded their investigation."

Sloane looked at her carefully. This was a rich woman, obviously accustomed to having her way. He remarked dryly, "I'm afraid Meg has not accepted his death as suicide."

"Since Adam's death has already been investigated, what do *you* plan to uncover? That perhaps Adam did not kill himself and was instead murdered?"

"It is a possibility," Sloane remarked. "I have to look at all angles."

"My son's death has been most upsetting, Mr. Sheppard," Helen said with genuine grief. "It is best for me not to discuss it," she added with finality.

Sloane coughed. "You were unconscious at the time of your son's death?"

"That is correct."

"Where were you after the fight erupted between your son and Mr. Faraday?"

"In that dining room, with my family, of course," Helen said with annoyance.

"In your chair?"

"No, I collapsed. Do you have a short memory, Mr. Sheppard?"

Sloane gave a professional smile; he was used to dealing with difficult clients. "No indeed, my memory is quite strong as I believe yours is too, Mrs. Cary." He paused. "And were there others at your table besides your family?"

"Yes, my servants, Ida Munson and Harmon Pendleton were at

the table." She paused and saw the expression on Sloane's face. "Yes, I invited them. As well as a friend, Grace Prescott. I wanted all of us to celebrate Adam being home. The evening started off well, the food was delicious, and the music and dancing were sensational."

Sloane nodded. "I'm glad to hear that, Mrs. Cary."

"Although I couldn't tell you anything else of what happened after the unfortunate fight, I was unconscious the whole time."

Sloane nodded again and made notes. He then looked up at Helen. "Why would Adam take his life, Mrs. Cary?"

Helen shrugged helplessly. "The police have asked me that many times. And I have asked myself the same question. We hadn't spoken since last Christmas." She hesitated. "Adam was obsessed with money, wouldn't you say so, Meg?"

Meg looked at Helen and was surprised she asked her opinion. "Yes, Adam was rather obsessed with money," she said. "He had a good job at the laboratory."

"Did you get along with your son, Mrs. Cary?" Sloane asked Helen.

"Yes, we did for the most part. We had disagreements, of course. I hadn't seen Adam or Meg since last Christmas. I really don't remember the discussion last Christmas. It was so long ago." She put her hand to her forehead as though trying to remember and found it too painful.

Sloane looked at her carefully and thought she could remember very well what occurred during Adam and Meg's Christmas 1926 visit but refused to discuss it.

"What made Adam upset on Saturday evening?"

"It may have been that he recognized Mr. Faraday, the man Meg met on the train," Helen said, casting a disapproving glance at Meg. "Adam wasn't glad to see him and wondered why, as we all did, that man and his mother came to the restaurant where we were dining."

Sloane thought of the many cases he had investigated over the years but did not remember one in which a family member, already wealthy in his own right and interested in women outside his marriage, committed suicide at the idea of his spouse showing possible interest in another man. Truthfully, he found that notion absurd.

Entering the room, Richard cleared his throat and introduced himself, his wife, and Iris and Bruce to Sloane. Sloane stood and shook hands with each of them. He beckoned them to sit and asked them if they could provide further details about the night Adam died.

"There was a time when we were all on the dance floor," Iris began.

"Yes, we were all dancing and enjoying the music," Elsie said.

"Except for you, Meg, you sat out a few dances and were alone at the table, weren't you?" Richard asked unexpectedly.

Meg looked at Richard and was surprised he would make that remark. "Yes, my back was to the table and I was facing the dance floor," she added as though she was under suspicion.

"And then, of course, there was a fight between Adam and Mr. Faraday," Elsie offered. "Adam was upset over seeing him."

"And then his mother collapsed," Bruce added.

"As did Mother," Iris said, looking sadly at her mother.

"Mr. Sheppard knows these facts already," Helen spoke up rather tartly. "And I don't believe he needs to hear them again."

Sloane cleared his throat. "From what I've learned about that evening, Adam became upset upon seeing Mr. Faraday and his mother approach your table. He started a fight with Mr. Faraday and needed to be removed from the dining room, where he was brought into another dining room to recoup himself. And it was there that he died."

Helen intervened. "I collapsed, so I can't tell you what happened after the fight."

"Ben's mother also collapsed," Meg said. "I don't know why."

Sloane asked everyone present if they knew why Ben Faraday's mother collapsed.

Nobody could offer a reason for her fainting.

"She just fell to the ground," Bruce said.

"After Helen collapsed," Elsie said.

"The fighting disturbed me," Helen said. "Although I can't speak for the other woman, I'm sure that's why she collapsed as well."

"His mother died on Sunday evening," Iris said. "She fell in front of a moving trolley and was crushed to death. It was in the paper."

"Iris, please!" her mother said firmly. "I find that too upsetting!"

"Adam must have thought that Meg and Mr. Faraday were involved," Iris went on, "and that he deliberately went to that restaurant to see her."

"What happened after that?" Sloane pressed Helen for an answer.

"Well, it all happened so fast. Adam started making accusations at Mr. Faraday and the next thing I knew they were fighting, and I collapsed onto the floor."

"Did you collapse when they started fighting or afterwards?"

Helen looked at Sloane strangely. "What does that mean? That sickly mother of his collapsed at the same time."

Sloane nodded, taking notes. "It wasn't the fighting that caused you to collapse?"

"I don't remember what *caused* me to collapse, or anything else, Mr. Sheppard. All I remember is waking up in the hospital with the most irritating nurse to attend me. I plan on reporting her to the administration as soon as possible."

"And Grace Prescott was there, too." Bruce added. "Where did she go after the fighting began?"

"She said she left afterwards," Iris said. "She didn't tell us because there was too much going on, with the ambulances arriving and the manager clearly in a dither."

"Why do you think she fainted?" Sloane asked Helen.

"I have no idea about that either, Mr. Sheppard."

"Who was your husband, Mrs. Cary?" Sloane said changing course.

Helen looked at him in surprise. "My husband? Why do you ask? I fail to see what he has to do with this."

"The late Mr. Cary," Sloane persisted. "His name, please."

Helen cleared her throat, clearly annoyed. "His name was Walter. He died several years ago, although I don't see—"

"In what year?"

"Mr. Sheppard, I'm sorry, but I do not wish—"

"The year, Mrs. Cary, please? Also, the attorney who handled his estate?"

Helen scowled. "In 1922, although I don't understand why you need to know that. His lawyer, I believe, was Mr. Luther Bernard." She looked intently at Sloane. "Why do you ask about my late husband and his lawyer? The estate was settled years ago."

"For the record, Mrs. Cary," Sloane explained, taking notes. "When I investigate a death, even a suicide, I need to know the family history and if I need to contact a family lawyer."

"Well, he wasn't a family lawyer," Helen said with contempt. "He was my late husband's lawyer."

"Your late husband died rather tragically, didn't he?"

"Yes, in a car mishap, but that has nothing to do with Adam's death," Helen said and closed her eyes as though deep in thought. "I refuse to discuss Adam's father."

Sloane did not think he could get any more out of Helen Cary; at least for now.

"The late Mr. Cary," Iris mused, "can mean my father or my brother."

AN UNFORTUNATE COINCIDENCE

"Iris, please!" Helen implored.

The doorbell rang at that moment. Harmon soon appeared in the doorway and announced Ben Faraday.

"Well, speak of the devil," Richard said, with a mischievous grin.

Harmon entered the living room, followed by a tall young man, impeccably dressed, wearing an Ulster coat, which he took off and handed to Harmon. As always, Ben was groomed to perfection; his immaculate Oxford shoes, pleated brown trousers, dress shirt, vest and tie made quite an impression. His black hair slicked back, and dark piercing eyes were penetrating. Helen, though, was not impressed.

"Sit down, Mr. Faraday," she said, only lukewarm. "I understand you're staying at a boarding house on State Street." Her tone implied it was convenient for him to stop by her house on Willett Street, only a block away.

"Thank you," Ben said and sat next to Meg. He was introduced to everyone and then Sloane turned to him.

"We've been discussing the events from last Saturday evening," he said. "Perhaps you can shed some light on what happened."

Ben cleared his throat and felt rather out of place. "Well, Meg's husband started making accusations. He swung at me and I had to defend myself."

"You shouldn't have fought him," Elsie said. "He didn't mean anything."

"Of course, he did," Iris spoke up. "Adam was livid and swung first."

"We're attempting to find a link," Sloane said to Ben, "if one exists, between the death of Adam and the death of your mother."

This time Helen did speak. She looked at Sloane squarely and her words were forceful and to the point.

"I have never heard anything so ridiculous. The idea is preposterous!" "And why do you say that, Mrs. Cary?" inquired Sloane.

187

Helen glared at him. "Adam was not acquainted with that woman. How could their deaths be related?"

"Were you acquainted with Janet Faraday?" he asked her.

"No, of course not. She and her son interrupted our dinner party." She paused and looked at Ben. "Isn't that correct, Mr. Faraday?"

"No, it isn't correct," Ben addressed Helen. "I didn't know Meg would be at the restaurant that night. My mother and I were trying to find a place to have dinner. Keeler's isn't far from the Ten Eyck Hotel where we had stayed so we decided to go there."

"And you just happened to see Meg?" Richard said incredulously.

"Well, yes, I did see Meg and went over to her." Ben paused. He looked at her and smiled, which did not go unnoticed by Helen.

"Do you know why your mother collapsed?" Sloane asked Ben.

"I have no idea," Ben told him. "I know she was extremely upset by the fighting. She did tell me she never forgets a face. I don't know what she meant, though."

"The fighting must have upset your mother," Bruce said to Ben.

Ben nodded. "Yes, of course. It caused her to faint."

Sloane thought Ben and Bruce had a point; the men fighting in a restaurant on what was supposed to be a happy occasion, could be enough to cause fainting or even a heart attack.

"Did your mother recognize someone at the restaurant?" Sloane asked Ben.

Ben shook his head. "We don't know anyone in Albany. It was our first time visiting."

"But she said she never forgets a face?" Sloane pondered. "That's interesting."

"Is there anything more, Mr. Sheppard?" Elsie asked irritably. "We are getting ready for Adam's wake this evening."

"I believe that'll be all for now," Sloane said and got up. "Thank you for your time and cooperation."

Helen's face held grief touched with anger. "Thank you for coming, Mr. Sheppard. You may contact me again if you wish."

Elsie went into the hallway and soon returned with coats for the two men. Sloane and Ben told Helen they appreciated her welcoming them into her home. Meg followed them to the main doorway.

"Thank you for coming tonight." She looked at Ben. "I'll see you Saturday morning at Union Station." Ben smiled and said goodbye.

The men descended the front steps, waved goodbye to Meg as she stood in the doorway, Ben walking to the right and Sloane, heading to the left.

By this time, the family was milling about, preparing to leave for the funeral parlor. Helen was alone in the living room. She spent many such evenings in peaceful comfort, but things were different now. The policemen, Adam's death, Janet Faraday's death, this Mr. Sheppard, making inquiries about her late husband's death. It was too much to comprehend.

She walked out of the living room, to the hallway and to the dining room. Ida and Harmon had returned to their rooms to dress for the wake. It was unusually quiet. As Helen glanced out the dining room windows, she saw it was still snowing, and light sleet battered the windows with quiet violence. It would be a cold evening for the wake. She shook her head sadly, dreading the evening ahead. She then went to the sideboard and opened a drawer. She turned on a lamp and rummaged around until she found what she wanted. A family photo album. Helen always found solace in looking at family photos. She felt she needed it more now than ever. She sat down at the dining room table and opened it. As she turned the pages, she clutched her hand to her chest and gasped for breath. She could not believe what she saw.

Page after page of photographs of Adam as a boy and his father were ripped off, leaving only jagged edges in place. Someone got to the album and removed photos of Adam and his father that were in it for years. She would wait for the right time to say something. First, she had to get through the wake this evening and the funeral tomorrow.

But who? Helen wondered, as she closed the album in dismay. She sat at the dining room table in shocked silence. Who would do such a thing and why?

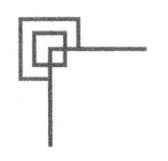

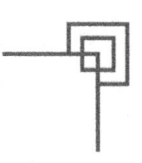

CHAPTER SIXTEEN

The snow was falling steadily as the cars returned from the cemetery. Meg looked out the car window into a sea of whiteness. She could hear Elsie and Richard in the backseat mumbling about the service. In the front, Helen sat near her but offered no sympathy or support. Only Iris and Bruce comforted her. Then the car abruptly turned onto Willett Street and stopped before the brownstone.

Adam's wake Thursday evening and the funeral Friday morning were not well attended. Grace Prescott was at both services, as though she did not want to miss anything. Community and church members, hospital volunteers who knew Helen attended out of obligation. They expressed their sympathy and wished Helen well.

The family gathered solemnly but Meg was glad when it ended, and she eagerly returned with the family to the house. She spent a quiet evening Friday, unwilling to talk with her mother-in-law, and went to bed early. She wanted nothing more than to return to the apartment in Manhattan and be away from her in-laws. As much as she appreciated Iris and Bruce, she found she needed to be alone. Adam's death was her burden and she had to cope as best she could.

She was content when Saturday morning dawned and she knew she would leave Albany, return to Manhattan, and hopefully spend time with Ben Faraday.

I CANNOT GO ON. I CAN ENDURE NO LONGER. I SEE NO OTHER WAY OUT.

Ben handed the note back to Meg after reading it several times and shook his head. They were sitting on a bench in the waiting area of Union Station on Saturday morning. Meg met Ben as arranged for the train back to Manhattan. Iris was there, to see Meg off.

"I don't know what to make of it," he told Meg. "Sounds like a suicide note. There's no name on it. You found it that evening?"

Meg put the note back in her purse. "Yes, when we returned from the restaurant. It was on top of the bureau in the guest room. There's a typewriter there, so he must have used it before we left."

Ben looked at her. Her mere presence, her sensitive mouth, touched daintily with lipstick, powdered cheeks and nose, accentuating her fine jawbone, her cloche hat, evenly placed on her lovely head, adding to the glamor she exuded, just enough perfume. Why would her husband not be enchanted by her?

"I don't remember anyone typing," Iris said. "Maybe he had it with him."

Meg shook her head. "I would have seen it. I packed our bags. Unless, he had it with him." She hesitated and looked at the busy station, people coming and going, trains being announced.

Iris smiled. "I wish we could have had a better weekend. I'm so sorry about Adam, Meg, I really am."

"Thanks, Iris," Meg said. "Monday, I go back to work." She paused. "I feel differently now, though. Things won't be the same."

The train bound for New York City was called. They left the waiting area and looked up at the departures board.

Iris pulled her heavy coat around her, her hat fit snugly and evenly on her pretty head. She gave both Meg and Ben a quick handshake and hastily made her way out of the station and to Broadway, where she caught the trolley to take her uptown.

"Well, this is it," Ben said. They joined the crowd on the platform, entered the train and found two seats. Meg commented she enjoyed sitting on the left-hand side, so that she could see the Hudson River and the West Point military campus. The conductor came around to collect the tickets. After putting the receipt in her pocketbook, Meg was reminded of the day she came to Albany for the library conference. When she first met Janet Faraday then. And Ben Faraday, the handsome young man by her side.

As the conductor continued checking tickets, Meg tried to put Janet Faraday out of her mind but, how could she? She thought of the chaos in the restaurant that evening. Although Adam was clearly upset, it seemed that Janet Faraday was the center of it.

The train soon pulled into Castleton and a few people boarded. Ben turned to her.

"Are you all right, Meg? You've been through a lot this week, with the wake and the funeral. Do you want coffee?"

"No, I'm fine, thanks." She paused, uneasily. "Ben, do you remember the night Adam and you fought?"

"Of course, I remember," he said rather irritably. "Your husband attacked me."

"Your mother was standing beside you, wasn't she?"

Ben nodded. "Then she fainted when we started fighting."

"Did she see something that caused her to faint or was it the fighting?" "It was the fighting, of course."

Meg nodded. Of course it was the fighting, what else could it have been? She then said she'd like that coffee he mentioned earlier.

They found the café car, where they bought coffee and sat at a table overlooking the Hudson River. While Ben was talking, Meg listened and smiled, but her mind was elsewhere. Naturally, it was the fighting that caused Janet Faraday to collapse and Helen, too. She continued looking at the handsome young man across from her, but her mind kept racing. She repeated to herself, it was the fighting, of course. What else could it have been?

"I don't believe it," Elsie said, finishing her third cup of coffee.

The weekend passed slowly enough. Helen waited to tell the family about the photo album as she was too worked up over the wake and funeral. Monday morning arrived cold and blustery, but things seemed to slowly be returning to normal, at least as best as possible.

Elsie sat at the dining room table, with Helen and Richard, looking at the photo album, with page after page of missing photographs. She and Richard looked at the album in disbelief, wondering how it got in such condition.

"How long had it been like that?" Richard asked, as he folded the morning paper, put it on the table, and took the photo album from Helen to look at it closely.

"I'm not sure," was Helen's answer. She was drawn and tired, Elsie noted, still in her housecoat and slippers, her face wrinkled and full of worry. After all she had been through now this? Elsie sighed and put down her coffee cup.

"I do have to get to work," she announced. "But someone's responsible for removing those pictures!"

"Who would do such a thing?" Richard pondered. "I remember seeing this album. Photos of Adam as a child are gone! Those of his father, too."

Helen nodded, too weak to speak. She reached for her coffee cup and the hot liquid restored some vitality in her.

"Perhaps Meg removed them," she said.

"Meg?" Elsie said in shock. "Whatever for?"

"For reasons of her own. I don't trust her." Helen paused. "And as far as Adam's death is concerned, I don't see why she wants a private investigator to look into it. After all, she is responsible."

"Helen!" Elsie exclaimed, again in shock. "Are you saying Meg is responsible for Adam's death? That she killed him? Then why should she have it investigated?"

"To clear her own name, of course," Helen said simply. "Meg's very clever." Elsie and Richard did not imagine that Helen's distrust went so far as accusing Meg of murder much less ruining personal property.

"You can't accuse her of anything unless you have proof, Helen," Richard told her. "And proof isn't easy to come by."

"Mr. Sheppard's here in Albany. Since Meg returned to the city, I may call him."

"What could you possibly tell him?" Elsie asked.

Helen set her mouth firmly. "I always felt Meg wasn't right for Adam. She ruined his life and drove him to suicide. Now she wants to clear her name by hiring an investigator. And notice how she took off with another man right away!"

"It does seem strange," Elsie agreed. She looked at the clock on the wall. "Oh, dear, I have to get going, or I'll be late!"

Elsie said goodbye to her sister and kissed her husband, went into the hallway for her coat and then hastily made her way to the front door, which she hurriedly banged closed behind her. Helen then turned to Richard.

"What are your plans today, Richard?"

"I may go downtown to Whitney's to shop for a new sweater. With this cold weather I certainly need it."

Helen agreed. "Richard, dear, would you ask Ida and Harmon to come in here?" He got up and took their coffee cups with the intention of returning them to the kitchen.

"Are you volunteering today, Helen?" he asked her before leaving the room.

"Tomorrow," she said. "I need to find out what happened to this photo album." Richard departed with the cups and soon returned with Ida and Harmon. They greeted Helen again and asked if anything was wrong. Having worked for Helen for several years, they could tell by her facial expression alone that something indeed was troubling her.

"Harmon, Ida, this photo album has been destroyed." She showed them the removed pictures, many pieces left as they were taken out in haste and asked them if they knew anything about it.

Harmon and Ida were speechless. They expressed their disbelief and remorse but knew nothing about it. Harmon asked the same question that Richard had asked, and Helen replied she wasn't sure how long it had been in that condition.

"Do you know anything about it, Harmon?" Richard asked as he stood next to him, looking at the album.

"No, I don't," Harmon protested. "I've never touched it." "And you, Ida?" Richard persisted.

Ida was clearly flustered, as she was not used to people looking at her, probing into her thoughts and even asking her opinion. She flushed and made to leave the dining room when Helen stopped her.

"Ida, you must know something about this. You always clean in here!"

"Bruce and Iris looked at it a few weeks ago," Ida said, reluctantly.

"Why would Bruce and Iris remove pictures from the album?" Harmon asked.

"Why would anyone remove photos from it?" Richard asked.

Helen shook her head, dismissing Ida and Harmon. "I'll speak to Iris and Bruce when they get home tonight." She paused. "May I join you to Whitney's later, Richard?" Richard was surprised that she'd want to go out, but he heartily encouraged her and said they'd take the trolley and eat lunch there, too. Helen told him that was perfect, perhaps she could find a new dress while at the department store. Ida came in and asked if Helen wanted anything. She looked at the maid and smiled briefly.

"I'm sorry, Ida, if I appeared a little brusque. I've had a rough time with Adam's death and the deplorable behavior of my daughter-in-law."

"Perhaps Meg is responsible," Ida said helpfully. "I did see her looking through the drawers of the sideboard the weekend she was here for the library conference."

"Why didn't you tell me that, Ida?"

"I didn't think anything of it. I assumed she was looking for an extra plate or a cup." She paused. "I'm sorry, Mrs. Cary."

Helen told Ida not to worry. She told Richard she would be downstairs in a few minutes, so they could go to Whitney's to shop.

"And I feel like spending money today, too!" she exclaimed. Then she walked through the hallway and up the stairs to her room to prepare for the day.

Bruce looked with contempt at the students in his literature class. It was the usual Monday attitude with the students. They were chatty and inattentive, and he found his efforts, as usual, to be fruitless. Soon the bell rang, signaling the end of class. With an inward sigh of relief that his day was almost over, Bruce gathered his textbook and exited the classroom, on his way to the faculty room.

He relaxed with a cup of coffee and chatted briefly with a few colleagues. He glanced at his watch and noticed it was almost three o'clock. He'd be glad to see Iris, as this made the first day back at their jobs, after Adam's death. Some teachers expressed sympathy over the death of his brother-in-law, but most didn't even acknowledge it.

Soon the three o'clock bell rang, and the students erupted out of the school like locusts. With his heavy coat on and winter hat pulled down over his ears, he eagerly caught the Washington Avenue trolley. As it came to the intersection of State and Lark Street, Bruce got off and crossed at the light. He continued onto Willett Street and soon arrived at the brownstone house. He was about to climb the steps when he spotted Harmon, who had just turned the corner from State Street.

"Hey, Harmon!" Bruce called to the older man. He noticed he was carrying several bags of groceries. Bruce went over and relieved his load.

"Thanks, Bruce," Harmon said, panting slightly, his breath visible in the extreme cold. "I just went to the market." He caught his breath. "Sometimes I think my age is catching up with me!"

Bruce took the bags. "Oh, come on, Harmon, you're a young man! Besides, what would we do without you?"

Harmon smiled. "Let's see what Ida has planned for dinner tonight."

As they entered the house and closed the front door, they found it strangely quiet. Harmon looked in the living room and the kitchen but did not see Helen, Richard, or Ida. He even went into his basement room. Bruce ran upstairs and took a quick look on each floor but saw no one.

"That's certainly strange," Harmon said, meeting Bruce in the hallway. "I know Helen and Richard went to Whitney's, but that was hours ago."

"Well, they should be back soon," Bruce said, looking around at the strange emptiness of the big house.

The phone in the hallway rang just then, startling both men. Harmon moved to answer it and discovered it was Grace Prescott.

"Hello, Grace," he said warmly. "Nice to hear from you. What can I do for you?"

"Well, I'd like to speak to Helen," Grace said pleasantly. "I plan to go to the hospital tomorrow to volunteer and was wondering if she planned to go there, too."

Harmon found it odd that Grace would want to see Helen in the first place as he knew there was no love lost between them. He told Grace he'd leave a message for Helen, who wasn't home yet from shopping.

Just then the front door opened and in walked Helen and Richard, their faces red from the cold. Helen was cheerful and even exuberant from a shopping expedition the result of which she held in her hands. A large hat box and two packages, each containing dresses.

"Well, that was quite an afternoon!" Helen exclaimed, catching her breath. "I haven't enjoyed shopping in so long! And we had a nice lunch, too." She took off her coat. "Where's Ida?"

Bruce commented they just arrived and found no one in the house.

"That's strange," Richard said and joined them in the hallway. "Did she have an appointment today?"

"No, she would have told me," Helen said, hanging up her fur coat and Richard's coat in the hallway closet. She looked at Richard, Harmon and Bruce and could sense something was different, some tension, some undercurrent.

"Well, I guess I'll get dinner ready for us." Harmon paused. "Grace called. She asked you to return her call."

"There's chicken in the ice box, Harmon," Helen said, dismissing the subject of Grace Prescott.

"It'll take a while to prepare," he said, admitting he was not the best cook, certainly not as good as Ida.

"I'll help you, Harmon," Bruce offered.

In the kitchen, Harmon and Bruce got plates, silverware, and glasses. Bruce brought them into the dining room, while Harmon took the chicken out of the icebox.

Elsie and Iris entered the front door, bringing with them a surge of cold air, stomping their snowy shoes on the door mat, looking pleased to be home for the evening.

"The cold does us good, doesn't it, Iris?" Elsie laughed, taking off her fur coat. She helped Iris out of her own. Iris agreed, her cheeks red from the frigid air.

The women laughed and entered the living room, to see Richard listening to the radio console, while reading the evening newspaper and Helen, knitting placidly. They greeted Elsie and Iris amicably. Iris sniffed and looked around.

"No one's cooking dinner?" she commented and sat down on the sofa. "Usually we smell Ida's cooking from outside the front door!"

"Harmon is cooking dinner," Helen said, looking up from her knitting. "And Bruce is helping him."

"What?" Elsie said in surprise. "Ida always cooks dinner!"

AN UNFORTUNATE COINCIDENCE

It was at that moment that Bruce entered, flustered and speechless. Iris greeted her husband warmly. But Bruce said nothing. He continued staring at them, immobile and clearly agitated. It was obvious there was something troubling him.

"Bruce, is there something wrong?" Richard was the only one to speak as he looked at the other's horrified expression.

"The kitchen," Bruce stammered. "In the kitchen…"

At first no one moved. Richard then put the newspaper on the floor, Helen put her knitting on the coffee table and with Iris and Elsie, followed Bruce into the kitchen. Upon entering, they saw Harmon sitting at the kitchen table, his face in his hands. He looked up as they entered but said nothing.

"What is it?" Elsie was horrified, as she realized something was indeed wrong. "The broom closet," Harmon barely got the words out. "In the broom closet…" Richard, Elsie, Helen, and Iris moved past Bruce and went to the broom closet.

Richard saw it was part way open but opening it further, motioned for the women to stay back. Suddenly feeling weak, he leaned on the door for support. On the floor, in front of him, was Ida.

An old sewing machine, which Elsie and Richard stored on an upper shelf, apparently came crashing down on her skull, knocking her unconscious, bringing her into eternal darkness.

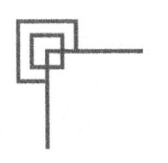

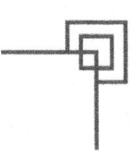

CHAPTER SEVENTEEN

It was a long weekend for Meg, and she was glad when she dragged herself to bed Sunday and fell asleep at last. Monday morning her alarm clock rang, and the routine of getting to work began. She knew she'd see Ben soon and with returning to work, she hoped some normalcy would return to her life.

She awoke to another cold morning. She had just entered the kitchen, to fix coffee, when the phone. Upon entering the hallway, for some dread reason, she expected the worse. It was ironic she realized she was not disappointed.

It was Iris, calling from Albany. They exchanged greetings, but then Iris drew her breath. She told Meg something she was certainly not expecting to hear.

"It's Ida Munson," Iris explained. Meg could hear her hesitate. "She died last night, Meg." She explained the circumstances surrounding Ida's death. She said nothing for so long that Iris asked if she was still on the line.

"Yes, of course. How could the sewing machine fall on top of her?"

"Apparently it fell off the top shelf. It landed on her head and killed her," she added bluntly as though only the grim facts were the only way to explain the misfortune that had befallen Ida. "She was taken to the hospital but never regained consciousness. The police were here, and her body was removed. I plan to call Sloane Sheppard. He should know about it, too."

Meg agreed. "And now another funeral to arrange."

Iris told Meg she had to go to work and hung up. Meg slowly replaced the receiver on the candlestick phone.

Ida, dead? Sounded like an accident. The sewing machine fell, and she just happened to be in the broom closet. Meg dressed quickly and was outside in minutes.

She had a nagging impulse. Was Ida's death unnatural? Could it tie in with Adam and Janet Faraday? But how? Joining the morning crowds on Fifth Avenue, walking steadily in the light snow toward the library, she pondered if the deaths were somehow connected.

Grace Prescott got off the trolley on New Scotland Avenue, in front of Albany City Hospital. She looked at the building with satisfaction. She was proud of this hospital and her volunteering meant much to her.

"Nice to see you, Grace," Mrs. Wilcox, the head of volunteers, smiled as Grace entered the volunteer office. She was a large, heavy-set woman in her sixties. She had gray hair and maintained a serious expression but was congenial enough. She told Grace her work for the evening involved visiting patients on various floors. Grace preferred this, rather than menial clerical work such as filing or stuffing envelopes.

AN UNFORTUNATE COINCIDENCE

As she was about to turn into a room to greet a patient, she saw a fellow volunteer, Edna, who, like Grace, was widowed, and eager to get out of her house.

"Oh Grace," she said rather breathlessly. "Did you hear about Helen Cary?"

Grace was taken aback. "No, I didn't," was all she said.

"Well, not with Helen Cary, but her maid, Mrs. Ida Munson. She died."

"Mrs. Munson died?" Grace was in shock. "How did it happen?"

"Well, I don't know the details," Edna said, obviously enjoying the gossip. "But from what I hear, she looked for something in the broom closet when a sewing machine fell and killed her! Of course, those old sewing machines weigh a ton! If one fell on top of you it'd kill you! Poor dear, and poor Helen!"

Yes, poor Helen, Grace thought bitterly. Rich Helen with her money and bossing people around, demanding this and that, ruining lives and creating havoc.

"Are you all right, Grace?" Edna said as she saw the other woman's startled face.

Grace blinked. "I'm fine, Edna dear. It's rather shocking."

Edna agreed. "I don't know Helen well, except when she volunteers here. I heard it from one of the nurses, who heard it from someone in the morgue. What a thing to happen to poor Mrs. Munson!"

Grace agreed it was terrible and offered further words of disbelief. She then excused herself from Edna and went to a patient's room. She greeted the young child in the bed, who was with his parents, having recently undergone surgery on his knee. Grace never asked what the reason was as she did not feel it was her business to do so, but she smiled and offered words of encouragement to the young boy and his parents.

After visiting several other patients on different floors, she retired to the lounge on the fifth floor, where she made a cup of coffee. She wondered about Ida Munson and Helen Cary and her strange household.

Well, Helen dear, another death to contend with, she thought wryly, sipping her coffee. She wondered how the Cary family would account for this death now, another scandal brought to book.

Meg arrived back at the apartment after five o'clock. A hectic but pleasant day at the library, busy at the reference desk and assisting patrons.

After preparing a light meal, she relaxed in the living room with tea and put on the radio. She decided to call Ben and as she entered the hallway, the phone rang. She was rather surprised to hear the voice of Sloane Sheppard.

"I received a call from Iris Bauer this morning," he said rather abruptly. "She told me the maid, Ida Munson, died unexpectedly last night."

"Iris called this morning to tell me, too," Meg said. "Do you think it's related to Adam's death? And the death of Janet Faraday?"

"I don't know yet. Iris also told me someone ripped photos of Adam as a boy, from a photo album her mother kept in her dining room."

"Who would rip out photos of Adam as a child?" Meg wondered, surprised.

He asked Meg if Adam knew Ben or his mother.

"No, he didn't know them. Neither did I until I came to Albany." She related to Sloane again the circumstances when she first met Janet Faraday and Ben.

Sloane mentioned when Meg would return to Albany. "I don't know, really," she told him. "I'd like you to continue your investigation, of course, Mr. Sheppard—I mean, Sloane. Let me know what you find."

Sloane told her he would be in touch soon and the called ended. Meg replaced the receiver on the candlestick phone and returned to the living room, deep in thought.

Three strange deaths in less than two weeks? And with Adam's death dismissed by the police as suicide, Janet Faraday's death an accident, would the police claim the same for Ida Munson? And then her mind turned again to Janet Faraday. Wasn't she the start of all this mess? And the arsenic. It was in Adam's coffee. How else would he have gotten it?

That rather pointed to someone who was at the table. There was a time when it was vacant, except for when she was turned watching the dancing. The poison could have been put in the drink then. But wouldn't she have been aware of someone at the table behind her? And there were other tables surrounding theirs. But the lights in the dining room were dim, and people were too busy enjoying themselves. It was unlikely someone from another table would have noticed anything.

The next morning, while she was preparing for work, the revelation came to her.

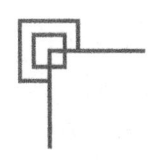

CHAPTER EIGHTEEN

Sloane Sheppard paused on the corner of South Pearl and State Streets in downtown Albany. The morning rush hour was in full swing. It was still cold but with enough layers, Sloane found the air invigorating. He wore a heavy winter coat, along with a scarf and hat, his trousers a heavy tweed and his Oxford shoes brilliant despite the slushy pavement.

He took the trolley downtown from his apartment on Madison Avenue. He avoided the crowds walking up State as he walked down, and hastily made his way until he came to Keeler's. He called the restaurant earlier in the morning and spoke to the manager, a Mr. Reynolds, who assured him he and his wait staff would assist if possible.

Sloane pulled open the door and stepped inside. It was warm and inviting, nicely decorated, with tables and chairs in the main dining room, a bar off to the left. Three larger dining rooms, in the back, were set apart from the main dining room, and were mostly used for private functions and dances, which usually occurred on weekends. Sloane spotted an older gentleman, busy cleaning a table and setting utensils and glasses. He glanced up and saw Sloane and spoke rather curtly.

"Sorry, but lunch doesn't start for another half hour."

It was a dismissal, but Sloane was not to be put off. Undaunted, he introduced himself and asked for Mr. Reynolds. The head waiter looked dubiously at Sloane, finished setting the last of the utensils and went in search of the manager. He returned with Mr. Reynolds, a large middle-aged man, with brown thinning hair, a rather red face, strong features and a pleasant, business way of speaking. He shook hands with Sloane, thanked him for coming and for his call earlier, and invited him to his office in the back. Sloane followed him past the back-dining rooms to a small office, with just enough room for a desk and two chairs. Sloane removed his coat and scarf, straightened his tie a little, his vest fitting snuggly with his dark hair, falling somewhat over his forehead as he removed his hat. He motioned Sloane to a chair, sat behind his desk and then looked at the man in front of him and ask what he could do for him. Sloane could tell he was not in the mood for an interrogation and chose his words carefully.

"Mr. Reynolds, I'm here regarding the death of a man who was a customer here. You may remember the Cary family. His name is Adam Cary."

"Yes, of course I remember," Mr. Reynolds replied, rather irritably. "It isn't my usual custom to call for ambulances to come to my restaurant." He paused. "It was quite a scene that evening, and I didn't like it at all."

"From a business viewpoint, I understand," Sloane said. "I'd like to ask you about that evening." He took out a small notebook from his jacket pocket, along with a pen, ready to write. Mr. Reynolds coughed slightly, clearly annoyed.

"I've spoken to the police, Mr. Sheppard. I don't know what more I can say."

"Start from the beginning," Sloane said.

Mr. Reynolds sighed impatiently. "There was a dance band here, which is customary for a Saturday evening. The one dining room was quite full, but the other two were not. I wasn't in the dining room when the commotion started, however, so I can only tell you what my wait staff told me and what I saw afterward."

"Please continue," Sloane encouraged him.

"Well, when I entered the dining room, I saw two men fighting and two women had collapsed. The entire scene was a chaos, chairs were overturned, the tablecloth was half off the table, dishes, cups and utensils were on the floor, there was broken glass just about everywhere." He paused. "It was quite a scene and very upsetting to me."

"Did you see the men fighting?"

"Yes, I did. Many patrons got up and left, that's how upsetting it was."

"Who broke up the fight?"

"A few men in the same party. My wait staff took the belligerent man and brought him to another dining room so that he could collect himself. It seemed to work, at least for a while. When I looked in that dining room, he was sitting calmly. Then I looked in again a little later, and he was on the floor, gasping for breath. And then he died."

"Did you see anything unusual? Other than what you already described?"

Mr. Reynolds shook his head. "No, I read about it in the newspaper. This is not good for business. We've always had a good reputation. It could be ruined."

Sloane smiled slowly. "I understand that, Mr. Reynolds. Keeler's is a fine restaurant. I don't think you need worry about the restaurant's reputation." He hesitated. "Anything else you care to tell me about that evening?"

Mr. Reynolds shook his head, clearly wanting to end the questioning. "Perhaps you care to speak to some of the wait staff. Rafael discovered Mr. Cary in the other dining room. Should I get him for you?"

Sloane knew he could get nothing more from him. "Yes, thank you."

Mr. Reynolds got up and went into the dining area. He returned with a young man, of no more than twenty, with slick black hair, looking every part the waiter, wearing a white shirt, a crisp bow tie, black pleated pants, black shoes and a rather serious expression. Mr. Reynolds returned to his seat behind the desk.

"Rafael, this is Mr. Sheppard. He's investigating Mr. Cary's death. He'd like to speak to you about that evening."

Rafael looked at Sloane and flushed. He explained his knowledge of English was not too good.

"I don't know too much," he told Sloane, somewhat frightfully. "I just see him dead on the floor, you know, and he no move."

"When did you realize he was dead?" Sloane asked him.

"Well, I brought him in that dining room, after they fought, you know. And he was sitting in a chair, in front of one of the tables and he seemed okay. When I went back in, he was on the floor, moving all around."

"What did you see before you brought him to the other dining room?"

Rafael frowned. "The men fighting, and they finally stopped, I brought him to the other dining room to cool down, you know."

"And did you serve that table, too?"

Rafael nodded. "Oh yes, generous, too. The lady she gives me a good tip for my service." He smiled at the remembrance.

"Was there tension at the table or was everyone in a good mood?" Sloane asked.

"Oh no. Everyone was happy and enjoying himself."

"Anything unusual happen before the fighting started?"

"Unusual?"

"Yes, something that stands out to you as unusual?"

"Stand out? No, I saw nothing different."

"And you took their orders, brought the food to their table?"

"Yes, everything was okay."

"Did everyone dance at once?"

Rafael frowned. "At once? Well, I think so. Although a young lady was sitting by herself for a little while. The rest were dancing."

Sloane assured him. "Rafael, what you've told me is extremely helpful and I appreciate the information. Thank you for your help."

Mr. Reynolds dismissed Rafael, who seemed glad to end the questioning. Rather hurriedly he left the office on his way back to the dining room to assist the lunch time crowd. Mr. Reynolds also stood, eager to end the meeting.

"Thank you, Mr. Reynolds," Sloane said as they shook hands. They walked to the front entrance. "You've been most helpful. If I need to speak to you again, I may call you later."

From his expression alone, Sloane could tell the last thing Mr. Reynolds wanted was to hear from this infuriating investigator again. As he held open the front door for Sloane, as though he could not wait to take leave of him, Sloane thanked him again and soon left the restaurant.

Walking up State Street in whirling snow, Sloane thought of Adam Cary, Janet Faraday and Ida Munson. Were their deaths related? Was there something he didn't see? He would speak to Meg again, and soon, but first he would send her a telegram.

During a lull in her work, Meg reached for the phone on the reference table and asked the operator to call Ben's number. It was almost noon and she did not think he would be at his apartment. He would be at work, naturally. She should have called him last night. She was surprised when he answered on almost the first ring.

"Ben, it's Meg. I'm so glad to hear your voice!"

Ben was relaxing in his living room, his feet up on his coffee table, a cigarette between his lips. Meg could tell from his voice that he was glad to hear from her.

"I hope we can get together again soon, Meg. I've missed you."

"I meant to call you last night, but I was so tired! You're not working today?"

He explained he was going in to work later in the day. He was busy arranging his mother's cremation and funeral service, for next week. Her body had already been returned to New York and was awaiting the cremation. It took a lot of time to complete the arrangements, he explained. He then asked Meg how she holding up, given the circumstances.

"Well, I'm managing. Sloane Sheppard called last night. He's still investigating Adam's death."

"What's he found out?"

"Not much yet. But he plans to talk to the manager at the restaurant and some of the wait staff there, too." She then told Ben about Ida's unexpected death.

"The maid died too?" Ben said incredulously.

"Iris told me a heavy sewing machine fell on her in the broom closet, killing her. It was on a top shelf. Somehow it got loose and fell on her."

Ben expressed his concern for her, alone in that big apartment. Meg smiled. At least she had him to confide in. She knew he understood and that he was there for her.

"Why don't we meet for lunch?" She paused. "There's something that's been bothering me." She hesitated, keeping her voice low. There were plenty of people walking back and forth in the reference room. "Ben, I can't talk right now, but it had to do with your mother. The reason why she fainted!"

"Of course, Meg," Ben said and lit a fresh cigarette. He took a long drag and hesitated. "The fighting was too much for her. Mother was overwrought. She wasn't used to scenes of violence."

"No, Ben, it was more than that!" Meg whispered into the telephone.

"What do you mean?" Ben asked in confusion. "What else could it have been?"

"I think," Meg began, "I know what it was that caused your mother to faint in the restaurant that night."

Harmon sat in the living room, looking out the window onto Washington Park. He was solemn, as though he was shocked into paralysis. It was dark now and the streetlamps showed brilliantly against the snow on the sidewalk.

Helen and Iris were there as well, trying their best to comfort him. Helen sat in her chair by the fireplace, knitting. Iris was in the chair opposite her mother, flipping the pages of the latest issue of *Vanity Fair*. As hard as he could, Harmon tried not to cry, but a few tears fell down his cheeks. He wiped them away, unashamedly. He remained quiet by the window, looking out at the falling snow.

"We'll plan for her funeral, of course," Helen spoke, breaking the silence.

Harmon turned from the window. He forced a brief smile. "Too much has happened lately in this family. First, Adam died, then that woman who collapsed, died and now Ida."

"You make it sound as though they are related," Helen remarked dryly.

"Meg thinks they might be," Iris said.

"Well, Meg does tend to have an overactive imagination," Helen remarked.

The doorbell rang. Harmon went to the front door to see who was calling at this late hour. Mother and daughter remained quiet in the living room, until Harmon reappeared, followed by Grace Prescott.

"Hello, Helen and Iris," Grace said and entered the living room briskly. She took off her coat and kept it with her, removed her scarf and hat and sat down on the Victorian sofa. She wore a black dress of no current style, no make-up but did look fresh and alert, with a slight gleam to her eyes. She looked at mother and daughter. Neither seemed particularly glad to see her and were not in much mood to converse. Grace, though, plunged into conversation, eager to get all the news straight.

"Yesterday at the hospital Edna told me about Ida. I'm so sorry, Helen."

Helen did not look up from her knitting. "Well, thank you, Grace," was all she said. "Ida was a fine person. She will be missed."

"What exactly happened to Ida?" Grace said, this time turning to Iris.

Iris finished with *Vanity Fair* and was listening to the news on the radio. She got up restlessly, watched people on Willett Street from the window. She turned and looked at Grace.

"Bruce and Harmon found her. One of Elsie's old sewing machines, fell and hit her in the head, killing her."

"She really died?" Grace said, like it was a mistake. "Did you call anybody?"

"Yes, of course," Iris said, trying to keep the irritation out of her voice. "There was nothing we could do. She was already dead when the ambulance arrived." She hesitated. "Her skull had been crushed."

Helen addressed her daughter. "Iris, that's enough. Such graphic descriptions are unnecessary."

Grace offered words of sympathy, but deep-down relished hearing the details and watching Helen's reactions. Perhaps it was time for her to talk after all.

"At first I didn't know whether to believe Edna," Grace said. "She likes to gossip, you know."

As if you don't, Iris wanted to say but resisted.

"I wanted to stop by to offer my condolences."

Helen then looked up from her knitting. "Thank you, Grace."

"Strange that a mother and son should suffer the same consequences…"

At that moment, Helen put her hand to her chest and gasped for breath. Her face turned ashen white. "I'm not feeling well, Grace. Perhaps another time you can visit." Iris went to her mother and took her hand, feeling her pulse.

Grace nodded again, sympathetically. She told Helen she was sorry if she upset her. She got up and gave her a hug and did likewise with Iris.

"I don't especially like to hear about death and suffering," Helen murmured.

Grace nodded, again pretending sympathy. "I'm so sorry, Helen."

Helen smiled wanly. "Please visit at another time."

"I'll see myself to the door," she said, leaving Iris to see to her mother.

She glanced back and saw Iris attending to Helen, as though she were an invalid on her death bed. She then walked to the front door and noticed the house had an eerie quiet to it. She glanced up the staircase. No one was about and Harmon must have gone to his basement room. She did not see Elsie, Richard, or Bruce anywhere.

Opening the front door and stepping outside into the cold, fresh air, Grace buried her chin in her scarf and fixed her hat lower on her head. She laughed to herself.

Well, well, Helen dear, how will you live this one down?

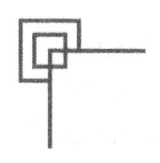

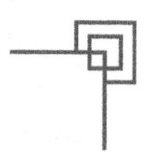

CHAPTER NINETEEN

At nine o'clock the next morning, the sun shining brightly on another cold day, Lieutenant Taylor and Inspector Harris of the Albany Police Department looked up from their desks and saw a tall, well-dressed man being shown into their office. The inspector put down a file he was reviewing, and the lieutenant stopped typing a letter.

The policemen shared a common space in the back of the police station, as the Albany Police Department was not a large one and space was at a premium. The cells and intake rooms were the largest areas and the offices, small to the extreme, were at the back. Inspector Harris smiled in recognition. "Well, Mr. Sheppard, long time no see. How's everything going these days?"

Sloane Sheppard returned the smile, took off his hat and coat and upon the lieutenant offering him a chair, sat down, facing the policemen. He was dressed in trousers of khaki brown, a well-pressed white shirt, tie, and suspenders, over which a brown jacket fit him nicely. His hair was slicked back and his brown eyes, eager and persuasive, were troubled as he began to speak.

"Well, there've been some strange deaths in Albany recently." He told them he wanted to discuss the late Mr. Cary. Also, the death of Janet Faraday.

"What more can we tell you?" Inspector Harris said. His face, coarse from years of police work, frowned and held a hard look. His thinning hair was parted on the side and his eyes, although alert, were downcast. "We've interviewed the family. Adam Cary left a suicide note. His wife found it later that evening."

"But to kill himself in a restaurant, where there were lots of people?" Sloane said. "In my work as an investigator and as a librarian doing research on unsolved murder cases, I've never heard of such a thing."

The lieutenant agreed, although reluctantly. "As far as Janet Faraday is concerned, she fell in front of a trolley. We've had that occur before, although this is the first someone's been killed."

The Inspector agreed. "Her son, and a witness, believes someone pushed her. But we have no evidence of foul play. Most likely, in her haste to board the trolley, she slipped on ice and before it could stop, the trolley ran over her. Unpleasant, but it does happen."

"Strange," Sloane said. "Also strange about Mr. Cary's death. The arsenic was in the coffee. It was put there, but not by Mr. Cary."

"That'd mean he didn't kill himself," the Inspector concluded.

"The dining room was dim," Sloane pointed out. "And it's common for people to put things in their drinks. People do it all the time these days, nobody would pay attention to it. With the cigarette smoke, dancing, and the loud music, it wouldn't be impossible for someone to put something in his drink."

"That still brings us back to the suicide theory," the Inspector said, rather firmly. "I believe, for reasons of which we'll never be certain, he took his own life. Perhaps as retribution to his mother, as I understand there was no love lost between them. Or his wife, either."

AN UNFORTUNATE COINCIDENCE

"We were called to Helen Cary's house earlier," the Inspector said. He told Sloane about Ida and the nature of her death. "I don't believe Ida Munson's death was anything but a freak accident."

Sloane mentioned Iris Bauer called to relate the news to him. He realized there was little more he could accomplish in speaking to the policemen. He thanked them for their time and made his way out the front entrance.

Once outside, Sloane paused, deep in thought. People passed by him, but Sloane kept thinking. Adam Cary, Janet Faraday and now Ida Munson. Was there a connection, somewhere, somehow?

As he waited for the trolley, he realized he had yet to send the telegram to Meg in New York City, which he meant to do yesterday. Resolute to his plan, he eagerly boarded the trolley. He'd go to the Western Union office on State Street, reviewing in his mind what he'd write to Meg. He would send it as urgent.

Albany Times Union
Monday, January 30, 1928

Mrs. Ida Munson has died at the age of forty-five. Mrs. Munson was employed as a cook and personal maid to the Cary family on Willett Street. Described as a hard-worker and sincere person, Mrs. Munson was a loyal servant and committed to the family she serviced. An unfortunate accident claimed the life of Mrs. Munson, who apparently has no immediate family. Funeral services are pending.

Elsie put down the newspaper and looked at Iris. They met for lunch at the cafeteria in the state capital, a favorite meeting place. It was busy with the lunch crowd. Elsie and Iris placed their orders, sipped coffee, lit cigarettes, and tried to relax.

"Poor Ida," she said sadly. She brushed back some auburn hair from her forehead, fingered the pearls around her neck. "Too good for Helen. I don't think she really appreciated her."

"Well, in her own way, she did," Iris said. "Mother has a strange way of showing her feelings." She was stylishly dressed in a dark beige dress with white collar and cuffs, high heels, with a slight scent of Chanel No. 5.

"How long had that sewing machine been in the broom closet?" Iris asked.

Elsie thought for a moment. "Over a year. I had no more use of it so instead of discarding it, we stored it on the upper shelf of the broom closet. It was heavy, but we managed."

"What are the chances of it falling when Ida was in there?" Elsie frowned. "I don't know. It was an accident."

"Did Ida know something? Did she see something and have to be silenced?" "Iris, this isn't a murder mystery! Ida's death was an accident."

"Like the Faraday woman's death," Iris said.

Elsie put her cigarette in the ashtray and looked at Iris. "There's something I've been wondering. It has to do with Mr. Faraday."

Iris waited for her aunt to continue.

"Something that caught my eye," Elsie continued.

"Like what? Other than the fact that he's so handsome."

Elsie agreed. "I've tried to figure it out. There was something about him, before they fought."

"Had you ever seen him before?"

Elsie hesitated, her cigarette halfway to her lips. "No, I don't think so." She shook her head. "Well, maybe I'm just imagining things. Too much on my mind, especially with Ida's death. Will you help me cook dinner tonight?"

Iris told her aunt she would be happy to help with preparing the family dinner. After more coffee and another cigarette, Elsie and Iris paid the check and left the cafeteria.

On the Washington Avenue entrance, Iris told her aunt she would see her this evening. They kissed cheeks and went their separate ways. Once outside, the wind seized Iris as she hurriedly crossed Washington Avenue to the state library.

Elsie then climbed the Million-Dollar staircase, the centerpiece of the state capital, to return to her office. Her mind was turning over the recent deaths. She wondered if there was something hidden. And if more deaths were soon to come.

Richard sat in the easy chair in the bedroom he shared with Elsie, reading the morning paper. He had breakfast with Helen as usual in the dining room and after Elsie left for the day, retreated upstairs and to solitude with the morning newspaper.

He saw the small obituary on Ida. He remembered when, over a year ago, he and Elsie put that heavy sewing machine on the top shelf of the broom closet. Of course, never thinking it would someday come crashing down and hit someone in the head. But how could that happen? The shelves were sturdy enough, he assumed, although later he decided he would check them out to see for himself.

His mind flew to Adam, causing a fight, lunging for that Ben whatever his name was, attacking him in the restaurant. He felt bad for Helen, who planned the evening and wanted it to be special for the family.

Adam, his lousy nephew, who borrowed five thousand dollars from him years ago and never repaid it. Well, dear Adam, now you never will repay me, will you? He was never fond of his nephew. He should have pressed him for the money at the time.

Helen, of course, made excuses for him, after all, he was graduating from college and needed to start work. Sometimes Richard could not stand his sister-in-law and mentioned to Elsie his desire to move out and find a place of their own.

The War made that almost impossible with the housing shortage, but this was 1928 and it was starting to improve, so perhaps he should mention it to Elsie again? The Willett Street house was a convenient location for her job; most times she walked to work, even in winter.

And Grace Prescott, that insufferable woman, always sticking her nose into other people's business. Well, she has nothing else to do, he thought. She was there that night; she could have seen something that the rest did not see. She was inquisitive enough to notice things.

Richard put his jacket over his narrow-striped shirt, adjusted his tie and vest and decided to go downstairs to check on Helen. However, upon searching the lower floor he did not see his sister-in-law anywhere. Upon entering the kitchen, he asked Harmon, who was busy cleaning, and said he had seen her go to the fifth floor, to Ida's room.

On the fifth floor, Helen was in Ida's room, carefully folding some of her clothes and straightening the furniture. It was pointless to do, as nothing was out of place, but doing it helped to overcome her nerves. She sat on the bed, deep in thought.

Helen spent part of the morning planning for Ida's wake and funeral to be held within the week. Her reverie was broken by Richard standing in the doorway. He asked what she was doing in Ida's room.

"Nothing, really, I guess I wanted to see it." She sighed and got up from the bed. "Did you need me for anything, Richard?"

Richard explained he found Harmon busy in the kitchen, who mentioned he had seen her go upstairs. There really was nothing for her to do right now, he thought. The house was empty, except for Harmon and he knew she missed Ida, like they all did. He suggested she contact the hospital to inquire if she could volunteer there later today, or perhaps take a walk in Washington Park, or possibly another shopping trip to Whitney's.

Helen forced a smile. "I'll be fine, Richard. Are you going to the library today?" Richard could not tell if that was a dismissal or just an inquiry. "Yes, I'm sure I'll bump into Iris. Care to join me?"

Helen thanked him but declined. He walked downstairs, gathered his coat, hat and scarf from the hallway closet and then rather quickly made his way to the front door.

"Poor Helen," he thought as he stepped outside onto the snowy sidewalk.

At the New York Public Library, it was business as usual. Meg was at the card catalog, assisting a woman in locating information on Italy. She noticed someone near the reference desk. She excused herself and hastily went over.

"Hello, Meg," said a familiar voice.

It was Ben, glad to see her. He was dressed in a dark business suit, vest, blue striped tie, pristine white shirt, well-tailored pleated pants, and those two-tone Oxford shoes. An impressive figure, tall, solid, rather self-confident but not arrogant. As opposed to Adam. But she would not think of Adam now.

"Ben, I'm glad you're here. I didn't call you last night," she lamented. "I was tired."

Ben told her not to worry, they were together now. She pushed in the chair and went for her fur coat. She joined Ben in the main entrance.

They walked outside, down the marble stairs, past the lions that seemed to guard the building and then mingled with the crowd on Fifth Avenue. Meg bundled her scarf tighter around her neck and pulled her hat lower on her head.

"I need to see you more often," Meg said, linking her arm through his.

"I've missed not seeing you," Ben agreed, as tiny snow pellets stung their faces. Meg smiled up at him. They continued walking, enjoying each other's company, feeling vibrant, the cold air making their faces blotched red. They came to the corner of Fifth Avenue and 59th Street, not realizing they walked so far.

"You live near here, don't you?" Ben asked, looking further down 59th Street.

There were in front of the Plaza Hotel. They almost blocked the main entrance and moved to the side to let people enter. Meg explained her building was just half a block up, on 59th Street and it was only appropriate to ask him over, which she did.

"I don't know this part of Manhattan well," Ben said, looking at the kiosks, shops, and small grocery stores. There were plenty of people and traffic, too, rush hour in full swing.

"We choose it because it's close to work," Meg explained, feeling carefree, not realizing Adam was no longer there.

They arrived at the building and as much as she liked James, the doorman, was glad it was someone else instead of him. In the foyer and up the elevator, a different elevator boy this time, too, to the tenth floor. Once inside, Meg turned on the lights and took off her fur coat, helped Ben off with his and invited him in.

"Make yourself comfortable, Ben," Meg called from the kitchen. "I'll see what I can make for dinner." After a few moments, she returned to the living room, where Ben sat on the sofa, smoking quietly. Meg sat next to him.

"I'm afraid I don't have much to offer," she said, accepting a cigarette from him. He lit it for her, and Meg blew a fine trail of smoke. "Why don't we send out for food? Or there's a small café just a block from here."

"Meg, I've been through so much on account of my mother. And now she's gone, and I'll never know what happened to her."

He put his cigarette in an ashtray on the coffee table in front of them and Meg did the same. They reached for each other, tenderly, full of understanding, and heartache together. Ben stopped and looked at her eyes again.

"Sorry, Meg, I didn't mean to be so direct like that."

"Don't apologize, Ben. Haven't we been through hell these last weeks?"

He went to the windows overlooking Central Park. It was dark out and the lights from the other buildings lit up the sky brilliantly.

"Ben, what's wrong?" Meg asked, turning to him.

He turned to face her. "Your husband committed suicide in that restaurant, leaving a note to find when you returned. My mother fell in front of the trolley, and now the maid was killed in the broom closet!" His handsome face was troubled, and Meg wanted nothing more to reach out to him, but she hesitated. She waited for him to return to the sofa.

"You believe these deaths are related?" he asked.

"It seems strange that Adam and your mother died within twenty-four hours and now Ida Munson, too." She paused. "I think your mother recognized someone from her past. Someone who was a threat to her."

Ben nodded. "My mother told me she never forgets a face. She didn't elaborate further. I don't know what she meant."

"That's what I'm wondering, too. I believe your mother recognized someone."

Ben looked at her intently. "But who, Meg? My mother didn't associate with many people. And as I've said, we've never been to Albany." There was an uneasy silence until Ben asked her if she was happy on her own.

Meg looked at him, somewhat surprised. "I haven't thought of it that way. Part of me misses Adam. The other part doesn't."

"Does the other part include me?" he asked, rather shyly.

Meg looked at him with compassion. "Ben dear, the whole part includes you." Instantly he had her in his arms. He then gently pulled away from her, smiled and reached in his pocket for his cigarettes. He realized he had smoked the last one.

"I didn't have the fifteen cents to buy another pack this morning!" he exclaimed. "There's a kiosk at the 96th Street Station but I thought I had enough!"

Meg went for her purse. "Here, try one of mine." She handed him one and she lit another for herself. Soon they were talking and relaxing again, enjoying each other's company and the pleasures of smoking.

It was while they were making plans to go out to eat, since Meg admitted she did not have much in the apartment except eggs and leftover chicken, that the telegram came from Sloane Sheppard.

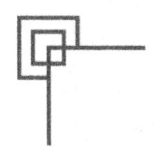

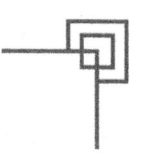

CHAPTER TWENTY

"Excuse me, Mr. Sheppard?"

The following morning Sloane got to his office early, to finish some last-minute work before the end of the month and to possibly leave early in the afternoon. It was after lunch time when a soft knock came on his office door.

"Mr. Sheppard? I'm sorry to disturb you."

Sloane looked up and saw a stout, middle-age female, wearing a heavy winter coat, dress, and cloche hat. She smiled, rather embarrassed. "I realize I don't have an appointment, but I just finished speaking with the detectives at the Albany Police." She hesitated as though that clarified her appearance. "About the late Mr. Cary."

Sloane was taken aback then regained his composure. "Please come in." He gestured to one of the metal chairs in front of his desk. As he looked at her, he wondered who she was and what she could offer about Adam Cary.

"My name is Mrs. Grace Prescott," she said pleasantly as though reading his mind. "I was at the restaurant the night he died."

Sloane looked carefully at the woman in front of him. She seemed the reliable type, nosy for sure, eager for gossip, but he knew these nosy parkers could provide valuable information. With nothing to lose, Sloane encouraged her to tell him what she knew.

"Well, as I said, I don't mean to interrupt you," Grace started as she unbuttoned her coat. She looked at the man before her, dressed in suspenders and white shirt with a formal tie, his suit jacket flung over his chair. His eyes, attentive and serious, were gentle as she spoke.

"That's all right, Mrs. Prescott. How may I help you?"

"Well, it's about the evening that Adam Cary passed away," Grace began, and Sloane could tell she relished being a storyteller. "I was there and saw the whole thing." She hesitated as though seeking his approval. Sloane simply nodded and Grace continued.

"After the fighting and the men were broken apart, I went out of the dining room, as I found it too upsetting. As I passed the second dining room, where Adam was taken to, I saw him sitting upright in a chair, in front of one of the tables, as though in a trance. I didn't think anything of it at the time, of course. Then I found out he died from arsenic poisoning, which must have been quite a strong dosage, for it to work so quickly."

Sloane agreed and asked her to continue.

"Well, as I was leaving, Ida Munson had gone to the ladies' room and passed by the second dining room. I noticed that she glanced there, too, and then returned to our table."

"How is this information helpful to me, Mrs. Prescott?"

She sat thoughtfully, as though she wanted to say something else. "Mr. Sheppard, the Cary family has plenty of secrets. Helen Cary's first husband committed suicide, due largely to Helen and her second husband leading him to it. As far as her second husband is concerned, he had several affairs. He may have fathered at least one child out of wedlock."

Again, Sloane didn't see what this information had to do with Adam Cary's death. But he assumed Grace Prescott would get to the point sooner or later, hopefully sooner.

"Of course, I tell myself now Grace, you must mind your Ps and Qs and not get involved with anyone else's business. On the other hand, I've known Helen Cary for years, so I'm rather concerned, you know."

"Of course," Sloane said patiently. "But I still don't see how this information is helpful to Adam Cary's death."

"Neither did I, at first. Walter Cary, Helen's second husband, was a womanizer. I remember when he died, although Helen never mentioned the details. Some car accident out of town. He had a quick burial and it was over and forgotten. But not by me. I never forget a thing."

No, I'm sure you don't, Sloane felt like saying. "If Walter Cary, Helen Cary's husband, fathered a child out of wedlock, how does that tie in with Adam Cary?"

Grace looked at Sloane sardonically, almost mocking in her expression and tone. "Really, Mr. Sheppard. Must I say it? Either Adam or Iris may belong to someone else!"

"Are you saying either Adam or Iris has a different parentage?"

"Well, I'm not sure," she responded truthfully. "Just what I've heard over the years. From women at the hospital, the market, and friends, you know."

"And you think Helen Cary put arsenic in her son's coffee that night?"

"Well, I can't say. Helen Cary and her sister Elsie are held in high regard in the community. After the war Elsie worked with refugee families and Helen was a Sunday school teacher." She paused. "Helen's also a hospital volunteer, active in church functions and charity events." She was deep in thought. "I hardly think either of the sisters is capable of murder."

Sloane glanced at his watch and noticed late afternoon was approaching. Grace saw him look at the time and although happy to continue speaking, realized she had outdone her welcome.

"Well, thank you for seeing me, Mr. Sheppard." She stood and shook hands with Sloane. He showed her to the door. "If I remember anything else from that evening, I'll be in touch with you again and the policemen, too."

Sloane thanked her for stopping by and closed the office door. He returned to his desk, thinking of the woman who just left. She gave him some things to think about.

So, Walter Cary, Helen's second husband, fathered a child or more than one, from another woman. Well, that's nothing new, he thought, happens often enough. But why would she tell him that in the first place? Was she trying to tell him something that she was reluctant to explain further? Adam or Iris, or both, had a different parent. It still doesn't tie in with his death. Or does it? Sloane shook his head, not understanding, yet seeing a pattern that was slowly forming in his mind.

His thoughts then flew to Meg in New York City. Had she gotten his telegram? She must return to Albany as soon as possible, so this matter could finally be put to rest.

As Grace left the Home Savings Bank Building and stepped out onto Pearl Street, it had started to snow again, lightly and the gray clouds threatened more as the evening progressed. She crossed the street at the light and waited on State Street for the trolley. After what seemed a long time, especially in the cold, the trolley finally came and Grace eagerly boarded, along with several other people. As it made its way up State, turned right at the bend in front of city hall and continued up Washington Avenue, Grace glanced out the window at the crowd about to board. Soon enough she noticed Elsie and Iris. Their eyes met immediately. Grace smiled and Elsie sat down in the empty seat next to her. Iris stood in the crowd next to them, holding on to the straps that hung from the roof.

"Well, hello Elsie and Iris," Grace said pleasantly. "Are you just off from work?" "Yes, a long day," Elsie smiled in return. "Sometimes we take the same trolley." "How are you, Grace?" Iris asked as she was jostled by a heavy-set woman making her way to an empty seat behind them.

"I'm fine, thank you, Iris."

"You don't usually take this trolley, do you, so late in the afternoon? Were you downtown shopping?"

"No, dear, I went to see Mr. Sheppard today."

Elsie looked at her carefully. "Mr. Sheppard, Grace? The private detective?"

"Yes, first I went to the police station. Well, anyway, they told me Meg hired Mr. Sloane Sheppard to investigate Adam's death." She looked at them. "I went there to tell him what I remember, and a few other things, too," she added with a mischievous smile, which did not go unnoticed by both Elsie and Iris.

"Was he at his office?" Iris asked her.

Grace nodded. "Such a nice man. I hope he can find out the truth soon."

"The truth?" Elsie said, perplexed. "What do you mean?"

Grace patted her hand. "I need to get going, dear. I want to pick up the new novel by Grace Livingston Hill at the library. Goodbye

Elsie and Iris, dear. So nice to see you both." She stood and made her way to the front of the trolley and exited, crossed the busy street at the light and disappeared down Dove Street.

"I wonder what that was all about," Iris said to her aunt, as Elsie moved to Grace's empty seat allowing Iris to sit.

"Grace is so nosy," Elsie said, in annoyance. "She should learn to keep her mouth shut. It could get her into trouble."

Iris looked at Elsie with concern. "Aunt Elsie, what do you think happened the night Adam died?" The trolley turned onto Lark Street, dropping off and picking up more passengers.

"I think I know what happened," Elsie said, looking Iris in the eyes. "But I won't say anything about it. I'd prefer to keep it that way."

After leaving the Harmanus Bleecker Library, Grace walked up State Street on her way home. Her Grace Livingston Hill library book was clutched in her hand, which she planned to start reading before bedtime. She stopped at the market on Lark Street, to pick up some chicken for dinner.

Passing the intersection with Willett Street, she glanced to her left and spotted Helen's imposing brownstone further down. It was a beautiful house, too good for her, she thought contemptuously. But then she wouldn't let thoughts of Helen Cary or her hideous family spoil her good mood.

Arriving home at last, she stepped inside. She entered her small kitchen, just room enough for a table, counter space, icebox, and a gas stove. She put her groceries on the table, removed her coat, and hung it in the hallway closet. She noticed the back door slightly open. Foolish of her, she was in a rush this morning to get to the police station and that Mr. Sheppard's office. She must have left it ajar after shoveling the back stairs. Grace never bothered to lock her doors. There was no need in her well-to-do neighborhood. Closing it, she set about making dinner.

While the chicken was cooking, Grace's thoughts turned to Mr. Sheppard and the policemen. She gave them plenty to think about. Walter Cary, Helen, even Ida and Harmon, too. And that sewing machine falling and killing Ida just as she entered the broom closet? She found it hard to believe, just like she found Walter Cary's car mishap hard to believe in 1922. And then Adam dying in the restaurant, and that other woman, too.

And there was Richard. He had to know secrets kept hushed over the years. After all, he did live with his sister-in-law, which Grace thought had to be intolerable. Why would they live under the same roof? Couldn't they afford to live elsewhere? Elsie, of course, would always defend her sister. She wondered if Iris and Bruce had their own secrets. With enough neighborhood gossip, Grace would find things out soon enough. She decided she would have peas with her chicken, which were kept, like all her tinned goods, in a pantry in the basement.

Wiping her hands on a dish towel, she turned off the gas burner and then opened the cellar door. Unexpectedly, the back door flew open. Before she could turn, she felt a hard, purposeful shove on her back. She lost her balance and pitched forward, screaming, cascading down and down the cellar stairs till she hit her head on the hard cement floor at the bottom, and everything was quiet.

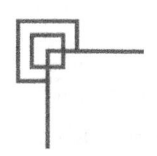

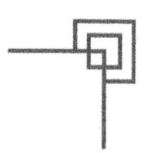

CHAPTER TWENTY-ONE

At about the same time that Grace Prescott knocked on Sloane's office door that afternoon, Meg was in the living room of her apartment, preparing to go to the library. Luckily, she was on the late afternoon shift. She spent a leisurely morning as she had not experienced before. Was it wrong to feel that way so soon after her husband's death?

She was slipping into high heels, zipping up her dress and fastening a string of pearls when Ben entered from the bedroom, barefoot but dressed, his hair tousled. He smiled at her and sat on the sofa, putting on his socks and his Oxford shoes.

"I hope no one notices my wearing the same clothes from yesterday," he said, always conscientious of his appearance. He felt the stubble on his face. "And I'm unshaven, too." He made it seem like being unshaven was a crime. Meg joined him on the sofa.

"I think you look just fine, even with a little facial hair," she said reassuringly.

He held onto her, touching her golden hair, looking tenderly into her eyes. "My mother liked talking to you on the train. She never opened up to anyone before, but she felt she could with you."

"I felt the same with her," Meg told him.

"The doorman will wonder why I'm leaving with you," he said, as he sat back on the sofa. He ran his fingers through his wavy black hair. "My boss wasn't keen on my taking another half day!"

"I don't care about the doorman," Meg said. "Ben, I want to call Sloane Sheppard in Albany first before we leave," she changed the subject. "That telegram sounded urgent. Maybe he's onto something." She went to the hallway and the telephone, Ben following. She spoke to the operator and asked her to put through a call to Mr. Sloane Sheppard in Albany. After a few minutes, the call was finally connected. Sloane recognized her voice right away.

"Meg, I'm glad you called. I sent you a telegram yesterday. Did you get it?"

"Yes, in the evening. I didn't think you were in at that time."

"That's quite all right. I'd like you to return to Albany, sometime soon."

"Yes, of course, Sloane, if it'll help."

"This weekend, perhaps?"

"When I get to the library, I need to check my calendar." She paused. "Is there something urgent?"

"Well, Mrs. Prescott was here to see me earlier today," Sloane told her about Grace's visit. He also told her briefly about Rafael, the waiter at the restaurant.

A million thoughts went through her mind. "I'll get back to you by tomorrow, Sloane. And thank you again for your help." She hung up and watched Ben as he fidgeted with lighting a cigarette. He offered her one and she eagerly took it. He then asked her about the call.

Meg walked back to the living room. "Well, he told me Grace Prescott went to see him today. He didn't go into too much detail. He also told me about a waiter at the restaurant that night." She blew a fine ring of smoke.

AN UNFORTUNATE COINCIDENCE

Ben puffed on his cigarette. "I wish I knew what to say, Meg, to make you feel better." He then glanced at his watch. "We better get going, otherwise we'll both be out of a job!"

Meg too looked at her watch and did not realize time had gone by. They got up together, raced for their coats, and then left the apartment. Down in the elevator—another new elevator boy, to Meg's relief—and out to the lobby, where James, the doorman, greeted her and said likewise to the handsome young man next to her. They walked on 59th Street to Fifth Avenue, and then down to the library, where Ben held her close, not wanting to let her go. Meg clung to him.

Ben watched as she walked into the public library, people falling in step behind her. He then joined the crowd on his way to catch the subway to work.

That evening, after ten o'clock, a call came into the Albany Police. The dispatcher radioed for patrolmen to go to upper State Street, across from Washington Park.

An elderly woman, Mrs. Marshall, called, frantic, that her neighbor, Mrs. Prescott, had not answered her phone, collected her evening newspaper, mail or milk bottles. She tried the front door, found it unlocked, and called for Mrs. Prescott. No, she did not go in, she was too frightened. Yes, we always keep our doors unlocked here, Mrs. Marshall explained. Patrols are frequent, and we never have problems, she added firmly. The dispatcher assured Mrs. Marshall they would have patrolmen there in no time.

When the policemen arrived at the house in question, it was quiet as usual in that affluent part of Albany. The first officer rang the bell and getting no response, tried knocking several times. As the dispatcher relayed the information, he found the front door unlocked and motioned to his partner to join him inside.

Upon calling her name and getting no answer, they looked throughout the small house, upstairs in the bedrooms, the dinette area, the living room, and the kitchen. Then the second patrolman noticed the basement door open. He flicked on the light switch and saw Grace lying at the bottom of the stairs, a crumpled heap. Quickly descending the stairs, they knew before touching her that she was dead.

The first patrolman grabbed his radio and contacted dispatch to send an ambulance to the house on State Street at once.

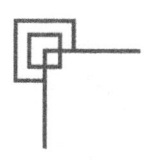

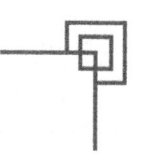

CHAPTER TWENTY-TWO

Elsie, Iris and Bruce were at the dining room table, having breakfast. The atmosphere was somber, and no one felt much like talking. The same thoughts were swirling in their minds, unspoken, yet so obviously present. Adam's death, Janet Faraday's death, and now Ida's unfortunate death. And, of course, the photos of Adam ripped out of Helen's photo album. There was an undercurrent of fear and suspicion, as though they wanted to look at each other, wondering if they knew of anything, but decided against it and kept quiet. Elsie poured another cup of coffee and lit a cigarette. Iris buttered a muffin and lit a cigarette. Bruce kept his head down, dreading the day ahead of him at the school, sleep still in his eyes. He also poured another cup of coffee, hoping the caffeine would give him some energy. Fortunately, he found it did.

"Well, I'm off to the library," Iris said, stubbing out her cigarette.

"I'm coming, too," Elsie said, more energized than her niece, doing the same with her cigarette. "Should we have lunch today, Iris?"

Iris told her lunch sounded like a good idea. They were about to leave the dining room and go for their coats when Bruce suddenly gave a sharp exclamation. Iris looked at her husband and asked if something was wrong.

Bruce was speechless. He unfolded the morning paper that Harmon had brought in with the coffee. He merely folded back the page and pointed it out to Elsie and Iris. He slurped his coffee, adjusted his tie, and stood. Giving a quick kiss on the cheek to his wife, he left the dining room, grabbed his coat from the hallway closet and sped out the front door, slamming it behind him.

"What's gotten into him?" Elsie said, looking after Bruce. They looked at the newspaper and saw for themselves what disturbed him so much.

Albany Times Union
Monday, February 6, 1928

Mrs. Grace Prescott has died, aged 50, at her home in Albany. A life-long city resident, Mrs. Prescott was retired from the Kenmore Hotel, where she was employed as a secretary. She was the widow of the late Sterling Prescott, who predeceased her. An unfortunate accident at her home claimed the life of Mrs. Prescott, who has no other immediate family. Funeral services are pending.

Elsie put down the newspaper, her mind racing. Grace Prescott, dead, an accident in her home? She turned to look at Iris, whose thoughts mirrored her own. As though in a trance, Elsie returned to her seat at the table, unable to speak.

"What could have happened to Grace?" Iris said thoughtfully. "She seemed fine the other day. An unfortunate accident in her house?"

"Maybe she had a heart attack," Elsie suggested but then discounted that as she knew Grace was strong as an ox. She then glanced at her watch and noticed the time. "I need to get going, Iris. You should too if you want to get to work on time."

Iris left the newspaper on the dining room table and together they got their coats, hats and scarves and left the house.

At about the same time that Iris and Elsie left for work, Helen was walking slowly down the stairs, feeling a rush of cold air from the front door. She walked along the hallway and entered the dining room, finding it bare except for Harmon, who was cleaning up and preparing a place for her and Richard.

"Is Richard not up yet?" she asked, sitting at the head of the table. She pulled her robe tighter around her waist and yawned. "Coffee, please, Harmon and one of those corn muffins, too."

"No, Richard hasn't gotten up yet," Harmon told her. "But Elsie, Iris and Bruce have already left." He paused. "Have you heard from Megan?"

Helen gave a snort of disgust. "No, I have not heard from her. I'm afraid my daughter-in-law does whatever she pleases, Harmon. She doesn't think of anyone other than herself."

Harmon nodded in understanding. "Here's this morning's paper." He handed it to her and left for the kitchen. Helen unfolded it and flipped through the pages. Not wanting to read about the upcoming primary in New Hampshire or the race for the White House, she skimmed the local news.

From in the kitchen, Harmon heard a gasp. Hurriedly, he entered and saw Helen, clutching her chest, unable to speak, merely pointing to the newspaper.

"Read this," she told Harmon, barely getting the words out.

Harmon took the newspaper and followed Helen's pointing finger. He read the article about Grace and her untimely death. He put the paper down, crestfallen, too numb to speak.

"Grace, dead?" he pondered. "What could have happened?"

Helen could barely speak. "It doesn't say what happened, but then obituaries usually don't go into too much detail."

With a yawn, Richard entered the dining room, fully dressed and ready for the day. He sat next to Helen and told Harmon he'd have coffee and toast. From the zombie like movement of Harmon to the shocked facial expression on Helen, Richard could see something was not quite right. She merely showed him the obituary on Grace, too upset to speak. Richard put down the newspaper and stared ahead of him. Neither spoke until he finally cleared his throat.

"What kind of accident? Heart condition?"

Helen disagreed. "Another death, Richard."

"What do you think of it?"

"Well, I don't really know. But someone removed photos of Adam from my photo album." She spoke as if that were more tragic than the recent deaths. "I'd like to know who did it and why."

Harmon entered at that moment with Richard's toast and coffee, which upon receiving it, found he wasn't too hungry. He only sipped his coffee. He turned again to Helen.

"What should we do?"

"What do you mean, what should we do? We don't know what happened to Grace. We must plan Ida's funeral." She paused uncertainly. "I think, Richard, if you don't mind, I'd like to be alone right now."

She stood up and before leaving the dining room, turned back to her brother-in-law. She spoke with a certain dignity, her proud head erect, her words coming with unexpected strength and resolve. "This has been too much for me. I must face these matters on my own." She turned and left the dining room, leaving Richard to stare after her.

AN UNFORTUNATE COINCIDENCE

The next morning, Meg was about to leave the apartment when the phone rang. After work, she wanted very much to see Ben again. Was it scandalous to be with another man so soon after her husband's untimely demise? Her mother-in-law would have a fit. But then she was no longer my mother-in-law, Meg thought happily.

As she brushed her hair in the hallway mirror determinedly, a rather hard look to her face, she applied lipstick carefully. The night she and Ben shared was precious, and it meant so much to her. And what would Adam do if it were reversed? How long would he mourn? She doubted whether he even would, with the countless women he had been involved with.

She took a final look at herself in the mirror. She was about to put on her fur coat when the phone rang, stopping her momentarily. She was startled when upon answering she heard Sloane's voice.

"Meg, I'm glad I caught you at home. This is Sloane Sheppard in Albany. I need to talk to you again. You need to be aware of some recent events."

Meg sat in the chair next to the phone table. "Of course, Sloane."

"This is important, Meg." Sloane told her about Grace Prescott's death.

"I spoke to the Albany police this morning," he continued. "They told me Mrs. Prescott was found dead in her home, at the bottom of her basement stairs. Her neck was broken. They haven't determined if she fell or if she was pushed." He hesitated. "Her doors were unlocked, so anyone could have entered her house."

"Pushed?" Meg said, raising her voice, horrified. "What are you saying?"

Sloane hesitated and loosened his tie. "Grace Prescott had a bad habit of finding things out, of knowing things from the past."

Meg was lost in deep thought. "Have you spoken to the family yet?"

"No, but I plan to later today and again when you and I are there. I believe I've figured out things, Meg, but I need to verify them first."

"I have an idea what made Janet Faraday faint at the restaurant that night," Meg confided. "It may have been she recognized someone."

Sloane agreed. "We need to see the entire family again, to put all the cards on the table. That's why I'd like you to come back to Albany."

Meg hesitated. "What about next weekend? Saturday?" "Well, it could be too late."

"Too late? Sloane, what do you mean?"

"Will you speak to your sister-in-law soon?"

"Yes, I keep in touch with Iris."

"You can stay with your in-laws again. Let me know when you'll be here." There was urgency in his voice, which Meg didn't quite understand. She told him she needed to get going. She hung up, grabbed her pocketbook and keys, locked the door, caught the elevator, and made her way to the main lobby.

As she was walking to the library, Meg tried to think of Ben but found her mind pushing him aside, at least momentarily. She thought back to the phone conversation she had with Sloane. He wanted her to return to Albany soon, to get all the cards on the table as he put it. And Grace Prescott, falling down her basement stairs, or was she pushed? What made Sloane think she was pushed?

He must have figured this mess out. But then came something else. She shivered, more from fear than of the cold. He said she needed to return to Albany soon. Before it was too late.

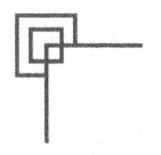

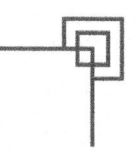

CHAPTER TWENTY-THREE

"I don't know, Helen. I feel Ida's death could have been suspicious. Maybe Grace, too. There must be something we aren't seeing."

Elsie and Helen were in the sewing room on the fourth floor. Elsie's usual glowing face was now full of worry, her dark hair covering her forehead, rather messily, her blue dress wrinkly. Helen, also, was downcast, her dark eyes anxious and the bright dress she wore did little to alleviate her mood.

It was early the next afternoon, and the sisters were deciding on clothes that needed hemming. Helen handed Elsie a blouse that had a torn neckline. Elsie realized she was rambling on and on, which she knew her sister despised, so she decided to be quiet.

Elsie took the blouse and fit it into the sewing machine. She remained silent, giving herself time to think. As she started sewing, she asked Helen her opinion of Ida's death. Helen looked at her sister with surprise.

"What do I think? Well, Elsie, what is there to think? Ida suffered an accident, poor dear. I don't know why you and Richard stored that old sewing machine up in the broom closet, anyway. It was bound to fall sooner or later."

"It was up on the shelf for over a year, Helen," Elsie pointed out. She glared at her sister, almost missing a stitch in the blouse. She made it sound like it was their fault that the sewing machine fell on top of Ida.

"Grace must have suffered a heart attack," Helen said, changing the subject.

"Well, I find that hard to believe. Grace was always strong."

Helen agreed with her. "And Mr. Faraday's mother, too."

"You mean Megan's new boyfriend?" Elsie said with derision. The sisters looked at each in mutual understanding.

"So, you feel the same," Helen remarked dryly. "I don't care to see Megan. She's already involved with another man," she added contemptuously. "I've never heard of such behavior!"

Elsie looked again at Helen. She wanted to say it wasn't too long before Helen got involved with Walter Cary after Arthur, her first husband, committed suicide, but decided against it. From Helen's tone, she could tell that her sister deplored that behavior in others, but it was acceptable for her.

"We can't get involved in Meg's business," she said. "She lives in New York City, not Albany, and what she does there is no concern of ours."

"Perhaps not," Helen said acidly. "But she carries the Cary name. She's still a member of this family."

"Well, perhaps she never really was a member," Elsie said with tight lips. She took a pair of Richard's pants that needed hemming. Helen's gaze wandered over to the windows overlooking the park.

Elsie put down the pants she was about to sew. She could see Adam and Ben, with Meg standing between them. The fight about to erupt, and that sickly-looking woman, Janet Faraday or whatever her name was, looking at everyone. And everyone looking back, at Adam and Ben, and at that Faraday woman, too.

Something that was familiar and yet, so incredible! They were all stunned and astonished at the scene before them. Ida, numb, her face ashen. Helen stood transfixed, eyes disbelieving, also in a state of paralysis. And Iris, looking aghast, her mouth open, speechless and in shock.

Elsie knew there was something familiar. It seemed so remote, so beyond belief, and yet, in her own mind, she could see it, for she realized it must be true.

Richard stood in the broom closet in the kitchen, staring at the collapsed shelves. He collected them and stood them up against the right side. He shook his head in disbelief, not sure of what he was looking at or what to think.

Not one to probe into matters, especially after a police investigation, he was drawn to the closet again. He loosened his tie and unbuttoned his shirt at the collar. Even though it was still cold out, he felt warm, even over-heated as though he couldn't breathe. That's what Adam's death and the subsequent events had done to me, he thought grimly.

The closet was not large but roomy enough for five shelves each on both sides and three shelves on the far wall. The shelves on the right had more room for storage in width and easily fitted things such as an iron and even Ida's small ironing board. There was plenty of room on the top for Elsie's old sewing machine, which, the shelf being wide enough, fit perfectly.

He went back into the kitchen and, as he had done previously, took a chair from the table and brought it back to the broom closet.

He stood on it, looked carefully at the wall that contained the right sided shelves and wondered.

Was it just Ida's misfortune to open the broom closet door, and have that shelf containing the sewing machine fall on her? No, there was nothing wrong with the nails, holding up the shelves. Unless, a nail was removed, which would have caused the sewing machine to be too heavy for the shelf.

As he stepped down from the chair and was about to return it to the kitchen table, his eyes glanced up at the inside of the closet door. Nothing unusual there. He was about to enter the kitchen with the chair, when his eyes fell on a piece of string, hanging from a nail. He looked at the piece of string hanging from the back of the door. Wouldn't the police have seen that? Or the rest of us, he thought. Attached to the string was a set of spare keys, which Ida kept in the broom closet. He remembered Helen wanted extra keys made some years ago. So, after all, that string meant nothing, so Richard closed the pantry door and returned to the kitchen.

He stood at the kitchen window, looking out, his mind racing with wild thoughts. He looked back at the broom closet door. That string, even with the spare keys tied at the end, could have been affixed to an upper shelf hook so that upon opening the broom closet, and stepping inside, the sewing machine would come crashing down on the person standing underneath it.

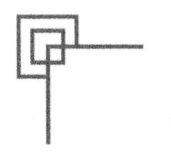

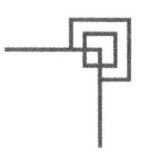

CHAPTER TWENTY-FOUR

The next morning, Sloane Sheppard left his office at the Home Savings Bank Building on his way to the Harmanus Bleecker Library.

As he stood on the corner of State and Pearl, in front of the Ten Eyck Hotel, his thoughts turned to Adam and his apparent suicide by arsenic at Keeler's restaurant. He shook his head as snow pellets stung his face. Meg was not satisfied by the conclusion reached by the police and neither was he. He found it difficult to believe a man like Adam Cary would kill himself and, in a restaurant, so open to the public.

He caught the trolley uptown and in no time arrived at the corner of Washington Avenue and Dove Street. He entered the Harmanus Bleecker Library, Albany's new public library. He was greeted by a librarian he knew well.

"Well, hello, Mr. Sheppard," said a pleasant middle-aged woman named Mrs. Sawyer. She recognized Sloane from his numerous visits. She was busy at the circulation desk, handling magazines and answering phone calls. She checked out a few books for a patron and then turned her attention to Sloane. "How can I help you today?"

"I'd like to look at some newspaper articles," Sloane explained. "From the fall of 1921 and January 1922."

"This way, please," Mrs. Sawyer said and smiled.

She led Sloane to a small room where various file cabinets were kept, each holding past issues of Albany, Schenectady and Troy newspapers. She asked Sloane if it was the Times Union, Albany's major newspaper, and he replied that was what he wanted. He sat at a table while Mrs. Sawyer retrieved from two file cabinets the issues of the Times Union, dated October to December 1921 and January 1922.

He thanked her and then started to flip through the pages of the Times Union for September, October, and November 1921. He found a few articles of interest.

Sloane read in September 1921 about the homicide in Kinderhook of a married man. The family requested names to be withheld. The man who committed the homicide was arrested. Sloane searched through countless pages for local stories, then looked at November 1921. There was a trial about the Kinderhook murder, but the killer was acquitted. So, Janet Faraday was proven correct, Sloane thought.

He then looked at the issue dated January 1922. On the last page of the local news section, he saw a small blurb about the death of a local man, also in Kinderhook.

He read about the man, although his name was withheld by police, and the woman the man lived with and who found his body, and whose name was Janet Faraday. The man apparently fell asleep in the garage and was overcome by fumes and died. Sloane wondered why the man's name was not reported, but the paper clearly named Janet Faraday. It also was withheld at the request of the family.

So, Janet Faraday's lover was acquitted of murder, but murdering who? The article was so vague he was surprised it was even reported. Janet Faraday's lover was Ben's father.

And the part about Janet killing him, closing the garage door so that he'd be overcome by fumes, as Meg told him, was accurate. Janet Faraday told Meg about it herself, although it wasn't put like that in the newspaper, of course. She escaped police notice but apparently in the six years since she had trouble accepting her deed and lived a life of remorse and paranoia. And made it hell for her son, who could never live a normal life with a schizophrenic mother. Ben planned to have his mother committed to the state psychiatric hospital in Albany. But then she fell in front of the moving trolley and was killed. What bearing did this have on Adam's death, if his death was a suicide?

Sloane finished with the newspapers, returned to the circulation desk, thanked Mrs. Sawyer again and walked out onto Dove Street. Where to now? He decided to stop at city hall, at the office of vital records.

He hopped on the next trolley and got off in front of city hall. From his previous investigations, he got to know people at the office of vital records, so his work was made easier. The pleasant, elderly woman, Mrs. Endicott, who had worked at city hall for many years, recognized Sloane and greeted him with a smile.

Of course, Sloane knew birth certificates were a matter of privacy, state law, but since he was an Albany investigator who used their services before, and under a police probe, too, she was able to confidentially accommodate his request. Sloane asked for the birth certificate of Adam Cary, born in 1900 in Albany and Benjamin Faraday, born in 1901, but he was unsure of the city. She told him it may take a bit of time, she welcomed him to a chair in the waiting area. While she was in a back room, looking at past records, Sloane picked up a magazine and thumbed through it, restlessly. She returned in about twenty minutes, having exhausted countless files kept in archives.

"I'm sorry, Mr. Sheppard, no records for those names," Mrs. Endicott exclaimed. "Are you sure you have the names correct? Perhaps they were born in another state?"

"No, I believe they are New York State residents," Sloane said.

"Well, I double-checked the files for those years, including 1899 and 1902. There are no records with those names, I'm sorry."

Sloane thanked her and left the office. On his way downstairs, to the lobby and outside city hall, he looked straight ahead, at the state capital, at Albany Academy, oblivious to the cold and the light snow falling.

He decided to return to his office, but instead of taking the trolley, he walked, deep in thought, his mind going over what he just learned about Adam Cary and Ben Faraday. Did they even exist?

Meg returned to the reference desk and saw it was almost time for lunch. She gathered her fur coat and walked to the main entrance. She saw Ben, waiting near one of the lions. He smiled when she approached him.

"Meg, I'm glad to see you," he said, embracing her. "Ready for lunch?"

They joined the crowd, walking down Fifth Avenue toward a new café Meg wanted to try. They found a corner table and ordered sandwiches and coffee. After the waitress left, Ben asked her about Sloane's investigation. Meg told him Sloane's recent call and Grace Prescott's sudden death. Ben looked at her in disbelief.

"He wants me to return to Albany," she explained. "He made it sound urgent."

"Are you going?" Ben asked, lighting her a cigarette and then his own.

Meg shook her head. "I really don't want to. I don't know how or if Grace Prescott's death and Ida Munson's death are related to Adam."

Ben agreed. "You told me you think Mother fainted for other reasons beside the fighting. What do you think made her collapse?"

"I think she saw someone from the past," Meg said, knocking ash from her cigarette into an ashtray.

The waitress arrived with their sandwiches. Meg asked Ben about his work, and if he liked his apartment on 96th Street. He asked Meg about living without Adam in the big apartment and if she had heard from Iris and more about her library work. Meg then asked him what he remembered about that night.

"Well, mother and I wanted to eat out. We saw Keeler's restaurant. It looked like a good place, so we decided to enter." He took a long drag on his cigarette. "I didn't know you'd be there, Meg. How would I have known that?"

"I believe you, Ben," Meg said tenderly. "Apparently Adam didn't. His reaction was so typical, he was very jealous." She paused. "You mentioned you and your mother didn't know people in Albany. I wonder if your mother recognized someone she knew."

Ben shook his head. "We're from the city and didn't have any reason to go to Albany. Mother did live for a while in Kinderhook, where she killed my father."

Meg nodded sympathetically. "I understand, Ben. Don't think of that now." She put her hand on his, causing him to look into her eyes.

"Remember, I'm here for you," Ben smiled. "Maybe Mother did slip on the ice and Grace Prescott lost her balance and fell down the stairs."

"And Adam killed himself with arsenic at the restaurant that night?" Meg said. "I doubt it, Ben. Adam would never have killed himself."

"Well, I didn't know your husband," Ben said, and his tone implied he would not have wanted to. "I mean, the way he attacked me that night."

"Adam was moody at times. He thought of himself only."

"How was your husband's service?" Ben asked. "Was it difficult for you?"

"No, I managed. Iris and Bruce were supportive." She paused, drawing on her cigarette.

"So, the nightmare isn't quite over yet then?" he asked her.

"Not until I return to Albany and hear what Sloane wants to tell me."

"Why can't he tell you on the phone? Or send another telegram?"

"It's urgent. I think he may be on to something."

Ben glanced at his watch. "I have to get back to the office soon. My office is in mid-town, so it isn't too far."

"Do you like accounting?" Meg asked him.

Ben shrugged. "It was my major at Union College. I had to find a job to support mother." His mind was reeling from the past, unpleasant episodes of his mother.

"I'll make a nice meal for us tonight," Meg said persuasively.

"I can help you cook, if you'd like," Ben said with a smile.

He told her he would stop by after work, about six o'clock, and then motioned the waitress for the check. They paid at the cashier and walked out of the cafe, on their way back to work.

Her shift ending at five o'clock, Meg left the library promptly. She told Ben she had an icebox full of food when in truth she had extraordinarily little. Since Adam's death and all the strange happenings since then, she had little to no appetite. Perhaps having Ben for dinner would help to change that, she thought making her way down the stairs and onto Fifth Avenue.

She stopped at a small market to buy groceries, steaks, vegetables, and an apple pie with vanilla ice cream for dessert.

As she got off at her floor, keys out of her purse, she could not open the door fast enough to get in, put the groceries in the kitchen and start to cook for Ben. She kicked off her shoes, threw her fur coat, scarf and hat on the hallway chair and entered the kitchen.

With the steaks cooking on the burner, the vegetables heating, and the apple pie in the icebox along with the ice cream, Meg lit a cigarette and sighed contentedly.

The doorbell rang and Meg eagerly went to answer it. To her dismay it was not Ben, but a Western Union man, holding out a telegram. He asked her to sign for it, which she did. She thanked him and closed the door. She looked at the telegram and saw it was again from Sloane Sheppard in Albany. It must be urgent if he'd send another telegram. She ripped it open and read it, standing motionless in the hallway.

MEG PLEASE COME TO ALBANY STOP NEED TO SEE YOU WITH FAMILY STOP HAVE FIGURED THINGS OUT STOP THIS WEEKEND?

She read it again thoughtfully. The doorbell rang again. She left the telegram on the kitchen counter, entered the hallway and upon opening the door, she saw Ben, holding flowers for her.

"Ben, you didn't have to get flowers!"

He looks like he came straight from a Saks Fifth Avenue window display, Meg thought. Exquisitely attired in a pristine white shirt, gray vest in which a gold chain held a pocket watch, blue tie, matching gray jacket and pleated pants. He removed his hat, coat, and jacket, left them on top of Meg's on the hallway chair and followed her into the living room.

"Something smells good!" he said.

"If I haven't burned it!" Meg exclaimed. She put the flowers in a vase she found in a cupboard and then went to the stove. With the steaks on plates and the vegetables ready to go, they sat at the kitchen table, preparing to eat. They spoke of pleasant subjects, summer activities, shows at Radio City, walks through Central Park, Jones Beach, trips to Atlantic City. Meg announced they'd have dessert in the living room.

As he was about to leave the kitchen, Ben noticed Sloane's telegram on the counter. He asked Meg what it was about.

"Then you are going to Albany?" he asked, still in the kitchen.

"I haven't decided. Tomorrow I'll call Sloane."

"Well, if you do go, I'll go with you."

"You'll come with me?"

"After all you've been though, I want to be there for support."

She carried a tray into the living room. Ben looked again at the telegram, rather perplexed. Meg handed him coffee and pie, lit two cigarettes, one for herself and the other for him. She put the tray on the coffee table and sat on the sofa next to him.

While he was eating the pie, sipping the coffee, and puffing at his cigarette, he asked her what she thought of Ida Munson, Grace Prescott and the telegram from Sloane, which he put on the coffee table in front of them.

"Oh, I don't want to discuss those people or Adam. Tonight, belongs to us. And the whole world can go to hell as far as I'm concerned!" She glanced out the balcony windows, as though all the madness, turmoil, conflict, and pain they experienced were shut out and they were together, insulated in their own world. She took a long drag on her cigarette. Ben looked at her, rather shyly, and smiled. He felt flustered and full of anguish.

"I never had the chance to have relationships," he said softly, almost in a whisper. "Mother always took up so much of my time. I never knew when she would explode or create a scene." He loosened his tie and unbuttoned his vest, he felt rather warm, with her so close to him. "I lived my life not knowing when she'd become unhinged." He paused, almost in tears.

Meg touched his handsome face, pushed back some black hair that had fallen across his forehead. "Let's not think about that now, Ben." She moved closer to him. "I don't want to talk about Adam tonight."

She reached out for him. In that moment, his right arm was around her. As he stubbed out his cigarette in the ashtray on the coffee table with his left hand, Meg did the same. He enveloped her in his strong arms.

She then took his warm hand and gently led him out of the living room, to the softness of the mattress underneath them. She felt his soft hair touch her face, inhaled his fine cologne, and felt the firmness of his muscular body. She pulled him closer to her. She knew they were together and if Ben was with her, she need not fear the unknown again.

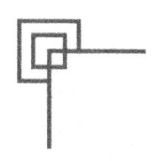

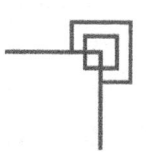

CHAPTER TWENTY-FIVE

Sloane Sheppard lit a cigarette, sipped his coffee, and looked at the files on his desk. It was early, not quite nine o'clock. His attention was drawn to the late Mr. Cary.

He reviewed his notes from the library. The newspaper articles were a disappointment. Although he read about Janet Faraday's lover and his death by carbon monoxide, there was nothing else of interest. There was never any breath of suspicion on Janet and if there was an investigation, and from the article it did not appear that there was, she was cleared of any wrongdoing.

The article regarding the shooting that took place in late 1921 was also of little help. Again, it mentioned Janet Faraday, but not the name of her lover or the name of the man he allegedly shot. It did mention at the request of the family, as well as the police, the name of Janet's lover, Ben Faraday's father, was withheld. Was he someone prominent in the area? If his name were revealed would it create further scandal? He was brought to trial and locals would obviously know who he was, but his name was not mentioned.

Was there a connection between Janet Faraday, Adam Cary, and Ida Munson? Adam's death was ruled a suicide, but anyone could have slipped arsenic in his drink, with the dim lights, the crowds, the music, the dancing. No one would have paid attention to their table. Unless, Grace Prescott saw something or Ida Munson, too. Grace's death was ruled an accident, as she supposedly fell down her basement stairs. Ida's death also was considered accidental, as the sewing machine fell off the top shelf, killing her.

He would go to see the Cary family again. He would go there today and this weekend with Meg, as he felt he was coming closer to the truth. He picked up the phone on his desk, asked the operator to put through a call to Mrs. Helen Cary on Willett Street and after a few moments, it was answered by Helen herself. He told Helen he would like to stop by again to speak to the family.

"Well, everyone has left for the day, Mr. Sheppard," Helen told him curtly, having recently finished breakfast and not wishing to be disturbed at such an early hour. "Richard and I are here, but I always take my walk." She paused. "What was it you want to see us about?"

"About Adam's death and the subsequent events. The police are investigating Mrs. Prescott's death, whether she fell down her basement stairs or was pushed." Before Helen could interrupt Soane continued. "I'd like to look at the broom closet where Mrs. Munson met her death."

"I don't know what you'll find. The police have already been here."

"I understand, but I'm investigating this for Meg, and I plan to wrap it up soon."

Helen gave a tired sigh. "Mr. Sheppard, my daughter-in-law is not rational. She is a disgrace to this entire family!"

Sloane could hear the animosity in her voice. Obviously there was no love lost between Meg and her mother-in-law. "Perhaps later today, after four o'clock?"

Helen hesitated, rather irritably. "I'll be back by then. That's fine."

AN UNFORTUNATE COINCIDENCE

Sloane thanked her and hung up. He turned back to the notes when a knock came on his office door. He saw a young man holding a telegram. He signed for it and ripped it open. It was from Meg, in Manhattan. She was coming to Albany on Friday evening, leaving to return on Sunday, and she planned to bring Ben Faraday, too. If Sloane wanted her there to clarify the events of the last month, she will be there. Sloane nodded in approval. He picked up the phone again and this time asked the operator to dial the Albany Police. Within moments, he was speaking to Inspector Harris. Sloane asked if he learned anything new about the deaths of Ida Munson and Grace Prescott. The Inspector was negative on both accounts.

"We spoke to the family at length," he told Sloane. "And looked at the broom closet where the shelf fell. We saw the sewing machine on the floor, an older model, and quite a heavy one, too. From the height of the shelf from which it fell, it would cause considerable damage and even death upon falling onto someone underneath it."

Sloane was reluctant to agree. "And Mrs. Grace Prescott?"

Sloane could hear him rustle some papers before speaking. "Mrs. Prescott was found at the bottom of her basement stairs. Her neck was broken. She could have been pushed or some struggle could have taken place, but there's really nothing to suggest foul play."

"Her back door was unlocked," Sloane pointed out.

"As well as her front door. Many people in that neighborhood don't lock their doors. Crime is rare in that part of town. Mrs. Prescott was held in high regard in the State Street community and volunteered at the city hospital, too. She lived in her house for many years. We are still investigating Mrs. Prescott's death. She didn't have any enemies, at least none that we are aware of."

"On Saturday afternoon, I'd like you and the lieutenant to come to Mrs. Cary's house," Sloane told him. "Megan Cary will be present as well as Mr. Faraday." He hesitated. "I plan to address the family with my findings. It's imperative you and the lieutenant, as investigating officers into these deaths, are present."

Sloane could hear disbelief. "Yes, we will be there. About one o'clock?"

Sloane mentioned he planned to speak with Mrs. Cary this afternoon. He would verify Saturday's time and then call him back when it was confirmed. After a few more words on the case, Sloane hung up and fiddled with the folder on his desk.

Did Grace Prescott know something that if revealed could cause considerable damage to the sisters? And Ida Munson. From his experience, maids were dowdy and unassuming, but vigilante. Ida could have seen something and was silenced. Did she also have information that could destroy someone in the family?

Sloane believed that Janet Faraday was the answer to this case. Janet Faraday moved slightly and then collapsed, leaving a clearing where the rest of the occupants could see her, and she could see them. Although the fighting was upsetting to someone like Janet Faraday, in her fragile condition, there was something else that added to it. She had to recognize someone who could destroy her. But then it was Janet who died the next day, having fallen in front of the trolley.

Sloane made a few more notes, then put his pen aside. He had to see Helen Cary and soon. He got up, put on his coat and after having lunch at the local diner, he caught the trolley uptown to Willett Street.

AN UNFORTUNATE COINCIDENCE

The radio console was playing jazz in the living room. Duke Ellington's music was uplifting to Helen and Richard and even Harmon admired the tune, whistling as he was busy cleaning.

"Mr. Sheppard will be here shortly," Helen said to her brother-in-law. "He wants to see us again, although I can't imagine why. We've answered enough questions."

Richard agreed. "Has he nothing else to do with his time?"

Helen sipped her coffee. "He's still working for Megan." Her tone held strict disapproval. "He mentioned the police are investigating Grace's death. He thinks she may have been pushed down her basement stairs, where the police found her."

"That's highly unlikely," Richard remarked dryly. "And what will he gain by speaking with us again? Adam killed himself, he left the suicide note."

"Richard, please," Helen said. "It's bad enough rehashing everything."

"Then why did you tell him he could come?"

Helen shrugged. "Perhaps if we comply, he'll leave us alone."

"Perhaps," Richard said with the coffee cup to his lips.

At that moment, the doorbell rang. Harmon went to answer it and from the living room, Helen and Richard could hear voices and then the door closed, letting in a swirl of cold air.

"Is he here already?" Richard inquired.

Harmon entered carrying a telegram and gave it to Helen. His face wrinkled in consternation. "It's for you," he said. "It's from Megan, in New York City."

"Megan?" Helen said, taking the telegram, clearly surprised. Why would her daughter-in-law send a telegram? Richard and Harmon looked at her as she read, not wanting to disturb her.

"Well, so that's that," she said in finality. She put the telegram on the coffee table. She said nothing until Richard asked her what it was about. She took time in replying.

"She plans to come here on Friday evening. Mr. Faraday, too."

"What?" Richard was incredulous. "Why would she bring him? He was here once already."

"I don't trust her," Helen said quietly. She looked at Richard and then Harmon, as though all hope was lost. "She's up to something. I just feel it."

"You may be overreacting," Harmon said. Upon seeing the reaction on her face, he wished he had kept quiet.

"I hardly think I'm overreacting, Harmon," she said icily. "My daughter-in-law is conniving and ruthless. She's already involved with another man."

"Why don't you send her a telegram telling her not to come?"

"No, that won't do. Mr. Sheppard wants to see her. I suppose she'll have to stay here. How horrid if she stayed at a hotel with that Mr. Faraday."

"Helen, this is 1928, times have changed, you know," Richard told her.

Helen looked at her brother-in-law with contempt. "I don't care what year it is. Her behavior is totally out of line. She should be in mourning for her husband."

Richard realized he could not rationalize with Helen. He glanced at her and could tell her mind was racing, fuming, clearly agitated. They heard the front door open again and could hear Iris and Bruce, laughing and talking, slamming the door behind them.

"Must you slam the door, Iris?" her mother said as soon as Iris entered the living room, Bruce following.

Iris looked at her mother and could tell something was wrong. "I'm sorry, Mother. Bruce and I saw each other on Willett and made a race for the door!"

"You act like children, Iris?" Again, her mother spoke acidly.

Iris and Bruce sat on the sofa, helped themselves to coffee and then Iris turned to her mother. "What's wrong?"

"You're home earlier than usual," her mother said dryly.

"Yes, I left a little bit earlier," Iris said and wasn't sure why her mother asked. Richard looked at his niece and didn't quite understand the young women of today, the flappers. They were rather forward in their approach, too abrasive at times, too forthright. When he courted Elsie, women were more demur but with the right to vote and the suffragette movement things had certainly changed.

"Mr. Sheppard will be here shortly," Helen said to her daughter. "He wants to speak to us all about Adam."

"About Ida and Grace, too?" Bruce asked.

Helen looked at her son-in-law as though resenting his interruption. "Yes, Bruce, that's correct. I don't feel there's anything more for him to look into."

Iris agreed. "What else, Mother?" She knew her mother too well to know it was just one thing.

Helen showed her daughter the telegram from Meg. Iris read it carefully, Bruce reading over her shoulder. They looked up at Helen at the same time.

"She plans to bring Mr. Faraday," Richard said.

"They'll stay here, of course," Iris said, putting the telegram on the coffee table. "Reluctantly I'll agree to that," Helen retorted. "They're not married, Iris. What shame and disgrace she brings to this family." She paused, fuming.

"Mr. Sheppard told Helen he's still working for Megan, regarding Adam's death," Richard told Iris and Bruce. "He mentioned Grace may have been pushed down her stairs."

"What?" Iris said in disbelief. "Who would push Grace down her stairs?"

"Hello everyone," a voice called pleasantly from the living room entrance. It was Elsie, looking pretty and feminine in a gray dress, heels, and lovely pearls. She approached her husband, kissed him on the cheek and then helped herself to coffee.

"We didn't hear you come in, Elsie," her sister said.

"Well, you were talking so intently," Elsie said, smiling and sat next to her husband. "Am I interrupting something, Helen?"

Bruce told Elsie that Sloane Sheppard would be stopping by to see them any time now. Elsie almost spilled the coffee on her dress.

"You don't know the worst," Helen said. She reached for the telegram on the coffee table and passed it to Richard to give to Elsie. "Read that, Elsie."

Elsie took the telegram and her expression alone was enough to convince Helen, Richard, Iris and Bruce that she, like her sister, disapproved of Meg's weekend visit.

"She's bringing Mr. Faraday with her," Elsie said. "She hasn't wasted any time."

"I'll say," remarked Helen dryly.

"Mr. Sheppard told Mother the police are investigating Grace's death," Iris told her aunt. "That she may have been pushed down the stairs in her home."

"Pushed?" Elsie also was incredulous. "That's hard to believe, Helen."

As four o'clock approached, the family was getting restless, anticipating Sloane's visit. The doorbell soon rang, and Harmon answered it, letting Sloane enter and bringing him to the living room. They greeted him cordially and Helen welcomed him to sit and have coffee and cake. Sloane handed Harmon his coat, hat and gloves and helped himself to coffee. He sat next to Bruce on the sofa and looked at the assembled faces before him.

AN UNFORTUNATE COINCIDENCE

"What can we do for you, Mr. Sheppard?" Helen asked him, coming to the point. Sloane also came straight to the point. "I'd like to take a look at the broom closet, where Mrs. Munson died," he said as he put down his coffee cup.

Helen and Elsie started to protest but Richard told Sloane he would take him to the pantry. Bruce and Iris also accompanied them. In the kitchen, Richard stood aside while Sloane entered the broom closet.

"This is where we found Ida," Bruce said, from behind Sloane. "The sewing machine was on top of her and there was blood on her forehead."

Sloane nodded. "Falling from that height, a heavy sewing machine would cause injury or death." He looked at the old sewing machine in the corner. "Who does this belong to?"

"My wife," Richard said from in the kitchen. "She used it years ago but recently purchased a new one. She didn't want to part with it, so we stored it on the top shelf."

"There was never any problem with it," Iris said.

"There's something else," Richard said, surprising even himself. "In back of the door." He pointed to the string, attached to a nail, with several keys on the end.

"Strange, we didn't notice that before," Bruce said, looking at the string.

"I'm surprised the police didn't say anything," Iris commented.

"Maybe they saw nothing wrong with it," Bruce said. "I remember your mother told Ida to go to the locksmith on Lark Street for an extra set of house keys to be made." He paused, looking at the string with the keys on it. "She put this nail here, tied the string with the keys onto it, so that she'd always know where to find the extra set."

Sloane again took his time before commenting. "It could have been fastened to one of the shelf hooks, so that upon opening the door and stepping in, the sewing machine would fall."

269

"Are you saying the string was deliberately tied to one of the hooks that holds up the shelf?" Iris said incredulously.

"It's a possibility." He hesitated. "Why don't we rejoin your mother and aunt?" They returned to the living room and saw Helen quietly knitting and Elsie reading the newspaper.

"What did you learn, Mr. Sheppard?" Elsie said, folding the paper.

"Nothing, really. The old sewing machine is quite a beautiful machine."

Elsie smiled. "I couldn't part with it. My husband and I decided to store it on the top shelf."

Helen nodded. "It was fine there." She paused, looking at Sloane. "Is there something wrong with keeping a sewing machine in a broom closet, Mr. Sheppard?"

Sloane met her gaze and mentioned that there was certainly nothing wrong with it. He did find it peculiar, though, that the shelf would collapse after so long.

"So did we," Helen said. "I'm still not over it. I don't care to discuss it."

"Perhaps we should discuss Mrs. Prescott," Sloane said.

"There's nothing to discuss," Elsie said flatly. "She fell down her stairs. Perhaps if she were more careful that wouldn't have happened."

"Apparently, she always kept her doors unlocked. An intruder could easily have pushed her down the stairs. The police ruled out a robbery attempt. There was nothing taken from the house."

"I don't care to discuss Grace any further," Helen said with firmness. "Are you quite finished yet, Mr. Sheppard?"

"Not quite yet, Mrs. Cary," Sloane said equally firmly. "This brings me to Janet Faraday."

"I fail to see what that has to do with us," Elsie said with tight lips.

"A witness claimed she saw someone push Janet Faraday in front of the trolley. She made a statement to the police."

"This is most upsetting," Helen said, nervously, catching her breath. "And highly unlikely. Must we hear about this?"

"Mr. Sheppard, someone removed pictures of Adam from Helen's photo album," Elsie said as though that was the most important thing.

Sloane looked at her and then at Helen. "When did you notice this?"

"Recently," Helen spoke before her sister had the chance. "Every photo of Adam as a child as well as my late husband was ripped out."

"And you think that is significant, Mrs. Cary?"

"Well, of course, Mr. Sheppard."

"How does it tie in with Adam's death?"

"I don't know. But it was done deliberately, and I want to know why."

"I asked Megan to return to Albany this weekend," Sloane said. "Is she staying with you?"

"Yes, she is," Helen said rather regrettably. "She sent a telegram, letting me know of her arrival. She's bringing Mr. Faraday."

Sloane nodded and stood. "I'll return on Saturday at one o'clock." Richard offered to show Sloane to the door. As the men walked out, Elsie turned to her sister.

"What's going on? Now, he's making assumptions about Ida and Grace!"

"I don't understand it," Helen said, almost on the verge of tears. Her face was a mixture of anger and remorse.

"Try to relax, Mother," Iris said soothingly. "Maybe Mr. Sheppard will realize there's nothing to look into."

Bruce agreed. "After all, Adam did commit suicide. Ida was an unfortunate accident. And Grace, well, she just fell down her stairs." He made it sound like falling downstairs was an everyday occurrence.

Bruce and Iris then went to their room upstairs while Richard helped Harmon clean up in the kitchen. Elsie continued reading the evening paper and Helen worked on her knitting.

Meanwhile, the fire burned softly, emitting a fine radiant glow and plenty of warmth. As evening arrived, a quietness settled over the house, a stillness that was both welcomed and frightening.

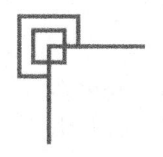

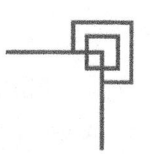

CHAPTER TWENTY-SIX

At the state capital the next day, Elsie paused on her way up the Million Dollar Staircase. From below she could hear people talking in the atrium, a reverberating sound, as the capital was full of voices that echoed off the high ceiling. Elsie never tired of the majestic beauty of the building, the ornate layout, and the historic staircase. She glanced at her watch. It was not yet four o'clock, so her workday was not quite over.

As she returned to her office, an assemblyman handed her meeting minutes that needed typing. Part of her routine although as she sat at her desk and inserted a fresh sheet of paper into her typewriter, she found it hard now to concentrate on her work.

More than one male had looked appealingly at Elsie over the years. She gave a pleasant appearance and, had she been a different sort of woman, would have encouraged the compliments she received from the many politicians. Her brown hair, worn neatly in a fashionable bob, her gray dress highlighted her slim figure and the elegant pearls showed her cream-colored skin at its best. But she was married, she told herself, and her devotion was to her husband, Richard.

Her mind flew to her nephew, Adam, a strange sort. He attracted animosity and admiration in equal amounts. Her sister's mental health was important. Too many scandals over the years. And Grace Prescott, that repulsive woman. Always sticking her nose in other people's business, that Grace. Well, she was out of the picture, forever.

Elsie struck the keyboard with a combination of anger and loathing. A few politicians stood outside her doorway, discussing the latest bills that needed approval by the state senate. Governor Smith was somewhere in the building. There was talk he would run on the Democratic ticket this year, although she personally preferred Roosevelt.

Mr. Sheppard would stop by Saturday. She sighed at the thought of another interrogation. She was prepared for Ida's service on Thursday evening, which would be difficult, but she would support her sister, no matter what.

With renewed vivacity, she continued typing, thoroughly engrossed in her work. She refused to think of her nephew. He would not disturb them anymore.

It was early evening and Sloane Sheppard was still in his office. A perfectionist and intent on finishing his task, he had one more card to play in the case of the late Mr. Cary. There was something more he needed, the missing link.

He reached for the Albany directory and thumbed through the yellow pages until he came to lawyers. He found the listing, although at a quick glance at his wall clock, doubted whether anyone would be available. He asked the operator to put through a call to the law firm of Mr. Luther Bernard and after several rings, he was about to hang up when to his surprise it was answered by a crisp sounding older male. He asked for Mr. Luther Bernard and was told, "Speaking. Who is calling please?" And his tone implied, after business hours?

"Mr. Bernard, my name is Sloane Sheppard and I am a private investigator here in Albany. We may have met years ago on a case." When no recognition came on the other line, Sloane continued. "I'm looking into the death of Adam Cary." He explained to the attorney the facts of Adam's death. Mr. Bernard asked Sloane what he could do for him at this late hour.

"Adam Cary's father was Walter Cary. You handled his estate in 1922."

Mr. Bernard acknowledged that fact and waited for Sloane to continue. "I'd like to know how Walter Cary left his assets, and any information on his estate."

"Mr. Sheppard, I do not give information over the telephone."

"I understand, Mr. Bernard. As you are probably aware, there have been several deaths in Albany recently. I believe they're homicides. The murderer is still at large."

From the other end Sloane could hear a sharp intaking of breath. "You're a private investigator you say? I think I do remember you now, Mr. Sheppard." He paused. "Give me a moment, please."

Sloane could hear opening and closing of file cabinets. He then heard the rustle of the phone receiver as the lawyer picked it back up. Although he reminded Sloane he did not usually give such information over the phone, the fact that he remembered Sloane Sheppard from years ago and the Walter Cary case was already resolved, he relayed to Sloane the details of Walter Cary's will and who inherited upon his death.

"He'd been in trouble with the law," Mr. Bernard remembered the case, flipping through pages in the folder. "He shot a man but was acquitted." He paused. "Oh yes, here's the inheritance part. Adam Cary's mother inherited the bulk of his estate."

"Who inherited, Mr. Bernard?" Sloane wanted to get the information straight.

"His son's mother, Mr. Sheppard. It was a strange provision, but we wrote it the way he wanted it. His major inheritor was his son's mother, but her name does not appear in the will." Sloane could tell he was reading the documents pertaining to the estate.

"His wife attempted to claim the inheritance." He paused reflectively. "She wasn't successful, though, as it would be in this file. Mr. Cary stipulated to receive her inheritance; it'd be paid only upon Adam Cary's death. Notwithstanding any last will and testament Adam Cary may have drawn up, of course. It's unlikely a mother would outlive her son, but that's the proviso he wanted." He paused again. "Certainly, an unusual clause but he had the right to do as he wanted with his estate."

"Were there other inheritors, Mr. Bernard?"

The old lawyer shuffled pages. "His children and even the wife received a trust fund. Since Adam Cary died recently, the mother can inherit, provided she shows proof of maternity."

"Thank you, Mr. Bernard," Sloane said. "You've been most helpful."

He hung up, his mind racing. He looked at the file on Adam Cary. Well, that clinches it, he thought and closed the folder with finality.

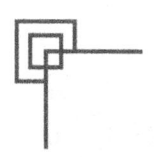

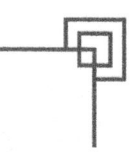

CHAPTER TWENTY-SEVEN

Ben lay back against the sofa, his long legs stretched comfortably, a cigarette dangling from his lips. He felt relaxed, having gone out to dinner with Meg after work and coming back to her apartment to spend more time with her.

It was Thursday evening, and another cold night settled over the city. The dinner was fabulous and although a dance band was scheduled, Meg and Ben choose to leave for her apartment, to talk about the weekend.

She entered the living room with two cups of coffee. She handed one to him, and then joined him on the sofa. She took a drag on her cigarette and got closer to him.

"Are you happy, sweetheart?" she asked, curling her legs underneath her.

Ben took her hand in his. "Yes, Meg, I couldn't be happier."

"Ida Munson's wake is set for this evening," Meg said, rather distracted.

"You knew Mrs. Munson?" Ben asked sipping coffee.

Meg shook her head. "No, just that she worked as Helen's maid."

"What do you know about Elsie and Richard?"

"Elsie is Helen's sister, but other than that, I don't know them. Richard is rather quiet. They take good care of Helen. They seem protective of her."

"It's strange they all live in the same house," Ben observed. "After the war there was a housing shortage, but things have gotten better. Has Iris mentioned she'd prefer her own place?"

"I don't know that either," Meg admitted, taking a sip of coffee. "They live with Helen to keep her company, especially since her husband died six years ago."

"How did he die, anyway? Seemed like a big secret."

Meg agreed. "They never mention it. Adam never talked about his father." They were quiet then; Ben puffing at his cigarette, Meg drinking her coffee.

"Should we meet at Grand Central tomorrow after work?" he asked. "I'll pack a bag when I get back to my place."

Meg said she planned to do the same. "That means you'd need to leave early in the morning."

Ben put down his coffee and took her hand in his again.

"Meg, your husband has been dead just a month. Should we take it more slowly?"

"Take it more slowly!" Meg was appalled. "Ben, I want to be with you!"

He reached for her as he had done so before. She was in his arms again, passionately. He held onto her even tighter and Meg felt her body giving way, yielding to the passions that were smoldering inside her.

It was a cold evening for a wake. Ida's service was soon over. The family made their way to the car, speechless and shivering from the chill air. Harmon carefully pulled onto Central Avenue on the way to Willett Street. Light snow dusted the windshield and was mixed with sleet. Harmon paid attention to the road and ignored the comments around him.

"It was a pleasant service," Elsie said to no one in particular. She glanced at her sister, dressed in the appropriate black, her face a mass of contradictions, grave, and angry. Helen murmured it was nice but said nothing else. She merely looked out the window, too numb for speech.

"Do you want anything to eat, Mother?" Iris asked. They got out of the car as Harmon parked on Willett Street. "I'll make a sandwich for you."

Helen thanked her daughter but declined. She reached for her sister and brother-in-law. They assisted her in walking to the steps. Once inside, they guided her down the hallway to the living room. Bruce went to the living room to rekindle the fire. Iris turned the lights on in the kitchen and washed plates, cups, and saucers.

As she entered the living room after Bruce, Elsie noticed how her sister looked up at Harmon. Their eyes met, briefly, but she could not identify the expression: remorse, candor, indignation? She brushed it off. Was there something between Helen and Harmon? Past secrets, perhaps? She wondered.

Her golden hair was spread on her pillow. Ben held her in his arms, not wanting to release her. "I love you, Meg, even when we first met on the train. Do you remember?"

Meg smiled at the recollection. "Darling, how could I forget? I met your mother then, too. We confided in each other."

He looked at her still figure. "You understand so much."

"That's just the librarian in me," she said and drew him to her.

They were lost in each other; their love comforting, and Meg had never felt such emotion. It was not long before daylight slowly began to fill the apartment and the alarm clock went off. The inevitable workday was upon them.

As Ben needed to return to his apartment to pack for the trip, they got up early. They enjoyed breakfast, listened to the latest hit songs on the radio, drank numerous cups of coffee, and smoked numerous cigarettes.

The blissful pre-dawn period, when the city was at its most quiet, came slowly to an end. They soon left the apartment, Meg taking her small suitcase with her. It was cold as they expected, but they decided to walk toward Fifth Avenue, instead of taking a cab.

The city started to come alive, cars and trucks rolled by and pedestrians began filling the streets. It was close to eight-thirty. Soon they arrived in front of the New York Public Library. Ben held onto Meg so tightly she thought he would not let go. She touched his face with her gloved hand.

"I'll see you at Grand Central later today," Meg said.

Ben told her he would be there. He hurried off to the subway on his way to his apartment on 96th Street. Meg looked after him then turned to enter the library.

At five o'clock, she gathered her fur coat and suitcase, and once outside hastily made her way to Grand Central Station. It was still early, but she told Ben she would meet him near the information counter. She almost ran in her haste to cross the concourse to reach him.

"I left work early," he explained as she approached him. People were coming and going in all directions, but Meg felt as though she were alone with Ben at that moment, as though no one else even existed.

"I see you have your suitcase, too," Meg said and then looked around. "Why don't we get something to eat since we have time?"

Ben agreed, and they walked over to the cafeteria and bought sandwiches and coffee. Lighting cigarettes and sitting back on his chair, Ben asked how she was feeling about returning to Albany.

"Well, Sloane feels it's important," Meg said. "He wouldn't have sent the telegrams."

"Can you trust him, Meg?" Ben asked.

"Absolutely. He told me if I ever needed his assistance, to call him."

"Our train should be posted soon, it's almost six twenty-five." He glanced at the departures board to find the track for the Empire State Express to Albany. "Track 4, Meg, let's go."

Meg gathered her suitcase, put on her fur coat and as she walked, slipped her left hand through his arm. Confidently, they entered the train, unaware of the revelations and incidents that awaited them this weekend.

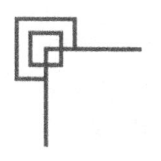

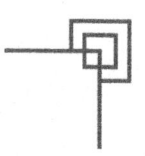

CHAPTER TWENTY-EIGHT

After a signal delay at Poughkeepsie, the train arrived in Albany, and passengers were eager to disembark. Meg and Ben gathered their belongings. Union Station was crowded. Upon entering the concourse, they spotted Iris and Bruce. Walking through the busy station, Iris commented how glad she and Bruce were to see them.

"There was a signal failure in Poughkeepsie," Meg said as they stepped out of the station onto Broadway. "But other than that, it was fine."

Light snow was falling, but the streetlamps on Broadway and around Union Station made a pretty glow, brilliantly illuminating the night sky. They crossed Broadway and waited, along with a sizeable crowd, for the trolley to take them uptown. Upon arriving at the corner of Lark and Washington, they got off and crossed at the light, on the way to Willett Street.

"I'm afraid everyone has gone to bed," Iris told Meg as they walked along Lark Street, their footsteps crunching in the snow.

"No problem, Iris," Meg said as she linked her hand through her arm "I'm glad to see you and Bruce again. We'll have the chance to talk more too."

"Thank you for letting me stay at your house," Ben said to Iris as they arrived.

Iris smiled. "Well, your Meg's friend which is fine with us," she said opening the front door with her key. Harmon was there in the hallway to greet them. He eyed the tall, handsome young man behind her.

"Hello, Mr. Faraday," he said, holding out his hand.

"Please call me Ben," he said, shaking Harmon's hand gratefully. "Thank you for letting me stay here."

Bruce helped them off with their coats. Iris left their suitcases in the hallway. They then entered the living room, where the fireplace was still smoldering, a pleasing warmth.

"I'm afraid everyone's gone to bed," Harmon told them. "Helen said she'd see you in the morning." He paused. "Do you want anything to drink, coffee or tea?"

Neither Meg nor Ben wanted anything to drink, so Harmon excused himself. They sat on the sofa, near the fireplace. Iris and Bruce joined them, took out cigarettes, offered them to Meg and Ben and settled down in the chairs near the sofa.

"Meg, what does Mr. Sheppard want to see us about?" Iris asked, taking a large draw on her cigarette. "Has he come up with something new?"

"I don't know yet. He sent me telegrams, saying it was urgent. I sent your mother a telegram, letting her know I was coming this weekend."

"Yes, we got it," Iris said.

"We can take in a movie at the Majestic tomorrow," Bruce suggested.

"Yes, that's a good idea!" Iris agreed. She crushed out her cigarette, eager to plan a night on the town in Albany.

"Are there a lot of theaters in Albany?" Ben asked.

Iris nodded. "*My Best Girl* with Mary Pickford is playing this week."

Small talk ensued for about a half hour until Meg stifled a yawn. She told them she was ready for bed.

"Thanks for meeting us at Union Station," she said to them. "We'll talk more in the morning before Sloane gets here."

Iris nodded. "Did you need help with your suitcase?"

Meg stood up, gave Iris and Bruce a hug, said she would carry her suitcase herself. Bruce began settling the room for the evening. Iris smoldered the fire and turned off the lights.

"Good night, Meg and Ben," Bruce said, as he appeared in the hallway.

On arriving at the third floor, Meg showed Ben the extra guest room and the one she would be in for the weekend. She pointed out the typewriter in the far corner. Ben shook his head but said nothing. They walked to the room he was using.

"I'll see you in the morning," he said, putting down his suitcase. He reached for her, drawing her further into the room.

"Ben, please, my mother-in-law is only two doors down!" Meg whispered.

He held her a moment, then watched her walk to the other guest room. Ben went into his room, wondering if he did the right thing by coming to Albany this weekend.

"Good morning, Meg," Elsie said pleasantly. Upon entering the dining room the next morning, Meg poured coffee and sat down at the long dining room table.

She realized the entire family was already there. She was dressed in a comfortable blue and gray dress, with pink pearls, her hair worn back in her usual bob. She decided to dress instead of coming downstairs in her robe. Looking at the rest of the family, most not even awake, she did not think it would have really mattered.

She saw Richard, already dressed, crunching a slice of toast, and looking at the morning edition of *The Times Union*. Next to him was Iris, still in her robe, sleep in her eyes, finishing a muffin. Bruce, opposite his wife, looked as though he had not slept a wink, also in his robe and slippers, finishing a bowl of corn flakes and sipping coffee. Elsie was next to her sister, who Meg just realized was there. Her mother-in-law was unusually quiet, as though the recent ordeal with Adam caused her to reflect on her disposition and possibly redirect it to a more congenial, gentler persona. Although Meg rather doubted that could be the case.

"Good morning, Meg dear," Helen said with a weak smile.

Meg smiled. "Thank you for having us this weekend."

The "us" seemed to hang in the air, undefined. No one spoke until Elsie asked Meg if she wanted more coffee. Meg thought she looked scared, as though her talking was a way to deflect from the undercurrent running through the room.

"Sleep okay last night?" Helen said Meg. "What about Mr. Faraday?"

Meg said she slept fine. She was aware of the undercurrent. Ben. Of course, what else could it be? They knew he was here and had yet to come downstairs for breakfast.

"I'm sure Ben slept well. I haven't seen him yet," she added as though her mother-in-law's look warranted such a comment.

Richard commented that Sloane Sheppard would be at the house today, as if the rest of the family was not aware of it. Helen looked at him rather crossly.

"We know that Richard, dear," she said. "He's expected about one o'clock. Although I hardly consider it a social visit."

Elsie agreed, her cup to her lips. "What more does he want from us?"

At that moment, Ben appeared at the dining room entrance. As though on stage, they turned their attention to him. Ben walked in and greeted everyone.

"Thank you, Mrs. Cary, for having me this weekend," he said earnestly.

Elsie glanced at her sister and knowing her too well, spoke up.

"It's a pleasure. Help yourself to breakfast on the sideboard."

Ben poured coffee. Bruce asked if he slept, Iris offered him a cigarette and Richard gave him the morning paper.

"How are you holding up?" Helen asked Ben, which surprised Meg.

Ben buttered a muffin. "I'm doing better, thank you. Meg's been helpful over the last several weeks." He looked at her next to him and smiled.

"Do you know why Mr. Sheppard is coming here today?" she asked him.

Meg looked at Helen with surprise. Why would she ask Ben that? Up to her old tricks, she thought, trying to hide her annoyance.

"No, I don't," Ben admitted, sipping the coffee. "Meg received telegrams, saying he wanted to see her as soon as possible. I told her I wanted to come, too."

"How appropriate," Helen said dryly.

"Did you want the fire lit in the living room, Helen?" Richard said as he stood. Helen told her brother-in-law that she would appreciate a fire. From the living room, Richard threw logs in the fireplace and turned the radio console to a station playing swing music.

The morning wore on, each occupant of the house waiting for the arrival of Sloane Sheppard, as though their anticipation was a cover-up for a more dreaded feeling.

Within the next two hours saw the family idly eating lunch. Elsie and Harmon set up the sideboard with chicken, salad, coffee, and iced tea.

Still in the dining room, after Richard, Iris and Bruce finished eating, Helen suggested to Meg that she and Ben take a walk along Willett Street. Meg, sensing the awkwardness in the air, as though her mother-in-law wanted them out of the way, at least for a while, agreed that was a good idea. She turned to Ben, who agreed.

"I don't know Albany too well," he said to Meg, finishing his second cup of coffee. "I'd like to walk around, see some of the city."

As you did the evening of our dinner, Helen thought contemptuously. And ruined it for us, too.

"Sounds like she wanted to get rid of us," Ben said once outside. Meg linked her hand through his arm. She bundled her coat around her, her scarf half covering her face.

"I'd rather be alone with you, anyway," Meg told him.

They crossed Madison Avenue at Willett, observing the fine brownstones and the cars buried in snow. After a half hour, they decided to return to the house. As they approached Willett Street, Meg noticed Sloane Sheppard just getting out of his car.

"Hello, Meg," he called, closing the car door. "Hello, Mr. Faraday."

"I'll freeze if I stay outside another minute!" Meg said, her teeth almost chattering. Soon they were at Helen's house, with Meg ringing the bell for Harmon to let them in. Elsie instead opened the door and at first did not see Sloane as he stood behind Ben.

"Is it one o'clock already?" she asked, rather irritated on seeing Sloane. "I didn't realize time had gone by. We're just clearing up after lunch." Her tone implied it was inconvenient although she knew of his arrival.

"It's almost one," Sloane said. "I'm here to see the family."

"Yes, I know," Elsie said, again rather irritably. "Come this way, please." She included Meg and Ben. Soon they were settled in the living room, Elsie going to the kitchen for coffee to offer to Sloane.

Helen and Richard were also in the living room, Helen knitting and Richard listening to a news broadcast. Helen looked worn out in a simple gray dress, with a gold chain, her hair tied back, rather carelessly, no make-up. Richard was dressed conservatively as usual. Neither spoke when Meg, Ben and Sloane entered. Only Richard commented that Sloane was present and motioned him to sit on the sofa. Helen merely glanced at him and put down her knitting.

In a moment Iris and Bruce entered. They greeted Sloane, lit cigarettes, and sat in the chairs near the sofa. Elsie soon returned with a tray on which reposed cups and coffee. Harmon entered and was surprised to see Sloane, greeted him cordially and was about to turn to leave when Sloane asked him to remain. Harmon turned and glared at him, then at Helen, as though seeking permission. Reluctantly he sat down on the extra chair in the corner, by the radio. Realizing all were present, Sloane cleared his throat and proceeded to address them.

"Thank you, Mrs. Cary for having me today," he first spoke to Helen, who merely nodded and tried to hide her annoyance. "I know what a difficult time this has been. I'd like to present what I've learned about Adam's death."

"What is the point?" Richard said. "This undue stress isn't good for Helen."

Elsie agreed. "If you have something to tell us, Mr. Sheppard, don't beat around the bush!"

Sloane lit a cigarette and helped himself to coffee. As he put the cup on the coffee table, he looked at Meg.

"Meg wanted me to look into her husband's death. At first, after hearing about it from her and speaking with the investigating officers,

I didn't see a cause for investigation. They concluded Adam took his own life. The note seemed to confirm that was the case." He paused. "However, after speaking with the restaurant staff, and the death of Janet Faraday, I began to see something different. Perhaps Adam did not kill himself."

"But Meg found the note upstairs!" Bruce exclaimed.

Sloane cleared his throat. "I've been told that Adam Cary was a difficult person. He argued frequently with his mother. He also rarely came here."

"He borrowed five thousand dollars from me," Richard commented, "and never repaid it."

"Must you mention that, Richard?" Helen said irritably.

"Meg stayed here for the weekend while she and Iris attended the state library convention. While on the train, she talked to a woman. She said her name was Irene Hanson, but her real name was Janet Faraday." Sloane looked at Ben. "She told Meg about the death of Ben's father."

"Mr. Sheppard, please," Elsie said. "We know all this!"

Sloane continued. "Meg listened to what Janet Faraday told her, not believing it, but somehow believing it. When she returned from the café car, Janet Faraday was gone. I assume she fled to another car out of fear." He looked again at Ben, who simply nodded. "For the dinner at Keeler's, Mrs. Cary invited Mrs. Munson, Mr. Pendleton, and Mrs. Prescott. But Mr. Faraday and his mother appeared, and Adam Cary became enraged when he realized who he was."

"Of course, he was upset," Helen spoke up. "He thought he was there to see Meg."

"I didn't know Meg was there," Ben spoke up, rather firmly.

"No, I don't believe you did either," Sloane continued. "However, Adam did. He swung at you, causing quite a scene. He was removed to the other dining room."

"Why are you telling us something we already know?" Richard interrupted.

Sloane finished his coffee. He butted his cigarette in the ashtray on the coffee table, holding everyone's interest as they waited for him to continue.

"After learning about Adam, his parentage, his father, and the circumstances surrounding his birth, I realized what actually happened."

"Mr. Sheppard, this is more than enough," Helen intervened.

"What kind of man was Walter Cary? Was he a good husband and father? What were the circumstances surrounding his death in 1922?"

"Walter Cary was an evil man," Elsie spoke before Helen had the chance. "He caused misery in our lives. But what does that have to do with Adam's death?"

"I'm afraid it has everything to do with it," Sloane continued. "Six years ago, in 1922, a man in Kinderhook died from inhaling carbon monoxide. That man was Walter Cary."

"What are you saying?" Richard asked.

"I'm saying that Janet Faraday killed Walter Cary, the man with whom she had a child. She gave him sleeping pills, and then closed the garage door after he started the car, letting him suffocate by inhaling carbon monoxide."

"Well then, that would mean…" Bruce started and then stopped.

"Now I see what was so familiar!" Elsie exclaimed. "I knew there was a resemblance between Adam and Ben Faraday. Of course! They're half-brothers!"

"And I'm his half-sister," Iris said. Her eyes filled with tears. "You're my brother, Ben. I don't believe it!"

"Iris, that's enough," her mother said sharply as though speaking to a child.

"What does that have to do with Adam's death?" Richard asked.

"The police tested the cup that held the coffee. It contained rat poison. The autopsy confirmed that. And Mrs. Cary told the police there was rat poison here in the house."

"Who would put poison in his coffee?" Elsie asked, clearly perturbed.

Sloane blew smoke from another cigarette. "It was Ida Munson, his natural mother."

Exclamations of disbelief, shock. Everyone started to speak at once before Sloane cleared his throat to continue. He looked at Helen who slowly nodded.

"I believe you have some explaining to do, Mrs. Cary."

Helen sighed and looked at the family. "It's true that Ida was Adam's real mother," she explained regrettably. "We kept it a secret from the time he was born and never had the birth registered, so there would be no record of it. Ida went away to have the baby by a midwife. I never legally adopted him. I raised Adam as my own child. My first child was stillborn, and I was devastated I could not have a child. Walter had gotten Ida pregnant, when she was living in Kinderhook as he did Janet Faraday. He promised Ida money if she gave up her baby. That was in 1900, the year of Adam's birth. It was a long twenty-eight years, but Ida still wanted the money. She managed to keep it a secret, but in 1921, her husband found out. He pulled a gun on Walter, there was a struggle and it went off, killing Ida's husband. Walter was put on trial but he was acquitted. He had an excellent lawyer."

She paused, deep in thought. Everyone looked at her, speechless, immobile, not believing what they were hearing.

"Ida went away for several years. She found out Walter left her the money in his will. He never gave it to her directly, as she assumed he would. Eventually she came back to Albany and was destitute. She had no job, no money and no family. I hired her as my maid, which worked well for us. I told her I had nothing to do with Walter's will or the money he promised her for giving up her baby. But it was true; he stipulated that Ida—Adam's birth mother—could only inherit upon Adam's death."

"That sounds like Walter," Elsie remarked. "Cruel to the end."

"Ida Munson wanted the money," Sloane continued. "It didn't matter that Adam was her natural son. She had no relationship with him. He didn't know it anyway. She took enough of the rat poison to the restaurant. When no one was looking, she put a hefty dose in her own coffee cup. When the table was clear and everyone was dancing, she switched her cup with his. And as you all know, he was dead within the half hour."

"But why would Ida do something so cruel?" Iris asked.

"Because your father condemned her to a servant's life. She had no money of her own, no other family. Walter killed her husband and she had no children, except for the son she had by your father, who, of course, was Adam."

"And Janet Faraday got away with killing him?" Richard asked, looking at Ben.

"I wouldn't put it like that," Sloane said. "You, Mr. Faraday, realized she couldn't live a normal life. You arranged for her to be admitted to the psychiatric hospital here in Albany."

Ben nodded. "Yes, she suffered because of him. I never really knew my father, except that my mother killed him."

"Who ripped out the pictures of Adam in mother's album?" Iris asked.

"Most likely Ida," Sloane said. "She wanted to erase anything dealing with Adam's childhood. I'm sure she planned to see a lawyer, with proof of maternity, to claim her inheritance."

"She could prove it without a birth certificate?" Bruce asked.

"There are other ways to prove parentage," Sloane commented.

"She had other opportunities to do this," Elsie said bitterly. "Why did she wait until that night?"

"Meg and Adam rarely came to Albany. At a busy restaurant, it was easier, especially these days when so many people put things in their drinks. If someone saw Ida, I doubt if anyone would have paid the slightest attention. After all, it was dim in the dining room, the music was loud, and people were dancing. After Meg finished dancing, she returned to the table and watched the couples on the dance floor, with her back to the table. It was while Meg's back was to the table that Ida put the poison in her cup. She then switched her cup with Adam's cup.

"Janet Faraday collapsed because she recognized you, Mrs. Cary, as the wife of the man she had a baby with. And she recognized Ida as the woman who lived near her in Kinderhook." He paused. "Mr. Faraday mentioned his mother told him she never forgot a face. That made me realize she must have recognized someone at the restaurant. She felt terrified and collapsed."

"As did I," Helen said sadly. "I didn't know Ida would kill Adam for the money."

"I believe you," Sloane said.

"Then Mr. Faraday's mother died as did Ida and Grace."

"Yes, that is correct."

"Then who was responsible?"

"Very simple," Sloane said carefully, "You. Either you or Mrs. Munson were responsible and since Mrs. Munson is dead, I concluded it was you."

Helen choked slightly, then spoke hoarsely. "Are you serious, Mr. Sheppard?'

"Indeed, Mrs. Cary, quite serious."

AN UNFORTUNATE COINCIDENCE

For a few seconds, a shocked silence permeated the room. Everyone looked in horror at Helen as she sat transfixed in her chair. Only Elsie was brave enough to speak.

"This is outrageous," she said in contempt. "You have no proof!"

"In fact, I do," Sloane said. "The police told me about a witness who saw her push Janet Faraday in front of the trolley. She'd recognize Mrs. Cary as that person."

"That is ridiculous!" Elsie said, her face flustered.

Sloane continued to address Helen. "You were afraid Janet Faraday would talk because you knew she recognized both you and Ida. And you recognized her. As you told me, you're fond of taking walks by yourself. By chance you saw her walking with her son. It was easy to push her in front of the trolley. You're a remarkably strong woman, even having just come out of the hospital. You're also a well-respected member of the Willett Street community. You wanted nothing to interfere with your good standing. It was risky, but your name and reputation were worth the risk."

"Helen couldn't walk far in this weather!" Richard intervened.

Harmon agreed. "Helen and I have walked together for years. Although…" Sloane turned to him. "Although there were plenty of times when she walked alone, as she did on the evening Janet Faraday was killed. Is that what you were going to say?" Sloane returned his gaze to Helen and the rest of the family.

"It was when you discovered the pictures of Adam as a child ripped out of the photo album that made you realize Ida killed him. You knew seeing Janet Faraday unhinged her, too. She was extremely paranoid. You feared she'd admit she was Adam's real mother and expose the scheme she and your late husband created so you could have a child. It was easy to tie the string to the hook holding up the shelf with the heavy sewing machine. The sewing machine crushed her skull. She didn't stand a chance."

"Mr. Sheppard, I've heard enough of this!" Helen said firmly.

"The same for Mrs. Prescott," Sloane continued. "Grace Prescott was nosy; she too would talk and ruin your reputation. You knew she kept her doors unlocked. You also knew when she got home, since you volunteered at Albany Hospital. You must have been waiting on her back porch for a while. When you saw her in the kitchen, opening the basement door, you saw your chance. It was getting even more risky, but you were desperate for the truth never to come out."

"Mother, this can't be true!" Iris almost screamed at her.

Richard, Elsie, Iris and Bruce looked at Helen in shocked silence. Meg and Ben also were speechless. Only Harmon in the far chair spoke.

"I knew Ida was Adam's real mother," he said gravely. "She confided in me a long time ago. I promised her I wouldn't say anything. Walter Cary made that will to hurt Ida. He used her, like he did Janet Faraday. Ida was obsessed with the money, but I never knew she'd kill for it."

Another terrible silence followed broken only by the ringing of the doorbell. Harmon went to the hallway, and soon returned with Inspector Harris and Lieutenant Taylor. There was an air of professionalism as they entered, as though they were there to see justice done. They looked at Sloane and at the family. Sloane then turned to Helen as she sat quietly in her chair by the fire.

"Mrs. Cary, it will be much easier…" he started to say.

Helen then spoke, hoarsely again, barely getting the words out. She reached over to the end table and took something out of the drawer.

"You are foolish, Mr. Sheppard," she managed to say slyly, "to think you have won over on me." Her right hand went quickly to her mouth. Sloane started to move forward but could not reach her fast enough. Helen swallowed something.

Everyone was up at once. Elsie quickly went to her sister, while Harmon rushed to the telephone to call an ambulance. Helen's face turned a horrible red, her body withered in spasmic convulsions, and then she collapsed heavily onto the floor. Iris and Bruce knelt next to Helen, assisting Elsie. She pushed on her stomach, but it was to no avail. In Helen's hand were small remaining pellets of rat poison.

As they tried in vain to resuscitate her, Sloane looked at the still figure on the floor, and shook his head. He then felt a hand on his arm. It was Meg, with Ben next to her. She looked at him, tears about to fall. Sloane placed an arm around her. It's over, he told her grimly, it's over.

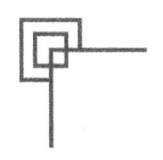

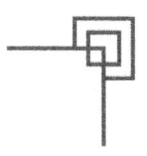

CHAPTER TWENTY-NINE

It was several hours later after the climactic scene in the living room. Meg, Ben, Bruce, and Richard sat around the large dining room table. After Helen collapsed from the poison, her doctor was called along with an ambulance. A stomach pump was used, but the poison already took hold and Helen was soon pronounced dead. The ambulance removed the body and the policemen also departed. Only Sloane remained, also seated at the dining room table, a cold cup of coffee in front of him. He looked at Bruce across from him, absently putting sugar into his cup.

"One thing I wonder," Bruce said. "Why the fake suicide note?"

"Ida would have typed it. She knew Meg would find it later that evening."

"Was Ida insane?" Richard stammered, clearly shaken by events. "What made her think she would get away with it?"

"Ida was consumed with the money Walter Cary promised her. She took advantage that Adam and Meg came here that weekend. A clever plan and it worked, too. The dinner, the dim lights, the music, dancing, and the crowds all played a role."

"When did she put arsenic in the coffee?" Meg asked. "I was sitting at the table after dancing. I would have seen something."

"Remember, your back was to the table while everyone was dancing, except Ida. Upon returning from the powder room, she had the opportunity to put the arsenic in her own cup and then switched hers with Adam's cup. No one noticed a thing."

Ben frowned. "It was unfortunate my mother and I chose that restaurant."

Sloane nodded. "An unfortunate coincidence. Adam believed you were there to meet Meg. He finished the poisoned coffee when he returned to the table. By the time he was removed to the other dining room, it took effect."

"Poor Adam," Meg said sadly. "All for money!"

Sloane nodded in sympathy. "Helen grew fearful Ida would talk. She realized Ida killed Adam. She also realized Ida had to be silenced. She saw her opportunity in the broom closet. With Richard out of the house, Harmon running errands and Ida cleaning upstairs, it was easy to tie that string to a hook. No one saw her do it since she had the first floor to herself during the day. As the kitchen was Ida's domain, it was she who opened the broom closet, and that sealed her fate."

"I knew Walter Cary," Richard said. "Elsie warned Helen not to marry him. He cheated on her almost from the beginning. And now we know he had an affair with Janet Faraday and fathered a child with her, who was Ben. And he fathered a child with Ida Munson, who was Adam."

"Were you and your wife aware of this?" Sloane asked him.

Richard shook his head vehemently. "We knew nothing about her scheme and that Adam was Ida's son."

"Grace Prescott surmised the truth, that Adam was Ida's son," Sloane continued. "She volunteered at the hospital and listened to gossip."

"Helen really killed her?" Meg asked still in shock.

Sloane nodded. "Helen feared Grace would talk, too. She knew Grace didn't lock her doors. She waited on her back porch. When she saw her open the basement door, she rushed in, and shoved her down the stairs."

Sloane turned to Richard with concern. "How is your wife?"

Elsie and Iris were given shots of morphine and were resting comfortably in the living room, heavily sedated.

"It was a shock to hear these revelations about her sister," Richard said.

They went into the living room to check on Iris and Elsie. Iris was on the sofa, a blanket around her, her head on a pillow. She blinked and smiled when she saw Meg and Ben. Bruce sat next to her, his hand over hers.

"Ben, how are you?" Iris asked, smiling. "I've gained a new brother!"

Ben smiled back. "Fine, my new sister!"

"You know something, Meg?" Iris spoke weakly. "If you and Ben get married, you'll still be my sister-in-law! Isn't that the cat's meow!"

Meg went to Iris and hugged her. "I'll always be your sister, Iris."

Elsie stirred restlessly. "Richard, dear," she said weakly. She was covered with a blanket, resting comfortably in a deep armchair. "What happened to Helen? Walter Cary, that bastard who ruined her life! She deserved so much better! Poor Helen!" Richard put his arm around his wife and comforted her.

In the hallway, Sloane looked at Meg and Ben. "Take care, Meg," he said and shook hands with her and Ben. "We'll be in touch." Harmon held the front door open and wished him good evening.

"Long day," Ben said, taking her by the hand and leading her upstairs to the guest rooms. "I'll see you in the morning, Meg." He kissed and held her tight. Meg then entered the guest room, wondering about the unknown future looming up before her.

Sunday morning Meg looked out the guest room window while getting dressed. She noticed it stopped snowing. She brushed her hair and closed the lid on her suitcase. Upon descending the stairs, she placed it in the hallway and entered the dining room.

She was glad to see Iris, Bruce, Elsie, and Richard already up. Harmon asked what she wanted for breakfast. He supplied her with coffee and a blueberry muffin. Meg asked Iris and Elsie how they were feeling.

"After yesterday's shock," Elsie said to which Iris agreed. "It'll take time to adjust to life without Helen. In time this will heal." She paused looking at Meg. "The same for you, Meg dear. In time it will heal."

Ben entered at that moment, fully dressed, his suitcase in hand. He set the suitcase near the sideboard and sat next to Meg. He poured coffee and helped himself to a corn muffin.

"What will you do now, Ben?" Bruce asked him.

"Well, I still have my accounting job. And Meg." He looked at her and smiled.

"You've been through a lot," Iris said compassionately.

"I'll see a lawyer about the money Walter left Ida," Elsie said. "It should go to you, Meg. I'll have the details worked out and will let you know."

"Elsie, shouldn't it go to the family?" Meg said, astonished.

"You *are* family," Iris said and agreed with her aunt. "Bruce and I will visit you in Manhattan. And of course you're always welcomed here. This is your second home!"

"And Ben, *you* are family, too," Elsie added sincerely.

Ben smiled. "I've never had a family. I feel like a new life has been given to me!"

Meg squeezed his hand and smiled. "We're all family now, Ben."

Elsie poured another cup of coffee and lit a fresh cigarette. She commented that she and Richard would also visit them in Manhattan in the near future.

"Any date for a wedding?" Richard asked.

Meg hesitated. "Well, I…"

Ben smiled again. He put his arm around Meg and his actions alone verified his love and commitment to her.

Harmon entered at that moment and told Meg and Ben that he would take them to Union Station in the car. After eating, they entered the hallway for their coats. Iris, Bruce, Richard, and Elsie joined them, gave them a reassuring hug, Iris telling Meg and Ben they would hear from her soon.

On Willett Street, it was sunny but still cold. As Harmon drove down State Street, past the state capitol, Meg thought of all the turmoil she and Ben had been through. She thought of Janet Faraday, and that first train journey to Albany. It seemed so long ago now. And then Adam and even Ida and Grace. Her thoughts were broken as they arrived abruptly at Union Station. Harmon shook their hands, and then gave them both a warm embrace. He offered to carry their suitcases but Ben told him they could manage. Harmon got back in the car, waved goodbye and drove off. Upon entering Union Station, busy even on a Sunday morning, they saw the Empire State Express arrived early from Schenectady.

Their train was soon announced. Waiting with a rather long line of passengers, Meg and Ben boarded and with their suitcases on the overhead rack, they settled down, together. As the train started on its journey, Meg felt at peace, with Ben by her side. As Elsie pointed out, in time it will heal. And with Ben, Meg knew she would be happy.

THE END

Made in United States
North Haven, CT
23 November 2024